UNFAIR GAME

UNFAIR GAME

SUSAN RENEE

PAGE
—&—
VINE

Page & Vine
An Imprint of Meredith Wild LLC

Paperback ISBN: 978-1-964264-16-5

To cock rings and the men who wear them.

Disclaimer:

This book is intended for adult readers only and is not appropriate for minors. The story includes adult language and adult sexual content. This story also makes mention of domestic abuse, childhood cancer, and adult infertility issues.

CHAPTER 1

Milo

"Did you just spank my monkey?"

Dex cackles. "Damn right I did. Felt pretty good, too!"

"You wait, Milo," Colby mumbles next to me. "I'm gonna bone him so hard he won't know what hit him."

"HA!" Dex hurls his whole body to the right instead of simply turning his controller. "You're jealous, Colby, because you don't have a monkey for me to spank."

"That's because his monkey belongs to me!" Carissa bellows from the kitchen. A minute later, she places bowls of chips, veggies, and some assorted dips on the coffee table in front of us and then gives Colby a peck on the cheek. "Don't worry baby, if you need to bone someone later, I'm all yours."

Colby tosses his controller on the couch. "Fuck it, I'll take that bone right now. Take over, Quinton."

"What the fuck?" Quinton scrambles to pick up Colby's controller as he and Carissa canoodle their way down the hall, her giggles still heard from a couple rooms away. "Am I on the top or bottom?"

"Depends, man," Hawken says with a smirk. "You want to watch her drive or not?"

My phone dings on the coffee table with an incoming text message, but my eyes are too glued to the screen to look away. It's most likely my sister, anyway.

"Last lap, suckers!" Dex laughs. "I'm about to smoke all of you!"

I watch my Donkey Kong character roll through the hieroglyphic square and end up with my favorite power-up. Hitting the button on my controller, I smile to myself as I fly through the air. "Make way for Bullet Bill!"

"Dang!" Colby laughs, having rejoined us in the living room with his wife. "He brought you to the end fast and hard."

Carissa playfully swats her husband's ass. "Never underestimate those bullets, babe."

Watching Dex hit the finish line only a half second in front of me, I sit back against the couch, my controller in my lap. "Well, at least I wasn't last."

My phone dings again.

"Who could possibly be texting you?" Hawken asks me. "All the dudes you hang with are in this room."

"Not Elias," Colby states. "Or Zeke."

I nod, reaching for my phone. "True. They're probably up to their elbow in baby blow-outs."

Turning my phone over, I glance at the text on the screen.

> **Daveed: Hey man. You busy? I need a favor. Pretty big one.**

"Oh. It's not Elias." I tap my thumbs across my phone, returning his text.

> **Me: Veeeeeed!! Long time no talk! Not busy. What's up?**

Daveed Bryce is an old friend and teammate. He played for the Red Tails for about four years before he was traded to Seattle a couple seasons ago. It's been several months since any of us have heard from him, though. Staying in touch with anyone during a busy hockey season can prove difficult.

Daveed: Will call you in a minute.

"It's Bryce," I tell everyone, my brow furrowed. "Says he needs a big favor."

"Son of a bitch." Dex chuckles. "Tell him no, Wongs will not deliver to Seattle, nor will it stay fresh in the mail. That dude has to be going through withdrawal as much as he loved their food." There's no question that Wongs has unequivocally the best Chinese take-out in the city, and when Daveed was on the team, we were eating that deliciousness multiple times a week.

Quinton shrugs and grabs a tortilla chip, dipping it in the bowl of salsa in front of him. "I'm sure there's equally good Chinese food in Seattle...somewhere."

"He didn't say what the favor is?" Colby asks.

I'm about to answer him, but my phone rings in my hand. Holding it up and standing from the couch, I respond, "He will now, I guess." I tap the button on my screen to accept the call. "Veed! How are you, you big son of a bitch? Nice of you to keep in touch."

"I know, I know. My apologies. The move was a lot mid-season, and Jada and I were house-hunting and dealing with all that bullshit. It's been a busy year."

"Nice game last night. Heard you guys obliterated Miami."

"We sure as hell did." He laughs. "Ten to one. And that one was a pity goal because I slid the wrong way and swear, I somehow crushed a nut in the process. Hurt like a bitch."

"Ouch." I wince out of sympathy. "All right, you're forgiven. Hey, the guys are all here. You should say hi!"

"Oh, man, I'm sorry I'm interrupting—"

"No, no, no. It's all good. We're literally hanging out at Colby's and dicking around with Mario Kart and snacks. We have a few days off and none of us wanted to deal with the weather tonight, so we're staying in."

"Sounds like my kind of hangout."

"How's Jada?"

"She's great. Really great. Found herself a sweet job at the hospital and seems to be loving it."

"Good! I'm really glad to hear that. Anyway, what's this favor you need help with? Whatever it is, I'm in."

"Well, you might want to hear me out before you say yes."

Dex calls out, "Ask him if he needs my nut juice!"

"What the fuck is he on about?" Daveed chuckles.

I flip Dex my middle finger. "He called for me, asshat. If he needed your nut juice your phone would be ringing right now and oh, look at that...it's not."

Daveed laughs on the other end of the line. "Tell that fucker I'll take his nut juice any time he wants to send it to me."

"I wouldn't throw that gauntlet down, Veed. He may very well pick it up."

"You're right." He's silent on the line for a second and then says, "All right, well, I'm just going to rip off the bandage here."

Uh oh. That sounds ominous.

"All right."

"Jada and I have a friend who needs a place to stay. You still living in that monster penthouse?"

"Absolutely, man. I've got tons of space. You know that."

"Yeah, but I'm not talking just a few days. We could be talking weeks, or maybe even a month or more, Milo."

"Hey, if you know someone who needs help and you trust it won't be a problem, then it's all good. It's not like I don't have the room. Is everything okay? Is he suspended? Injured? Being traded? What's going on?"

The guys are now watching me as I have this conversation with Daveed.

"Uh, yeah, everything will be okay, I think. And no, she's perfectly healthy. She needs to get out of a messy situation until she can figure things out on her own."

She...

"She? Veed, we're talking about a girl?"

"Oh shit. Yeah, it's a girl. Fuck, I should've asked first. I'm sorry. Are you single? I don't want to put you in a precarious position if you have someo—"

"Yeah, no. I'm single, Veed. It's fine." *Is it fine though? Am I really okay with this? Living with some girl I don't know, sharing my space with a stranger?* "So, what are we talking about when you say messy situation? She in trouble with the law? Because you know that would be a hard pass given our reputations."

"She's squeaky clean, I swear. It's nothing like that. She wants out of an unhealthy relationship. She's a good friend to Jada, but the guy she's with is an asshole. She needs a clean break. I don't know if her financial situation is strong enough to support an apartment in the city or not. This is going to be a quick getaway, so she hasn't had time to apply for places to live yet. She has a job connection in Chicago though, so Jada and I immediately thought of you when she was talking about places she could go."

"You did? Why me?"

"Of course, we did. You're a good guy, Milo. You're honest and helpful and compassionate. Fuckin' boy scout as far as I'm concerned. I told Jada if she was going to help her friend, we had to talk to someone we both would trust with our own lives."

"Wow." Warmth spreads through my chest. "I guess I'm speechless. That's nice of you to say."

"I wouldn't say it if I didn't mean it. So, can you help? For Jada? For me?"

As Daveed and I are talking, I'm writing out a note on paper for the guys about the possibility of gaining a female roommate. The guys have been whispering question after question at me ever since.

"Is she hot?"

"What's her name?"

"What does she look like?"

"How hot do you think she is?"

"I take it she's single?"

"What if you think she's hot?"

"If she's hot, can I date her?"

"Where is she going to sleep?"

"You gonna give her your bed?"

"Wonder if she gives good head."

"Are you going to do it?"

"Are you saying yes?"

"Of course, I'll help out. You know me, Veed. Always willing to help a friend. Or, in this case, a friend of a friend."

"You're a good man, Milo. I owe you one. A big one."

"Don't sweat it, man. When should I expect err...what's her name?"

"Charlee. Her name is Charlee. And she and Jada will be in town tomorrow. They're already on the road."

I chuckle softly. "Motherfucker, was I that much of a forgone conclusion?"

"Nah. But I had a strong feeling you wouldn't say no. I'll give Jada your number so she can keep you updated in case of a delay."

"Sounds good."

"Hey, thanks again, Milo. I really appreciate this. And I know Jada does too."

"Sure thing, Veed. Happy to help." Well, I don't know if I'm that happy to help knowing I've now opened my home to a complete stranger, but when have I ever turned away a friend in need?

Never.

Daveed used to be one of our defensemen when Zeke Miller and I joined the team. He took us both under his wing and helped us get our feet wet in the NHL. I've always admired his leadership, but more than that, I've always looked up to his way of life. He truly cares about people. He's constantly giving back to his community and his love for hockey is unmatched. He's an all-around great guy. Someone I aspire to be like.

"So, you're shacking up with some chick?" Hawken asks, grabbing a handful of pretzels and tossing them into his mouth.

I smooth my hand down my five-o'clock shadow and nod.

"Yeah, I guess I am."

"So, what's the story?"

I shrug. "Some friend of Jada's, I guess. Needs to get away from a douchebag and wants to start over in Chicago. She just needs a place to stay while she does some apartment hunting."

Dex chimes in. "Did he say if she's hot?"

"I hardly think that's important."

In fact, it would be better for me if she's the ugliest human I've ever set eyes on. The last thing I need right now is a distraction from my job on the ice. Gaining a roommate when I've never had one is one thing. Gaining a hot roommate I struggle to keep my eyes off of is a whole other set of issues.

"Maybe not." Dex bobs his head. "But having something nice to look at once in a while ain't a bad thing."

Colby wraps an arm around Carissa's shoulder. "When is she arriving?"

"Tomorrow."

Everyone's brows shoot up.

"I know." I run a hand through my hair. "So much for preparing."

"Don't worry about a thing." Carissa waves off my concerns. "Your guest room is fine. As long as she has a place to sleep and a bathroom to clean up in, she'll be fine. And I'm happy to help in any way I can."

"Thanks, Carissa."

She gives me a reassuring smile as she takes Colby's hand in hers. "Absolutely."

"I guess it's not like my sister hasn't spent time at my place before. If I can handle her being all up in my business..."

Colby chuckles. "If you can handle your sister, you can handle any other woman who walks through your door."

God, I hope he's not wrong.

CHAPTER 2

Charlee

"One hour to go." I shake my hands out from gripping the steering wheel, nerves and anxiety finally settling in. Until now, this has been a fun road trip with my best friend. From Seattle to Illinois, it's been miles upon miles of snorting in laughter combined with singing almost every song we hear at the top of our lungs. At my request, we haven't spoken much about my reason for leaving town or what I'm giving up by doing so. I know it's for the best, as does Jada, and that's all that matters. My best friend has my back at all times. I'm lucky to have her. "Tell me again what he's like."

"Milo?" Jada quirks a brow.

"Mmm-hmm. Is it gonna be weird the minute I move in? Is he shy? Oh my God, is he clean? I don't think I ever thought to ask you that. Am I moving into a dirty man cave where I'll have to sift through piles of dirty socks and underwear to find a path to walk through? Should I expect posters of Playboy centerfolds hung up all around his place?"

"Uhh..." She scoffs out a laugh. "He's not eighteen, Char. He's only a couple years younger than Daveed, and if he still lives the way he was living a couple years ago, he's clean and tidy with a modern but super comfortable home. He has a sister who is married with young kids, and though I don't think he's had any serious relationships lately, he's definitely dated before, so it's not like he doesn't know his way around women. And trust me when I say he's a looker. You'll think he's hot."

I shake my head, cringing. "I don't need him to be hot. I'm over hot. Hell, at this point, I think I'm over guys in general." I glance at my best friend. "You want to hook up? You're hot. I would do you."

She laughs. "Right back at ya, babe, but you just said you're over hot. Anyway, I thrive on big dick energy—and you will too when you finally find the right one. In the meantime, Milo is a good guy. He's friendly and compassionate and can be a fierce protector when he needs to be."

"I don't need a protector. I need a bed to sleep in that isn't in Seattle, and I'll be fine."

"Mmmkay." She gives me some side-eye. "Whatever helps you sleep at night, but that shiner around your eye says otherwise."

This is where I usually say something like, "it was an accident" or "I got in the way" or "I did it to myself"...anything to not have to admit my reality—but those would all be lies. Not that any of my previous "accidents" were this bad. They weren't. A bruise here or there from hands that grabbed too hard, but nothing that came across as unnatural. I could hide or excuse away just about anything.

But not this time.

"This hot mess of a face," I say, circling my face with my pointer finger, "is the reason we're in this car, driving I don't even know how many states away from Washington, so he can't ever lay a fucking hand on me again."

Jada nods. "It's six."

"Huh?"

"Six states. Illinois is six states from Washington. Roughly thirty hours away." She pats my thigh. "And, for what it's worth, I think you're the bravest woman I know. When the team gets back, that asshole isn't gonna know what hit him, and I'll be damned if he thinks he's going to get info from me. I'll go to my grave with your whereabouts, sis. Daveed will too. Nobody on the team thinks Jared is a good guy. We're glad to see you rid of him. We're just sorry it's come to this. I wish you would rethink pressing charges."

"You know I can't do that."

"No," she says. "I know why you won't. It's not a question of can or can't, but I'll respect your decision for now. You're going to thrive in Chicago. I can feel it. The world is yours for the taking."

I grab her hand and give it a strong squeeze. "Thanks, babe."

We navigate our way into the city and finally pull into the parking garage—Jada having gotten a guest code from Milo—and make our way up the elevator to the top floor. The elevator dings, and when the door opens, we're a few steps away from the entrance to my home for the near future. Butterflies flutter around in my stomach, and my feet are stuck to the floor. Jada steps ahead of me, assuming I'm with her, but turns around when she notices I haven't moved. She comes back to me and tenderly wraps her warm hand around mine.

"Hey, you've got this, sis. You've come all this way. It's just one foot in front of the other."

"But my face—"

"Is beautiful." She gives me a reassuring stare, her expression really saying, "Don't you for one second think otherwise."

She places her hands on my shoulders and then tips my chin with her finger. "Listen to me, Char. He doesn't get to win this one. You win this one, okay? You did all the right things. You're here. This...here..." She gestures to the short hallway leading to Milo Landric's apartment. "This is all temporary. This is for your comfort and your security while you're finding your footing. That's all. Okay? No expectations." Her head bobs. "Plus, I already texted Milo and told him not to ask a damn thing about your face. He understands. I promise you he's a good guy. I got you, sis."

I nod hesitantly at first and then square my shoulders back and lift my chin a little more. "You're right. I've got this."

We walk together to Milo's door, and I raise my hand, knocking confidently four times. It only takes a minute for someone to answer, and when he does, there's only one string of thoughts that crosses my mind.

For the love of Christ!

When Jada said he was hot, I didn't think she meant panty-melting hot.

I'm so totally fucked.

Dressed in a pair of worn, ripped jeans and a Red Tails hooded sweatshirt, he greets Jada first, embracing her in a warm, friendly hug with mentions of the long stretch of time between visits. Then his attention shifts. I take in his warm smile, angled jaw, and trimmed facial hair. More than a five-o'clock shadow, but less than a full beard. It's nice. It suits him.

Jada gestures to me with a smile. "Milo, this is—"

"Charlee," I tell him, offering him a handshake. "Charlee Mags." My eyes pass to Jada, who gives me an understanding smile.

"Charlee Mags." Milo smiles, shaking my hand, and I have to remind myself to close my mouth so I don't come across like some puck bunny with a crazy crush on the big hockey player. "It's a pleasure to finally meet you." His hand is warm and strong wrapped around mine. An immediate difference from Jared's cold, dry hands. "Daveed and Jada have had nothing but wonderful things to say about you." He gestures inside his palatial apartment. "Welcome home."

My eyes widen at his words.

Home.

Welcome home.

"Uh, thanks." I try to give him a warm smile, though I probably look as awkward as I feel. "I really appreciate you giving me a place to crash. It's very generous of you."

Milo inhales a breath as he takes in my face. I know that's what he's doing right now. I can see all the questions swirling in his head that he wants to ask but has been told not to. He glances at Jada, who smiles, and then back at me.

"Of course. Any friend of Jada and Daveed's is a friend of mine. You're welcome here as long as you like. Really. The place is too big for one person anyway." He smiles softly, gesturing to his split-level luxury apartment, but then his face falls a little more serious. "Did you uh...come empty-handed, or can I help you with a bag?"

"No, I, uh...no, I didn't come empty-handed." I gesture out the door with my thumb. "I have a couple bags and totes in the car."

Milo nods. "Well, let me help you bring them up."

Together, the three of us head down to the garage and bring up everything I was able to pack in the short window I gave myself the moment Jared left with the team for their string of away games. My life is currently packed inside three suitcases and two totes. It only takes us one trip to move it all into someone else's apartment.

Sad.

I gave a few things to Jada that I knew I wouldn't use or wear anymore, and grabbed only my essentials plus a small number of keepsakes from my family.

Jared can do whatever he wants with what I left.

None of it means anything to me anyway.

We stash my things along the wall in the living room, and then Milo takes us on a quick tour of his place.

My place.

For now.

The opposite wall of the living room is nothing but floor-to-ceiling windows overlooking the rest of the city. It's gorgeous, but I'm also glad to see curtains hanging as well.

Do paparazzi hang around the Red Tails like they do the Sea Brawlers?

The open floor plan itself is exactly as Jada said it was. Modern but extremely comfy-looking, with an oversized couch I could see myself sinking into dividing the kitchen from the living room. A few comfy chairs square the space, and a television I swear is longer than me, hangs on the wall opposite the gray couch. The sheer size is impressive, and for a split second, I wonder if everything about Milo is oversized.

Everything.

The living room space flows right into the kitchen and dining area. The open concept has to be amazing when he's entertaining guests. Top-of-the-line chrome appliances sit amongst white cabinetry and gray marbled countertops. A kitchen island, long enough to seat six, provides ample space for food prep or display. It's absolutely stunning. A dream home so far.

"You have a wine closet?" Holy shit. I didn't even know penthouses had rooms like this.

"This is sort of my collection."

"Your collection? You're a wine connoisseur?"

He laughs softly. "Not really. I try to pick up a local wine or whiskey or bourbon—you know, whatever—in each city we play in. They're not all fancy, expensive bottles. But it's neat to look back at where we've been."

"That's a really cool idea."

"Thanks."

We climb the stairs, and he leads us down the short hallway.

"This is, uh... This is your room," he says, opening the second door on the right, the first being a walk-in pantry closet. "You can...you know, change anything you like. Decorate however you want. I'm sorry it's kind of bland. I haven't done much with this room since it doesn't get used a whole lot."

The room is more than enough for me. Spacious, with a queen bed, a comfy oversized chair in front of two bookshelves, one four-drawer dresser, and a closet big enough for—

"Damn, Char! I think the Kardashians could fit all their shit up in here!"

Yep. I guess it's big enough for the Kardashians.

"Well, if it's big enough for a Kardashian, it's big enough for me." I smile, and Milo chuckles softly.

"There's also an attached bathroom through there." He gestures to a door in the corner of the room.

"Thank you, Milo. So much. I really appreciate this."

His teddy-bear-like brown eyes nearly melt me, and I don't even know the guy.

"It's my pleasure."

We spend the next hour or so making small talk, and then Jada gives us both hugs before she takes our rental car and heads to the airport to fly back home. The team comes back tomorrow night. Once she's home, it'll be as if nothing ever happened. Nobody but Daveed knows we left and that's the way it'll stay.

Milo shuts the door when Jada heads out and then turns, his hands in his back pockets. The ballcap he wears backward on his head definitely adds to his appeal.

Why God, why?

Why does he have to look so good?

Why do you torture me like this?

"So, you hungry?"

My stomach rumbles audibly, answering him before I even get a word out. "I guess that answers your question."

Milo smiles. "How about pizza? Something easy? I figured you might want time to crash or unpack your things, but I can order whatever you want."

"Pizza sounds perfect."

"Toppings? Veggies? Meat?"

"Oh, I'm a meat girl." My eyes widen as I hear what just came out of my mouth. "I mean...I like meat. You know, on my pizza. Not that I don't like...well, you know. Shit. Shut up, Charlee. You're only making it worse."

Milo laughs softly. "Nah. It's all good. You should be proud of your big meat energy."

My eyes widen even more, and Milo's squeeze closed. "Shit. I'm sorry."

"Pfft!" I cover my mouth to hide my laugh, but it's no use. "You know what? You're right. I am proud of my big meat energy. Bring on the meatza."

"Meatza!" Milo beams, nodding in appreciation. "I like it. One super-sized meatza coming up."

The pizza box lying open on the counter, I pick at my second piece of pizza crust while Milo inhales his fifth slice. He probably shouldn't be eating pizza this close to a game day, but it was his offer. Who am I to question his diet? Besides, it's nothing an extra couple of miles on the treadmill or bike can't fix, not that I would tell him that either. He's a professional. He knows what he's doing.

He clears his throat after his last swallow. "So, are you originally from Seattle?"

I wipe my mouth with my napkin and shake my head. "No, I'm actually from Colorado. Born and raised in Boulder."

"Ah, yes. Home of the Bobcats."

Of course, he knows all the hockey teams. "Yep."

"Ever been to a game?"

I nod. "A couple times." That's a lie. I practically grew up on that rink watching my brother learn the sport.

Milo sits up a little taller, interested. "Does that mean you're a big hockey fan?"

Here comes lie number two. "Nah. Not really. I don't know that much about the sport. I mean, besides the fact that the players seem to like to pick fights all the time and ram each other into the wall."

His hand lands over his heart. "Ooh, I feel attacked with a comment like that."

"Sorry." I shrug with a timid smile. "I think you guys get paid a shit ton of money and already put yourselves at risk for injury with the kind of games you play. Why do something more that could literally break bones, knock out teeth, or even worse, by getting into ridiculous brawls on the ice?"

There. I said what I said.

Stupid hockey players.

Milo nods and huffs out a laugh. "Wow. Would you be offended if I told you that you sound like my mom right now?"

"Nope. Your mom is clearly a smart lady."

"That she is." He smiles. "And I see your point. Sometimes body checks happen because of the sheer speed at which we move. We can't always stop ourselves as swiftly as we want to or think we can."

I tilt my head and lift my brow. "But other times...?"

"Hockey is an aggressive sport. Fights happen. We look out for our teammates, and if one of them is wronged, we go all in." He lifts a shoulder. "We protect our own. No questions asked. If that means I suffer a bloody nose or a loose tooth, then so be it. Sometimes it's worth it."

I nod slowly, not knowing what to say to that except, "I guess sometimes it's nice to belong to someone. Otherwise, you have to protect yourself. Protect or sacrifice." Our eyes connect, and he shifts on his stool, his smile replaced with an empathetic cringe.

"Fuck, I'm sorry, Charlee," he says, shaking his head. "I shouldn't have said that. It was insensitive of me, and I'm sorry." His focus shifts to my eye, and my body tenses in response.

It's been a while since a man has apologized to me for anything.

"Are you apologizing because I currently have a black eye?"

He swallows. I have no doubt he's asking himself right now if he should ask what happened or take Jada's advice and not mention it.

"Do you, umm..." He clears his throat again. "Do you want to talk about it?"

Part of me wants to tell him everything. He's made this transition from one life to another so smooth today, easy.

Comfortable.

I feel as if I could tell him anything, and whatever I say would stay between us. But then I remind myself that we really don't know each other at all yet.

"What's there to talk about? He got one good hit." I toss my crust on my plate and wipe my hands on my napkin, shrugging like it's no big deal. But the way Milo is staring right now—listening, his eyes widened, his nostrils flaring—to him I can tell it's a major deal. "And one hit is all he'll ever get."

Milo shakes his head and softly says, "I'm sorry, Charlee. I'm so sorry that happened to you."

"You don't owe me any apologies, Milo."

He swallows again, his brows pinched. His hand shifts as if he's going to lay it over mine but then thinks better of it. "Nothing like that will ever happen to you here. You have my word. I won't let anyone hurt you. I can promise you that."

I want to tell him that's what Jared said when we first got together. I want to tell Milo about how big and bad Jared thought he was until he had one bad game after another, followed by too much alcohol. Instead, I picture the line from the last book I was editing two nights ago that caught my attention and share those words with him.

"Careful, Milo. Promise is a big word. It either makes something...or breaks everything."

CHAPTER 3

Milo

I've been around loads of women in my short lifetime. I've had women throw themselves at me, offer to suck me off—or whatever other kinky shit they think I might be interested in at the time. I get private messages via social media on the regular from single and married women who want a chance to get naked with me. As if, because I play professional hockey, I'm some sort of sex toy for the female population. Hell, maybe even a few males out there as well. Out of all those women who cross my path, I've never had a particular type. I've certainly sampled a good many. They're not all blondes or brunettes. Their bodies aren't all stick thin or physically fit. Each one has her own style, and I can admit many of them are eye candy I wouldn't mind looking at day in and day out.

That is, until Charlee Mags walks into my life.

I've had desperate, flirty women throw themselves at me, one after another, for years. But it took only seconds for someone to walk into my home and have me completely forget about any other woman I've ever met.

Holy shit, she's...wow, I don't even have the right word for what she is.

Pure?

Gorgeous?

Breathtaking?

Beautiful?

Simple?

Ugh, I imagine women don't want to be called simple...or

plain. I should come up with another word, but they're all evading me at the moment.

One thing is for certain, though.

Charlee Mags is one-hundred-percent my type.

She didn't show up here all dolled up like the women I meet at parties, or even at Pringle's Pub after a game. She was beautiful in the simplest way. She was dressed in ripped jeans that hugged her hips and legs, and a black sweater that hung off her shoulder. Not in a planned, fashionable way. More like a this-sweater-is-too-big-for-me-but-I-don't-fucking-care kind of way. Her dark, curly hair was pulled into a loose bun at the back of her head, a few tendrils hanging loose. A small amount of makeup on one eye, the other clearly having suffered a blow that makes me both nauseous and angry.

What fucker did this to her?

In all honesty, she looked tired, as she should have after a couple days of driving but, damn, all I wanted to do was look at her.

Talk to her.

Get to know her.

Take your time, Milo.

She clearly has baggage.

Once we finished eating, she wanted to spend the rest of her evening unpacking her things, so I gave her some space. Now that I've turned off the lights and climbed into bed, though, all I can think about is her.

It's my new goal to make her smile, because even the shy half-smile I got from her tonight melted me. I say shy, but in all reality, she doesn't come across as shy at all. Just the opposite, Charlee seems like a strong, independent woman. She's clearly hardworking. Her laptop and printer were the first things she hooked up this evening, so she could be ready to work in the morning. How dumb am I for not even asking what she does for a living?

Or maybe she didn't want to tell me?

The only small bit of unease I felt from her was when she talked about her eye, and even that she did with confidence and resiliency.

"He got one good hit. And one good hit is all he'll ever get."

Fucking hell.

The thought of some asshole putting his hands on any woman in that manner makes my skin crawl, but now there are feelings in me I can't exactly comprehend. Now that I know someone who has actually endured the pain, someone who has felt the sting of the punch...fuck. If that guy were here right now, whoever he is, I'm not sure I could control myself enough to not kill him for what he did to Charlee.

I've only known her for a few hours, but I'll be damned if anyone ever hurts her again.

My eyes are still open when my alarm goes off. I may have drifted off a few times throughout the night, but I am anything but rested. Spending hour after hour thinking about the woman asleep in my guest bed on the other side of my wall does not bode well for getting a restful night's sleep. And when you're wide awake in the middle of the night, the mind wanders to weird places.

Is she okay in there?

Is she asleep?

Is that mattress comfortable for her?

I knew I should've ordered those sleep number beds.

I never offered her any ice for her eye.

Dammit, Milo. Way to be a dick.

How did it happen anyway?

What happened that pissed him off?

Or is he a motherfucking dick all the time?

Did she get to hit him too?

I hope so. Fucker deserved it for sure.

I wonder what she sleeps in.

Sexy little satin number?

Nah. She's probably a cute sleep shorts-and-tank kind of girl.

If she's wearing shorts and a tank, is she warm enough?

Maybe I should turn the heat up.

Maybe I should offer her a couple blankets.

What if she's shivering and too afraid to ask for blankets?

But what if she's sleeping and I wake her up when I knock?

What if I don't knock and just walk in?

That's crazy. I can't do that.

What if I do that and she's awake?

Or worse...what if she's awake and naked?

I mean, that's not really worse.

That would be kind of amazing, actually.

Fuck, no. That would freak her out for sure.

Okay. Walking in equals bad idea.

Maybe I could lay a couple extra blankets outside her room in case she tries to hunt around for some and is afraid to ask me.

Yeah, that's a good idea.

We're totally trying out the new crisscross trick play at our next game.

I have to remind Colby...and Coach.

I could really go for some prime rib right now.

My left testicle itches.

Hmm, I think it might be a little bigger than my right testicle.

Big one, little one.

Is that normal?

Should I ask my doctor about my testicles being two different sizes?

Should testicles be identical?

Identical testicle...that sounds like a disease.

Or a cool band name.

I wonder how much a typical testicle weighs.

I should try to weigh mine sometime.

How would I do that? A food scale?

I wonder what testicles taste like.

I should ask someone who's been on Survivor.

They make people eat bull testicles on that show.

It's definitely been a while since my balls have been in someone's mouth.

I wonder if someone can tell if they're two different sizes.

I really need to sleep.

After I put some blankets outside Charlee's room.

I slap my alarm and turn my head to look outside, where the sun is beginning to lift itself off the horizon. The morning sunrise is one reason I chose this apartment. The view alone is as energizing as it is breathtaking, and helps a great deal on the days I don't feel like rolling out of bed.

"Shit, I never asked Charlee what she wants for breakfast," I mumble to myself.

Does she even eat breakfast?

So many people don't, but it's the most important meal of the day.

I could cook her something.

I make a mean omelet.

It's too early for her to be up yet.

I probably have time for a cup of coffee first.

Yeah, I'll do that.

After using the restroom and brushing my teeth, I pull on a pair of black sweatpants—sans shirt—and pad down the hall toward the kitchen to start the coffee pot. The apartment is mostly dark, except for the sunrise providing a soft glow in the living room area. Yawning, I scratch my chest and reach for the light switch, but a slight movement catches my eye and startles me.

It all happens so fast.

Charlee next to the living room windows.

Tight black leggings that form to her body like paint.

Red sports bra.

Her hands on the floor, her body lifted into the air.

Her magnificent ass staring right at me.

Holy shit, that ass is...toned...shapely...gorgeous.

I stare like any man would, yep, even a semi-tent growing in my pants.

"Fuck me, am I dreaming?"

"Oh my God! I...oompf!" A startled Charlee falls from the tantalizing pose she had herself in and lands in a heap on the floor, stirring me from my morning fog.

"Shit. I'm not dreaming." *That was fucking real?* "Charlee? Are you okay?"

"Yeah," she mumbles, rolling to her side and checking her wrist. "I'm good."

I'm at her side in seconds, crouched down beside her, my hands grabbing her arm to lift her up, but she flinches and recoils, and I hastily throw my hands up, shaking my head. My eyes wide. "I'm sorry. Shit. I'm sorry, Charlee."

"No, I'm sorry."

"I didn't mean to—"

"You didn't. Really. It's—"

"I was just trying to, he—"

"I know. I'm sorry, Mi—"

"Didn't know you were..." Her gaze lifts, and her eyes catch mine. "In here," I finish my sentence with a whisper.

God, she's even more beautiful than I remember from yesterday.

"It's okay," she says with a swallow. "I couldn't sleep anymore, so I thought I would get an early start on my day." She motions to the window behind us. "The view is as stunning in the morning as it is in the evening. You're very lucky."

The corner of my mouth lifts. "It's the reason I chose this place. Sometimes, I like to lose myself in the view."

I'd like to lose myself in this view.

And I'm not looking out the window.

Offering Charlee my hand, I ask this time, "Can I help you up?"

She slips her hand in mine, and I pull her up to her feet with ease. She steadies herself with her other hand on my chest, and it's right at this moment that I'm keenly aware I never slipped on a shirt.

And I think she becomes aware of the same.

Her hand is warm on my skin. The feeling might be long overdue, so I'm not hating it. The faintest of gasps comes from her lips, and I don't miss it. Her eyes trail up my body like she's devouring me with her mind, and she smooths her hand down my torso. I almost chuckle as I observe her blatant examination of me, from my bare feet to my six-pack abs.

What can I say? I work out like it's my job.

Hey, babe, my eyes are up here.

Just kidding. Look all you want.

I don't hate this.

I probably shouldn't be liking it.

But I don't hate it either.

I do wonder what she's thinking right now, though.

When she finally realizes what she's doing, she pulls her hand away, her eyes widening as she steps back.

"God, I'm so sorry." She chuckles and shakes her head, bringing a hand to her forehead, clearly a bit embarrassed. "I swear I'm not some sort of...weirdo...man feeler-upper...or whatever."

"Man feeler-upper." Trying hard not to laugh at her, I suck my lips in, but it's no use. I can't help it. She looks up at me with a worried "please-don't-think-I'm-psycho" expression, and I finally release the laugh I was holding. "That's definitely a term I don't think I've ever heard before."

"Well, you're welcome then. You learned something new today. Man feeler-upper. Apparently, it's a thing."

"It's really no problem. I'm sorry I didn't put a shirt on. I didn't think you would be up yet and was going to make some coffee." I nod toward the kitchen. "Would you like some?"

"Love some. Thank you." The tension in her body leaves when she sees I don't make a big deal of our awkward moment.

"Sure. Also, I realized when I woke up this morning, I never asked you what you like for breakfast, or if you even eat breakfast. I make a pretty good omelet and was going to make one for myself if you're interested."

"Yeah, that sounds good." She gives me an honest smile, and I almost swoon right in front of her because, dammit, her smile is not only beautiful, but also contagious. "And I'd love to help. You know, make me earn my keep and all."

"Want to grab the eggs and chopped veggies from the fridge while I grab a pan and mixing bowl? There might be some cheese in there too."

"Sure."

I crack a few eggs into the pan and then step to the side so she can sprinkle in some chopped veggies and cheese. While I finish our omelets, she makes coffee and sets us both a place at the island.

"So, what was that you were doing when I walked in?" I ask after inhaling a few bites of the best omelet I've ever made.

She tilts her head as she takes her bite, smiling as she chews. "Uh, it's this new thing. Hard to pronounce. I think they call it yo-gah."

"Oh, so she's flexible and she's a smartass too?" I mumble to myself and then give Charlee a wink. "Noted."

"Have you really never done yoga before?"

"Yeah, loads of times. That was just a pose I've never seen before. It's not like the ever-popular tree pose or downward dog or, you know, one of the easy ones I can actually do."

"True." She nods, "It's called the crow pose. It's great for opening the hips and strengthening the core muscles. You should try it sometime. Strengthens your forearms and wrists as well. Who knows, it could come in handy in a hockey game."

"For all those times I need to be able to skate on my hands, you mean?" My smile widens. "Also, if my teammate Dex were here right now, he would be making a comment about taking a puck or a stick up the ass in that pose."

She blushes like she knows what I'm thinking about right now, and she would probably be right. I did just picture her naked in that pose, ready and willing, with me standing right behind her.

Fuck, that would be incredibly hot.

"Well, I'm just saying." Her shoulder lifts. "Strong arms, strong wrists, strong core...those are all good things, so you never know."

"You're absolutely right. Maybe you can teach me sometime."

"Yeah. Maybe." How does she make a simple act like pulling a fork from her mouth look adorably sexy?

My eyes find the clock on the stove, and I lift off the stool with my plate in hand, carrying it to the sink. "I suppose I should get my stuff together and head to the gym. Morning workout starts in thirty minutes."

"Right." She waves me away when I offer to clear her plate. "Leave those. I'll do the dishes. It's the least I can do."

An uneasy feeling hits my chest, and before I retreat to my room to get dressed, I turn and lean across the kitchen island. "Charlee, you know you don't owe me anything, right? I'm not charging you any kind of rent to stay here, nor would I ever expect you to do anything. Please don't ever feel obligated, okay? I would feel terrible if you felt that way. I want you to be comfortable. Stay as long as you like. Do whatever you need or want to do. This is your place now too. Okay?"

She swallows as if she's nervous but gives me a reassuring and warm smile. She also reaches over and squeezes my hand.

Unexpected. But I'll take it.

"Thank you, Milo. Truly. But I don't like handouts. Consider us roommates, and I would expect a roommate to do her fair share. Please don't feel like you can't ask anything of me because I currently have a black eye."

I step back. "Is that what you think I'm doing?"

"Isn't it?"

"No. Not... I mean...no...I..."

She pulls her bottom lip into her mouth, trying to hide her smile, and now I have to take a breath and take ownership for my words.

"Okay, yes. Yes, that's exactly what I'm doing. I'm sorry."

"It's really all right." She stands and takes her plate to the sink, and I watch her every step. "I'm fine, okay? I'm stronger than you think."

"Doubtful."

"What?" Her eyes narrow.

"Right now, I think you're the strongest woman I've ever met."

"Because I got punched in the eye and lived to tell the tale?"

God, I wish she wouldn't mention her eye. The pit in my stomach grows every time I think about someone touching her like that. "No. Because you can do that bird pose you were doing."

Her eyes meet mine and I wink at her, making her giggle. "Get out of here, Milo. Get to work before they kick you off the team."

"Ha!" I almost cackle. "Fat chance of that happening. Hey, what do you do, by the way? Jada mentioned you work from home most of the time."

"Yeah. I'm a contracted book editor for Enchantment Publishing House. They're actually based right here in Chicago, but I've only had to fly here a couple times a year for our quarterly team meetings. They know they can save money if they don't have big office suites, so their people work remotely for the most part."

"Oh, so you've been to Chicago a few times then?"

"Yeah. Once or twice a year, at least."

"Where do you usually stay?"

Her eyes grow and a smile crosses her face. Her smile is easily one of her strongest features. I mean, besides her rockin' body in that yoga outfit. "I love staying at the Palmer House."

"Ah, yes. I know it well."

"It's so beautiful in there. Unlike any of the more modern hotels of the world. When I stay there, it makes me feel like..." She takes a deep breath. "Royalty. You know?"

"Did you know it's rumored that Mark Twain and Oscar Wilde have stayed in that very hotel?"

She nods. "I do. I mean, how cool is that? What if I've slept in the same room as some of the most popular authors of all time?"

"Yeah, that's pretty cool. Well, if you, you know, need

anything or an extra space to set up in, I don't mind moving my shit out of the way so you can work."

"It's totally fine." Her smile is endearing. "Anywhere my laptop can go, I can go. Nice perk of the job."

"Right." I nod. "Okay. All right then. I'll leave you to your day unless you need me for anything?"

"I'm good. I promise. Plus, Jada exchanged our numbers, so, you know..."

"Right. That she did. Good. Okay."

I can't believe I kind of don't want to leave. I wouldn't say no to staying in and chatting with her all day. She's easy to talk to. Fun, even.

And very easy on the eyes.

Especially in nothing but leggings and a red sports bra.

"Thank you again, Milo. And breakfast was delicious."

"You're welcome. Anytime. Oh, and uh, as long as you don't have anywhere to be today, we can go have another key made tomorrow. That okay?"

"Sounds great."

CHAPTER 4

Milo

"Well?" Colby watches me from the exercise bike next to mine. "Did she show up? Everything go okay?"

Already huffing from working my legs fast and hard, I glance around the room, the rest of the guys listening in, and nod. "She did. And uh, yeah."

He narrows his eyes. "That's very loquacious of you, Milo."

"Loquacious?" I pop a brow. "Do you even know what that word means?"

"That's really all you have to say? She did, and yeah?"

"What do you want to know?"

Colby shakes his head. "Who is she? Maybe start with her name. Does she have one of those?"

Hawken, overhearing our conversation, adds, "Is she nice? Pretty? What's her story?"

"Yeah." Zeke nods. "Do you think you guys will get along all right? And what about Jada? Is she still in town?"

Adding an incline to my ride, I continue to push harder as I tell the guys what I know so far. "Her name is Charlee. Charlee Mags. And she showed up at my door with a busted face, two bags, and a couple totes of her belongings."

"Whoa, whoa, whoa." Colby frowns. "Did you say a busted face?" The guys stop their workouts to focus on me, but I can't stop myself from moving because I know deep down, if I sit still for too long, I'll have to come to terms with my feelings about the last eighteen hours or so.

"Yeah. Huge ass black eye. Looked to only be a couple days old at the most."

"What's that about?" Quinton asks.

Whatever it's about, it fucking pisses me off.

I wipe a few beads of sweat from my brow. "She said he hit her. He got one good hit."

Dex's jaw drops. "What the fuck? Who hit her? Do we know the guy?"

I shake my head. "No. She didn't say. I don't think she's necessarily tied to anyone we know. She's a friend of Jada and Daveed's who needed a place to stay while she works out her next steps."

"But she's okay?" Colby asks pensively. "I mean other than the black eye?"

"Honestly, she seems great otherwise. Independent. Doesn't want to be a bother. Has a great sense of humor..."

"And?" Dex smirks.

"And what?"

"Come on, dumbass." He rolls his eyes. "You don't think we've all noticed how hard you've been pushing yourself since you walked in here this morning? Extra mile on the treadmill. Extra push-ups and weights on the barbell and look at you now. You're a fuckin' sweaty mess. It's what we all do when we're having a less-than-great day. What has your adrenaline so high?"

I steadily slow my pace, my arms hanging over the handlebars and my head bowed.

"She's pretty, all right?"

"Pretty?" Hawken blinks.

"Like...really fucking pretty." I wipe the sweat from my forehead with the bottom of my T-shirt. "And she edits books for a living. Fucking romance books, I'm assuming, given the publishing house she works for."

"Fuck yeah!" Dex laughs and claps me on the shoulder. "The universe is finally paying you back for being such an undouchey guy, Milo!"

Colby gives me a knowing glance. At least he gets it.

"Yeah, maybe. But she's coming out of some sort of bad situation. It's not like she's looking for any kind of relationship right now. I can't start boning the pretty stranger in my apartment. And what kind of a dick would I be if I tried to make any kind of move other than just being a supportive roommate when she needs one. If she needs one. It's like I'm automatically friend-zoned."

I lean back on my bike, wiping more sweat from my face with my shirt. "I mean, hell, she may choose to keep to herself and not want to be around me much for all I know. Or she may find a place and be out in a week. We haven't really talked about anything at all yet."

"All right, so you don't make any moves right now," Dex tells me. "But I feel pretty confident you can get yourself out of the friend zone when the timing is right, if that's what you want. You're there. She's there. So, if you're interested in something in the future, then now is absofuckinglutely the time to show her the kind of guy you are. That way she'll see what she could have. What she's missing. You've got nothing to lose, so why not? Besides, solid relationships are built on firm friendships, right?"

That might be the most intuitive thing Dex has ever said.

I mull over his instructions.

He's not wrong.

I can show Charlee who I am.

I can be her friend.

Get to know as much about her as I can.

"Yeah." I nod. "I can do that."

It might be hard as fuck, figuratively and physically. Especially if she continues to wear shit like the leggings and sports bra she had on this morning. And absolutely if she continues with whatever yoga pose she was doing in front of the window.

She needs to never do that again.

But I hope she does it again.

This is at least something I can do. Be myself. Show Charlee that not all relationships are bad ones. That there are guys out there, like me, who know how to give women the respect and love they deserve.

No way is this going to be easy, but something in me won't let me give up on the idea that Charlee Mags walked into my life for a reason.

After a long day of workouts, practice, and a few quick meetings scheduled by my agent, I stop by a local eatery and pick up some roasted chicken, salads, and dessert for Charlee and me. I feel bad that I never texted to make sure my dinner idea was okay with her or check that she didn't already have other plans. I suppose I shouldn't assume she's home waiting for me or that she'll be making dinner for us like one of those rich trophy wives.

Who am I kidding? Trophy wives probably order out as much as I do.

Really, I want to do whatever I can to make Charlee's adjustment here easier. No expectations. Whatever she needs, I'm certain I can provide. Dinner is easily something I can provide.

With my gym bag over my shoulder and two takeout bags in my hands, I hit the button in the elevator for the penthouse. When I reach the top, I hear music playing inside, and it brings a smile to my face.

At least she's comfortable and making herself at home.

I unlock the door and push it open, dropping my gym bag next to my shoes. When I carry our dinner to the kitchen, I find Charlee wrapped tightly in a blue bath towel.

A tiny blue bath towel.

Barely long enough to cover her whole body, the hem of her towel sits just below her ass. I know damn well if she dropped something on the floor and had to bend over to pick it up, I would get a show like none other.

Maybe I should drop this chicken.

Stop it, Milo.

"Oh, hey!" She smiles at me over her shoulder as she releases the pitcher to the blender and pours her drink into a tall glass, like it's no big deal that she's basically naked in my kitchen and I'm standing right here.

"I wasn't sure what time you would be getting home. Just finished a quick workout. Would you like a smoothie?"

When she turns, I have to willingly stop myself from gawking. *Holy shit.*

Her towel only barely conceals her tits, her cleavage on full display. For a second, I picture myself slipping a finger into that towel and releasing those beautiful globes, palming them in my hands, kneading them. Sucking them. Tugging them between my teeth while she whispers my name.

Fuck me.

My mouth goes completely dry, and I have to lean against the kitchen island in order to hide the evidence of my excitement because, like an idiot, I wore joggers home instead of jeans. "Hey," I squeak out, sounding like a young teenage boy.

Goddamn Milo. Get a fuckin' grip.

Clearing my throat, I try again. "Hey. Sorry about that. Uh, no smoothie for me, thanks. I had one after my workout." I lift the bags of food I brought home. "But I grabbed dinner for us. I hope roasted chicken and salad is okay with you. I'm sorry, I should've called or texted first to ask."

She smiles and turns back to the cupboards, opening one of the top ones and lifting up on her tiptoes to grab a few plates and bowls. When she does, her towel lifts up even more and fucking hell, I catch a glimpse of her ass cheeks. Of course, this is my luck. Of course, there is a beautiful woman naked but for a teeny-tiny towel in my kitchen and I can't do a damn thing about it.

Well played, Universe. Well played.

"Roasted chicken sounds perfect. Let me run upstairs and put some clothes on and I'll be right back down."

"Sounds good. I'll plate this up for us."

She moves upstairs, and I take a moment to breathe and

think about everything from dead puppies to Dex's farts until my hard-on eases and I no longer have to worry about embarrassing myself in front of Charlee.

While she's upstairs, I whip my phone from my pocket and text the guys, because if I have to keep my thoughts to myself, I might actually burst.

> **Me:** I don't think I can do this. How am I supposed to do this?

> **Colby:** Do what?

> **Quinton:** What can't you do?

> **Dex:** Yes, you can, big guy. It's easy. You just...fold it in.

> **Hawken:** LOL. Dude, what does that even mean?

> **Dex:** I don't know how I can be any clearer! You just fold it in!

> **Zeke:** OMG if you say fold it in ONE more time...!

> **Me:** This isn't about Schitt's Creek, you turds!

> **Hawken:** HA! I see what you did there.

> **Colby:** What's going on?

Me: I walked in to a naked woman in my kitchen.

Quinton: WTF?

Me: Yeah. Charlee. Wrapped in a teeny-tiny towel after a shower. You guys, I saw her ass cheeks. If she had bent over...

Dex: Niiiiice.

Me: It's not nice, Dex! I can't be walking around my own apartment with a fuckin' stiffy over my house guest.

Hawken: You could rub it out really quick.

Milo: I'm supposed to be plating chicken!

Dex: Tell her you got cock instead? *smirk emoji*

Me: Fuck you very much, Dexter. That's so helpful. *eye roll emoji*

Quinton: You could fuck her and get it out of your system.

Me: No go, man. She's literally been here two days.

Colby: Well, you could either set some boundaries and ask her not to walk around the apartment in a towel or you have to take one for the team, I'm afraid.

Quinton: Was she flaunting herself at you?

Dex: Tits in your face? Giving you the old Betty Boop?

Me: No. It wasn't like that.

Quinton: Ok then. She was just out of the shower. Did she know you were coming home?

Me: No.

Quinton: Then relax man. She didn't know you would be home. She was probably equally uncomfortable but didn't want to show it. I wouldn't worry about it.

Colby: Yeah, Quinton's right. Pretend it didn't happen but keep that visual in your back pocket.

Me: Pretty sure it's staying in my front pocket for life if you know what I mean. Ugh.

> **Dex:** Ding ding! New spank bank level acquired.

> **Me:** *eye roll emoji* Hey where did Zeke go?

> **Colby:** Don't know. He wasn't himself at practice. Probably home snuggling with his kid.

> **Me:** Right. Gotta run. Thanks guys.

I finally get our dinners plated and find us each a napkin and silverware just before Charlee comes down the stairs. "Smells great down here. I'm starving."

"Good. It's all ready for you."

I turn to hand her a plate and see her looking fresh and dry in black sweatpants and a pink T-shirt. Clearly though, she's not wearing a bra, as her hardened nipples are poking into the fabric and sticking out at me like two switches on a fuse box aching to be flicked up and down and up and down and dammit.

If every day is like this, I am fucked.

CHAPTER 5

Charlee

"Well, if this hasn't been a whirlwind couple of days," I mumble to myself. Sipping the coffee from my mug, I step into the living room and sink into the oversized chair, my eyes taking in everything around me. In all that was going on the last couple nights, I didn't take much time to properly look around at where I've landed. Closing my eyes for a moment, I take a deep breath and give thanks for Jada for making this liberating trip with me, for Daveed who called in a massive favor, and for Milo for simply saying yes.

Jared won't even be home until tomorrow.

Part of me wishes I could be a fly on the wall when he gets home and sees that I'm gone and left him no way to find me. He'll assume I'm with Jada and Daveed and that will undoubtedly be the first place he looks, but I trust my friends with my life. He won't get anything out of them.

I wonder how he'll react.

Will he panic?

Will he celebrate?

Will he care at all?

I suppose he'll have to at some point.

His reputation precedes him when it comes to his past relationships. He hasn't been seen in the best light in terms of how he treats women, but for some insane reason, I thought I would be different.

I thought I would be the one to change him.

But I was wrong.

And though he may pretend everything is hunky-dory for a short time, eventually, he'll have to deal with the fallout of yet another failed relationship.

His agent won't be happy.

His coach won't be happy.

The media will eat at him for weeks.

Part of me wishes it would destroy him, because he deserves every bit of shit that gets thrown his way. But the rational part of me knows that, regardless of what he goes through, I'm finally done.

I'm permanently out.

I was strong enough to walk away.

Throwing all my shit in a couple of totes and bags wasn't my original plan, but once his fist landed on my face, knocking me into the wall, I knew I could never look Jada in the eye and tell her everything was fine.

She reads me like a book.

And I don't like lying.

"Charlee Mags, you are one strong motherfucker, and I'm proud of you." I bring my mug to my mouth once again, feeling the warmth of its contents flow down my throat as I look around Milo's living room.

It's a cleaner space than I would've anticipated from a professional athlete, but then again, Jared had a housekeeper. Perhaps Milo does too. Everything about this place flows—from the chrome kitchen appliances to the gray sectional, white walls, and black balcony banisters. For an added touch of color, there is a red couch upstairs and red upholstered chairs line the black dining room table.

There's definitely a masculine vibe in here, but I like it. It's clean and modern, but comfortable. There are several pictures downstairs that I can only assume are of his family. A couple, I assume are Milo's parents, hangs in the center, with a collage of prints surrounding it. There's one of Milo with two kids, and there's another one next to it with the same two kids and, I'm guessing, their parents. Taking a closer look at that family picture, I remember Jada telling me Milo has a sister. This must be her. She shares many similar features to Milo.

"Niece and nephew, perhaps." He's clearly a family man and that makes me smile.

Having seen all the rooms downstairs, it dawns on me he never showed us his own room. I know it has to be the room next to mine because it's the only door he never opened when he was giving us a tour. It's probably a huge invasion of his privacy, but I'm alone in Milo Landric's luxury penthouse while he's in a few promo meetings this morning, and, well, curiosity hasn't killed the cat yet, I don't think.

But wait.

Are there cameras in here?

Could he be watching me right now?

If he sees me heading straight to his room now that he's not here, that could look very bad for me. Taking my empty coffee mug back to the kitchen, I sweep the area with my eyes, looking for any sign of a camera and then laugh to myself when I find no evidence of one.

"He would never risk someone hacking into an in-home camera," I remind myself. "They're normal people when they're off the ice."

Shaking my head at my own audacity, I purposefully climb the stairs and head past my bedroom to the next closed door. Tiny butterflies flutter in my stomach. I know I shouldn't be doing this, but I'm human and I can't help myself. I squeeze my eyes closed as I turn the doorknob, praying that some odd alarm doesn't go off and start shouting, "Intruder! Intruder! Get the fuck away from my stuff!" I don't need to be peeing my pants in fear today.

Slowly peeking into the room, I realize no alarm bells are ringing and no lasers are shooting across the floor, so I push the door fully open and gaze upon Milo's sanctuary. The same floor-to-ceiling windows take up the far wall, leading to a decent-sized balcony, but his room is obviously a corner room of the penthouse because there are also full-length windows to my left. With charcoal painted walls, silver sheath curtains shading the windows, and a king-sized bed with bedding in multiple shades of gray, the room should have a dark, dungeon-like feel, but the effect is the opposite. Perhaps it's the warm lighting, or the color of the wood flooring, or even the two green plants in the corner that offsets the darkened walls and bedding. Instead of dark and cold, the room has a calming appeal.

Plush.

Peaceful.

And damn it smells good in here. A mixture of freshly cleaned blankets and whatever cologne or aftershave Milo uses.

I'm impressed by the feel of his room, and when my eye catches a bookcase next to his bed, I'm intrigued.

Milo reads?

Curious, I step over to a set of books on the shelf, one set of book spines looking familiar. A slow smile spreads across my face when I pull the first of the set down to look at it.

"Milo reads romance?" And not just any romance, but one I actually edited! I mean, the book doesn't list me as the editor because I'm under the publishing company's name, but still. I know I edited this book.

Is it weird that Milo reads romance?

A professional hockey player?

A dude?

Yeah. It's a little weird, but only because I've never known a guy to sit and relax with a smutty romance book before.

"They should though," I murmur. "Would do them some good."

I finger through the other books on his shelf that range in genre from romantic comedies to mysteries, to historical biographies, and I'm seriously fascinated. Out of all the professional athletes I've met over the years, I can't say I've seen many of them with a book in their hands.

So, what makes Milo Landric so different?

Hopefully, I'll find out in the coming days, weeks, or however long it takes me to figure out what I'm doing with myself now that I'm here.

The first book I took off his shelf still in my hand, I open it to what I remember as my favorite chapter and read a couple pages. The story comes back to me quickly, and I laugh all over again at the scene where Chett delivers a purple box to Arya—who doesn't think he knows that the box contains a vibrating dildo called *The Oblivion*. Unbeknownst to her, Chett does know what's in the box because it's his sister's business Arya purchased it from, and he sees the boxes all the time. So, on his way to his delivery truck, he tells Arya to have a good night and winks at her, and that's when she knows that he knows.

After I read through the chapter, I sit down on Milo's bed, noting its softness compared to the guest bed I sleep on, and then skip around to some of my other favorite chapters in the book. Like the ones titled *Caution! Sticky Flaps!*, *Fanny Packs and Bird Attacks*, and *My Vagina Sounds Like John Stamos*. God, I loved this book. As any avid reader does, I get lost in the pages of the book, and my eyes grow heavy. I know I should get up, but I don't want to stop reading.

And that's the last thing I remember before my eyes close and I drift off to sleep.

When I open my eyes again, the book I was reading is resting on the bedside table, and my body is covered with a fluffy gray blanket patterned with hockey sticks. My first thought is how cute it is that Milo has a hockey throw blanket in his bedroom, but then my second thought steamrolls right over the first and smacks me in the face.

I didn't cover myself up with this blanket.

Which means somebody else did.

My body stiffens as I try to listen for noise coming from the penthouse, but then I raise my head to look at the door and find it partially closed.

"Shit."

"Shit. Shit. Shit."

I fly off the bed, cringing at myself and my stupid decisions. I didn't mean to fall asleep in here, obviously, but I shouldn't have even been in here to begin with. Ugh. And now Milo is home and he's been in here and he's seen me asleep on his bed and what the ever-loving fuck am I going to say to him?

"Hey, sorry I fell asleep in your room, but damn did it smell good in there."

"Sorry I peeked in your room. Who knew you read smut?"

"I wanted to know what your bed felt like. I swear I'm not a creep."

Ugh. No. I can't say any of those things to him and now I'm slightly panicking and embarrassed as hell. I glance at the clock that reads two in the afternoon and my eyes nearly bulge out of my head.

"I've been sleeping that long?" I whisper to myself. "Shit!"

Quietly placing the book I was reading back on the shelf, I fold the blanket Milo laid over me and softly tiptoe my way to my own room, praying I don't run into him. At least, not until I figure out what the hell I'm going to say. I click my door closed and grab a comfy hoodie to throw over the sports bra I was wearing for yoga this morning. I brush my teeth one more time and then run a brush through my bedhead before tossing it all up in a messy bun.

I guess that will have to do for now.

Standing at my door, I take a few deep breaths to calm my nerves before I head downstairs.

"It's no big deal, Mags. Just be honest."

And if all else fails, try to cry and tell him your black eye was hurting.

Sympathy points.

Pulling up my big girl pants, I swing open my door and head down the stairs. Milo's voice can be heard from the kitchen area.

"An eyeball fairy, huh?"

A little girl's voice comes through his iPad. "Uh-huh! She

takes your eyeball for you whenever it falls out and...and then she puts it in a flashlight so when people can't see because they lose their eyes, the eyeball fairy can give them new eyes!"

"Wow! That is really awesome of the eyeball fairy to help people like that."

"Yeah, and Mommy said I can draw you a picture of the eyeball fairy, so she's getting me a snack and then I'm gonna draw you one."

"Sophie, I cannot wait to see your drawing. You know what I'll do with it?"

"What?"

"I'm going to hang it up on my fridge so I can always see her and then I'll always smile when I'm in the kitchen."

Milo notices my movement in the living room. His eyes meet mine before he goes back to looking at his iPad screen.

"Hey, Sophie, I have to get going, so you enjoy your snack and then you draw me the best picture of the eyeball fairy you can, okay?"

"Okay."

"And can you do something else for me?"

"What?"

"Give your mom a hug and your little brother a kiss for me, okay?"

"Okay. Bye Uncle Lo!"

"See you later, Sophie."

He disconnects from his call and sets his iPad on the counter. "Hey, Goldilocks. How are you feeling?"

That comment alone breaks away some of the mortification I'm feeling. Shaking my head, I huff out a quiet laugh, covering my face in my hands. "Damn. I guess I deserved that one, huh? I'm so sorry, Milo."

He frowns as he nears the couch and sits next to me. "Sorry for what?"

"For totally invading your privacy. I swear to God, I'm not a creeper by nature, and I did not walk in there planning to fall asleep on your bed. I was just... Ugh, it was the only room you didn't show me before, and I was curious what it looked like. Then I saw the books on your shelf and oh, my God, you read romance! And not only do you read romance, you have Smooch on your shelf, and I edited that book! I loved it! It's now one of my favorites. So, I opened it and started reading some of my favorite parts and then the next thing I knew I was waking up covered with a blanket that I had never seen before, and I'm so sorry, and if you want me to leave, I completely understand." I'm nearly out of breath after all that.

"Whoa. That escalated fast." He chuckles. "First of all, I would never kick you out, so get that thought out of your head right now. You're not going anywhere. Secondly, don't be so hard on yourself."

"Milo—"

"No, I'm sorry too. I should've shown you my room the other night. It's no big deal. I don't have anything to hide, and I wasn't trying to keep anyone out. I apologize if I gave you that impression."

"You didn't." I shake my head. "I was being...obnoxiously curious."

"Well, for what it's worth, you looked way too peaceful when I found you. I wasn't about to wake you. Whatever you've been through," he says, glancing again at my black eye that of course looks worse as it heals. "You deserved some peace and quiet. I'm glad you were able to relax."

"Honestly? I don't think I've napped that long in years. I guess I needed it more than I thought I did."

"Good. You feeling okay?"

"Yeah, actually. Other than needing a shower later tonight, I feel refreshed. And I don't know if anyone has ever told you this, but your bed is perfect. Not too hard. Not too soft. It's just right."

"Ah." He grins, nudging my shoulder with his. "So, you are a real-life Goldilocks."

"Yeah, I guess I am." My smile broadens and I let out a laugh.

"Maybe I should dye my hair blonde, huh?"

"Hell no," he answers with no hesitation. "I mean...you know, your hair looks great as it is."

"Thanks, Milo." I glance down feeling a bit awkward, and try to come up with a change of subject. "So, that was your niece on the phone earlier? I wasn't eavesdropping, but I heard her call you Uncle Lo."

"Sophie? Oh, yeah. She's one of my sister's kids. The cutest little pip-squeak. She started kindergarten this year. Usually, the kids FaceTime me once or twice a week. It's a way for me to stay involved in their lives, especially when the team is on the road."

Does he not have any flaws?

"A nice guy and a family man. How is it you're single?"

Milo groans, wiping his hand down his face, but his smile doesn't fade, so at least I know I'm not offending him. "You're not the first person to ask me that. My sister asks me all the time."

"Hey, at least someone is looking out for you."

"Yeah, I guess. And to answer your question, I don't really know. I suppose I haven't found the right partner yet. But when I find her...I'll know." His eyes meet mine, and for the slightest nanosecond, something in my chest flips, but I swiftly swallow away the sensation.

"Our schedule keeps us pretty busy anyway." He shrugs. "I'm not sure it would be fair to ask a girlfriend or a wife to wait for me, you know? We're on the road for several days, sometimes weeks at a time. And then to bring kids into the mix?" He shakes his head. "I don't know how my buddies do it."

"So, you want kids?"

"Eventually, yeah. I'd love a big family. Seeing my sister get married and start a family, those were proud moments for me. I was so excited for her. Happy for her." He picks at nonexistent lint on his jeans. "Maybe when my hockey days are over, I can have the same thing. I would never ask my wife to raise our kids by herself. I want to be there right along with her."

"You'll be a great dad one day. I have no doubt." I smile, even though on the inside, I feel an overwhelming sense of emptiness.

Loneliness.

Frustration with the hand I was dealt.

Disappointment that my life ended up this way.

But grateful that I'm alive all the same.

It's an odd pairing of emotions, for sure.

At a loss for words, I stare off across the room. Silence falling between us.

Finally, Milo nudges my shoulder. "Hey. You okay over there? You got quiet all of a sudden."

I nod. "Yeah."

My phone dings with an incoming message.

"Yeah, I'm good."

I reach for my phone, my body stiffening when I see who it is.

Jared: Did you forget my mother was coming for the weekend? She says you're not there. Where the fuck are you, Charlene?

"Fuck," I murmur.

"Is everything okay?"

"Uh...yeah. It will be. But I'm going to need a new phone, stat." I glance at Milo, his brows furrowed. "Think you can help me with that? I need him to not have my number or be able to trace my phone."

Understanding exactly what I'm saying without having to ask questions, Milo stands. "We can go right fucking now, Charlee. Whatever you need. Whatever helps you feel safe."

I do feel safe.

He gives me a hand off the couch and then grabs his keys from the kitchen counter. "While we're out, if there's anything else you need, we'll get it too."

"Thank you, Milo." I slip my feet into a pair of tennis shoes by the door and grab my coat. "Wait!" My eyes bulge, well...one of them does, and my shoulders fall. "My eye."

Milo rests a hand on my shoulder, assessing the potential problem. "What about it?"

"If we're spotted out in public, it could be bad for you."

He frowns. "What? What do you mean?"

"Do you really want tomorrow's headlines to be about you beating up women? Because that's what people will think."

"I don't give a flying fuck what anyone thinks." He shakes his head. "Don't worry about me, okay? I'm a big guy. I can take whatever comes at me. Besides, I know where to go to be low profile, and I'll wear a hat. Nobody will know it's me."

I cock my head and give him a doubtful expression. He's Milo Landric. Everyone knows who he is. But he doesn't know that I know how famous he is in the hockey world. Because to him, I don't know much about hockey at all.

"Do you trust me?" he asks, slipping on his gloves.

"Of course, I trust you."

And it's true.

Though I've only known him a short time, I trust him completely.

"Then let's get out of here and have some fun. You've got to be hungry since you slept through lunch. If you like Chinese, I know just the place. It's a hole-in-the-wall little dive, but it's the best Chinese food I've ever had. Nobody will notice us in there."

I take a deep breath and let it out with as much of a smile as I can produce. "Sounds perfect."

CHAPTER 6

Milo

"Oh my God, this might be the best thing I have put in my mouth in a very long time."

I stifle a laugh at Charlee's comment. A small blob of sweet and sour sauce rests in the corner of her mouth. The part of me attracted to her wants so badly to reach out and wipe it away, but I fist my hand in my lap instead. The last thing I want to do is embarrass her.

Or come on to her.

"Well, it's not our famous Chicago deep dish, but Wong's is one of our favorite places for takeout. When Daveed was still with the Red Tails, he couldn't get enough."

"Now that you mention it, I think Daveed has talked about this place before. I'll have to let him know you brought me here."

"He'll be jealous as hell. Fair warning."

She grins. "Even better."

"So, how did you meet Daveed and Jada?"

"Oh, it was Jada I met first. She joined my yoga class and constantly bitched about having to contort her body into awkward positions that never led to a happy ending...as she so eloquently put it."

Fucking hell. I nearly choke on my drink.

Charlee laughs. "And we quickly became best friends."

I wipe my chin with my napkin. "I apologize. I guess I never thought of yoga as an aphrodisiac."

That's a lie.

I was thinking about it yesterday when I saw her ass in the air doing that bird stunt in my living room.

"Right?" She giggles. "I hadn't either until she walked into my life. Jada has a way with words."

"Oh, I know. The woman's got spunk, that's for damn sure. She kept on top of Daveed like nobody's business."

"Yeah, she's pretty great."

Charlee's gaze settles on me, and for once, I'm fucking speechless. Like, I can't string a group of words together to form a sentence. She's so pretty, and though I want to do nothing but stare at her face, studying every detail from the tiny mole under her good eye to the dimple in her right cheek when she smiles, I can't come across like some sort of lovesick puppy.

She sips her soda through her straw, and then lowers her cup, grinning at me. "So, tell me about you. I feel like I've done a lot of talking."

Phew. I'll take the save.

"What would you like to know?"

"Everything," she answers. "What's your favorite food?"

"Nachos."

She quirks a brow. "Nachos?"

"Yeah. With the works. The meat, all the gooey cheese, salsa, sour cream, and jalapeños on top. I don't get to eat it very often, but when I do, I'll devour it."

"All right, favorite animal?"

"Golden retriever."

"Oh, so not just a dog in general, but a golden retriever specifically?"

I nod. "Goldens are big floofers. Loyal, friendly, and easygoing. Great family pets and wonderful support animals."

Her face softens a bit, and she nods approvingly. "Do you identify with golden retrievers?"

I shrug, not giving it much thought. "Yeah. Sure. But I'm like the sexiest goddamn golden retriever. I'm not the wild retriever who jumps into every mud puddle with that crazed look in his eye."

She covers her mouth as she giggles. "All right. I guess we'll see about that one. Umm...ooh, I've got one for you."

"All right, let's hear it."

"Who was your teenage crush?"

I sit back in my seat, my eyes narrowing as I think. "I had three. Natalie Portman, Emma Stone, and Mila Kunis."

"Have you ever met any of them?"

"Nope." I shake my head. "Well, I was at a charity event not too long ago and Emma Stone was there, but I didn't take the chance to meet her."

"You didn't take the chance? Why not?"

"Do you ever hear people say sometimes you should never meet your heroes because you'll find out they're just normal, like you, and it's such a letdown that you don't consider them heroes anymore?"

She tilts her head. "Yeah."

"That's why. What if one of them is a diva or some mean-ass bitch in real life? I don't want to know that. It's okay for me to just say I thought about them in my bedroom on several occasions as a teenage boy and leave it at that."

What the fuck.

I shake my head. "Sorry. I think I forgot who I was talking to. I shouldn't have said that."

"Are you kidding? This is great information that I will save for a rainy day." She smirks. "Besides, if there's a grown man out there who didn't jack off as a teenager to the thought of some hot celebrity, I have yet to meet him."

"You kind of look like Mila Kunis, actually."

Her eyes narrow. "Are we talking like *That 70s Show* Mila, or more like *Black Swan* Mila?"

"*Black Swan* Mila was hot as fuck."

"I would have to agree with you there." She laughs. "I'm pretty damn sure she made every straight woman on this earth question their sexuality. *Black Swan* Mila, I am not."

Leaning forward on the table, I make sure I'm close enough

so she can hear me. "Charlee, you give Black Swan Mila a run for her money, and she pays millions to look like that. Plus, as far as I'm concerned, you're every bit the badass she is. Don't sell yourself short."

Her smile fades momentarily as her doe eyes stare back at me. "That's very nice of you to say."

I grab my drink and take a long sip. "Something else you should know about me, Charlee."

"Okay."

"I don't lie."

"What on earth is that?" Charlee all but guffaws when I walk into the living room wearing my favorite old sweatshirt. A Lakers-purple hoodie with a giant appliqué of Wile E. Coyote on the front. I tug on the bottom, glancing down at it.

"What?"

She covers her mouth. "I'm sorry. I totally shouldn't be laughing. That is not a sweatshirt I would've pictured you in or thought you would ever have in your inventory of apparel."

I shrug, lifting my hands out to the side. "Who doesn't like Wile E. Coyote? He's a classic. And this is my most comfortable and favorite sweatshirt of all time." I gesture to the sleeves. "Holes and tears at the wrists, and a hole or two on my sleeve, but I'll have you know this sweatshirt has been well loved over the years. This sweatshirt? It knows me."

"Oh, it knows you."

"That's right. This sweatshirt has seen some shit. This Wile E. and me?" I cross my fingers. "We're tight. I mean, this guy reveals no secrets. I'm just sayin'."

"It's very...purply." She sucks in her lips so she doesn't laugh too hard, but I see the jovial glint in her eyes.

I cock my head and challenge her. "I'm sorry. Would you tell LeBron James that his uniform is very purply?"

"Who's LeBron James again?"

My jaw drops.

Literally.

Like, on the floor.

Charlee lets out a belly laugh, and it's the greatest sound. "I'm totally kidding. I know who LeBron is, and hell yes, I would tell him. I'd be like, Hey! L. James! Your uniform is too purply, yo! Go put the yellow one back on."

Now she has me laughing.

I point my finger at her. "You're on. Someday in the future, I'm getting us courtside seats to a Lakers game, and you're telling LeBron James that his uniform is too purply."

"That's fine. Can you make sure we're sitting next to a hot celebrity, though? I know how much they like courtside seats."

She winks and I huff out an audible gasp. "Uhh, hello! Earth to Charlee. I am a hot celebrity. Do you not see how amazing I look in this hella fine retro statement piece?"

"Retro statement piece!" She cackles as I twirl for her, my hands running down my sides as I show off my hot, frumpy look.

Her hands come together in applause, and she whistles her approval. "Milo Landric, you are one fine piece of meat in that outfit." She holds up her phone and takes my picture. "If you ever create an online dating profile, puh-lease use this picture. You and Wile E. Coyote will bring all the girls to the yard."

Nice of her to say, but I don't think I want all the girls in my yard.

I kind of just want Charlee.

Me: I don't know what I did to deserve this, but I think I've set myself up to live in my own personal hell.

Colby: Uh oh. That can't be good. What happened?

Dex: She walking around your penthouse buck-ass naked now?

Me: No. *eye roll emoji* But she did sleep in my bed and now it smells like her.

Zeke: *eyeballs emoji* She's only been there for a short time, and you have her sleeping in your bed already? I thought you were taking this slow?

Quinton: I don't know, Milo. I hope you know what you're doing.

Me: You guys, she was asleep on my bed when I got home from my promo meeting, reading one of my books! She actually edited it by the way, because she indeed edits romance books for a living.

Hawken: So, let me get this straight. This hot girl is living with you for an unknown amount of time, she edits romance books... the kind you like to read, AND you found her asleep in your bed when you got home, but you can't make any moves because she has baggage.

Me: Ugh. That about sums it up, yep. Also, she didn't sleep IN my bed. Just ON my bed...if that makes any difference.

Colby: I guess it does a little.

Dex: Nope. No difference. She Goldilocksed her way into your room and napped in your bed, dude. That's kinda hot.

Me: Tell me about it! I covered her up when I found her and let her sleep. Also, she fucking teased me about my favorite sweatshirt, and her laugh is like...one of the best sounds I've ever heard.

Colby: Anyone would tease you for that old rag. I can't believe you wore that monstrosity in front of her. #nerdalert

Me: Hey, fuck nugget, you have no room to judge. Does Carissa even know about the Hooters T-shirt from your twenty-first birthday?

Colby: We don't talk about that T-shirt.

Me: Correction. YOU don't talk about it. But WE will talk about it for the rest of our lives. How many people have walked into a Hooters and walked out with one of the server's T-shirts right off her back? Your wife would be pissed to learn you still have it.

Dex: LOL. Now THAT is a challenge I can get behind!

Me: Anyway, so that's the predicament I'm in. I don't see myself sleeping much tonight.

Colby: You'll be fine. Run plays in your head until you fall asleep.

Quinton: It's not like you're in love with the girl, Milo. She's a pretty woman sleeping in your apartment. Many people could fit that bill. Your sister. Dex's sister. My sister. Carissa. Think of it that way and you'll be fine.

I guess he has a point. If I think about Charlee like she's another member of the family, maybe I won't be so attracted to her.

But she's not my sister.

She's not Dex's sister.

She's not Quinton's sister.

She's Charlee.

And her scent is all over my blankets. Vanilla mixed with some sort of fruity scent. Strawberry? Nah, that's not it. Peach? I don't know. It could be fucking kiwi, and I wouldn't know or care.

It smells amazing whatever it is.

So, for the first night in a fucking long time, I pull my blanket up to my face as I roll over, surrounding myself in her scent, and peacefully fall asleep.

CHAPTER 7

Charlee

"Well, how are you adjusting to Chicago? Is Milo being a gentleman?"

I smile, hearing my best friend's voice on the line. "Well, first week down, and everything has been relatively smooth so far. Except for falling asleep in his bed within the first couple days of my being here and the angry text from Jared when his mom came to town and couldn't find me. Milo was great about helping me out, so, new phone, who dis?"

Jada laughs. "That's right, asshole. She don't have time for your sorry ass no more. But let's back this truck up, sis, because what the hell you doin' sleeping in Milo's bed? Did he make a move? Do I need to slap him around a little? Or, you know, maybe congratulate him?"

"What?! No! He's been a perfect gentleman... Though I've caught him staring a few times."

"Uh, duh. I would be surprised if he hadn't. He's a man, and you're a fine-ass woman, *Charlee Mags*." She emphasizes my name. I'm sure it's taking a little getting used to for her as much as it has me.

"Well, anyway, I got too curious and wanted to peek in his room while he was at practice, so I did. And he reads romance books, Jada! One of the books I edited was on his shelf. My favorite one! So, I started reading it and sat down on his bed, and next thing I knew I was waking up covered in a throw blanket that I absolutely did not put there."

"Aww, he covered you up? That's so sweet of him. I totally forgot Milo reads romance books." She snickers. "I'll have to remind Daveed. He always teased Milo about his reading preferences."

"It's weird, Jada. Milo is the exact opposite of Jared. He's so..."

Compassionate.

Nice.

Friendly.

Comfortable.

"Chill. Like, he's easy to talk to. Easy to be around."

"Uh-huh," she says. "Easy to look at. Easy to drool over."

I chuckle softly because she's not wrong. "Okay, you might be right about that, but I just left my live-in boyfriend. The last thing I need is to start something with someone I barely know."

She's quiet for a moment and then explains, "You know him better than you would any guy you would meet in a bar or online."

True.

"All I'm saying is, he's not the worst guy in the world to end up with. Milo is a teddy bear of a man. He would treat you right or die trying."

"Jada, you know they're going to face-off before the season is over, right? If Jared finds out I'm living with Milo or that I even know him, he could make that game a painful one for the whole team. He's already tried to contact me on Facebook, Instagram, and through my email. I had to block him on every platform I could think of. I need to get my ass in gear and find my own place, whether that means here in Chicago or somewhere else. I don't want to be Milo's responsibility. That's not good for his game, either. He's used to doing his own thing."

"Has he not been doing his own thing?"

"He goes to practice, and his games and meetings, obviously. His agent keeps him relatively busy with sponsorship stuff, but when he's not busy, he's here. With me. I get the impression he doesn't want to leave me alone."

"Because he doesn't trust you?"

"No, no. I think it's more that he feels the need to make sure I feel safe."

Jada doesn't say anything to that, and I roll my eyes, knowing exactly what she's thinking.

"Okay, I can practically feel you smiling over there."

She squeals playfully. "I mean, come on. It's so cute! He wants to protect you."

"I don't need protection. I'm not a damsel in distress, Jada. Jared hit me one freaking time, and I was done."

"Yes, and I'm proud of you for that, you know that. But let's not forget how long he'd been an asshole to you before that hit happened."

Ugh.

She has a point.

"Okay, I get what you're saying."

"I'm not trying to push you into Milo's arms or anything. And this isn't me saying you need a man to be happy, because you don't. But out of all the guys I could possibly recommend to you, Milo could very well be the perfect one. So, while you may be telling yourself you don't think you're ready for another relationship, what I'm saying is, leave the door open. If you walk through it, you walk through it, but if you slam it shut and lock it up tight, you could miss a great opportunity. You deserve a happy ending at some point."

"He wants a family. Did I tell you that?"

"Milo?"

"Yeah. He's a big family guy."

"And that's a bad thing because...?"

A heavy sigh escapes my mouth. "You know why."

"Uh, no. I don't. You'll be the perfect mother one day, Charlene—Charlee. Sorry. Stop looking for flaws."

I huff out a laugh. "The man has zero flaws as far as I can tell. Seriously, he's like...walking perfection. It's almost disturbing."

She chuckles. "Yeah, well, you know those guys and their gym routines. At least Milo still has all his teeth."

"Ha! I guess that's true." Visions of Jared, smiling with a missing front tooth, swim through my mind. "I don't know what my happy ending looks like right now. I just know I'm happy being away from Jared. That asshole can rot in hell for all I care."

"That's the spirit!" Jada giggles. "I hope he gets himself full-body checked tonight. Serves him right."

"Trust me, once Milo finds out he's the mystery ex, I have a feeling he'll want to be the one to do it."

"Yes, that's right. I work from home, so I'm mostly interested in two bedrooms or even studio spaces large enough to have some sort of separate workspace."

"I see," the man on the other end of the line says with a thick Southern drawl, which is a bit shocking, given we're in Chicago. "I think I got wha'cher lookin' for. The house might be a little hard to find, but just look for the corner where the All Saints Graveyard and the sewage treatment plant meet. The house will be just down on the right. Now, I've got to go get some of them traps for vermin so you have a clean place to be, but I can meet you there tomorrow morning."

Vermin?

My face scrunches in disgust as the door to the penthouse opens. Milo walks in, tossing his gym bag on the bench inside.

"Uhh, on second thought, Mr. Flim, I think I'll pass. Thank you for your time."

I don't even give the man a chance to respond before hanging up, even more frustrated than I was when I started making calls this morning.

Milo takes a long sip from his water bottle, noting the irritation on my face.

"What was that about?"

"Nothing now," I tell him. "I called this guy about a house he put up for rent online."

"Yeah?"

"Yeah, he said it's hard to find, but if I look for the sewage treatment plant and the All Saints Graveyard, I'll find it. Oh, and he has to go get a bunch of vermin traps to clean the place up first."

Milo's brow arches "Vermin?"

"You heard me correctly."

"He didn't say what kind of vermin, specifically?"

I almost laugh. "Does it even matter? I'm not living in a place that has to be cleaned of disgusting pests before I move in." My body quivers. "Just the thought gives me the heebie-jeebies."

Milo laughs. "You know you can stay here as long as you need, right? I'm not kicking you out."

"I appreciate that. I do, but I don't want to rely on someone's generosity for too long, you know? I don't want to overstay my welcome. I came out here to get a new start. I just have to find the right place for the right price."

"Well, there's plenty of time, so don't feel like you have to rush into it. You're welcome here." His stare is almost pleading.

"Do you think..." I start as he climbs the stairs toward his room. He stops midway and glances down at me.

"Do I think what?"

"Do you think you might be willing to help me? I mean, when you can, that is." I lift my shoulder. "It might be nice having someone go with me to look at a few places."

He doesn't hesitate. "Of course, I'll help you. Whatever you want."

"Thanks, Milo."

"Sure. Anything you need."

I rock back on my heels, not sure what to do next. "So, what are your plans for the night? Have a hot date?"

There's something about his shy smile that makes my insides happy. "Why would I go out with someone I don't know when I can hang here with you? I mean, that is, unless you have plans."

"Nope. No plans here. Figured maybe I would relax and watch a movie or binge-watch something on Netflix."

"That sounds perfect. Want to get uncomfortably full on takeout that's completely bad for us, but love every minute of it?"

I return his cheeky grin. "I'm so in."

"Perfect." He nods. "I'll order food. You decide what we're watching."

Narrowing my eyes, I tap my chin and wonder out loud, "What would he say if I picked something like *Little Women*?"

Milo laughs. "I would say go for it, but if a dog dies in the movie and I end my night sobbing, I might never forgive you."

"No dying dogs. Hard limit for Milo. Got it."

He orders food and then joins me on the couch as I scroll through Netflix to find something to watch that would appeal to both of us.

"Ooh, 'You had me at hello,'" he says, quoting *Jerry Maguire* when it shows up on the menu. "That's always a good one."

"Ooh but look, what about *You've Got Mail*, when Meg Ryan's character says 'I wanted it to be you. I wanted it to be you so badly.'"

"Wow." Milo laughs. "Are we horribly weird because we remember sappy romance quotes?"

"What? Hell no! Romance is my job. Besides, it's good to remember good quotes. Never know when they might come in handy."

"That sounds like a challenge."

"Dude, this is a game I can win easily, so you better mean it if you decide to play."

A slow smirk spreads across his face. "All right, Mags. I'm in."

I give him a nod. "It's your turn then."

"So, we're just seeing who can recite a popular quote from any romantic show or movie?"

"Yep. First one to not come up with one loses."

He considers it for a minute and takes a look at the Netflix screen on the television. "Oh, how about 'The greatest thing you'll ever learn is just to love and be loved in return.' *Moulin Rouge*."

I swoon. "Ooh, that movie makes me cry. Okay, okay, ummm...let me think." I narrow my eyes at Milo and recite my favorite quote from *Bridgerton* Season Two. "You are the bane of my existence...and the object of all my desires."

He wags his finger at me. "That's a good one. Hot!"

I press my hand to my chest. "Seriously, it makes me swoon every time. To watch him deny his feelings for her time after time and then finally tell her how he feels. Ugh! It was so great. Such a great scene."

"All right, my turn. Hmm, how can I beat a *Bridgerton* quote?" He snaps his fingers. "Okay, so it's not super sexy but how about when Meredith Grey pleads to Derek, 'Pick me. Choose me. Love me.'"

I pretend to stab myself in the chest. "Argh! And then he doesn't choose her right then, and it's gut-wrenching!"

"Agreed. Even my super-manly romance-loving heart kind of shattered in that episode."

"Right? She redeems herself though with the prom episode. That was by far the best Meredith and Derek scene of them all. That scene was hot!"

"Yeah, but then Denny happened."

"Oh God." I grab my heart. "I totally forgot about Denny. Dammit. Shonda Rhimes definitely knows how to do romance." I notice another great movie title on the Netflix menu and jump up from the couch pointing it out. "Oh, but *Notting Hill* is one of my all-time favorites too." Turning toward Milo, I give him my best Julia Roberts impression and recite my favorite quote, even though I'm out of turn.

"I'm just a girl, standing in front of a boy, asking him to love her."

Milo stands, watching me intently, his eyes focused on mine until his gaze drops to my feet and slowly moves up my body. He swallows hard when he gets to my lips, and I wonder what he could possibly be thinking.

Oh, my God, is he going to kiss me?

He moistens his lips with the tip of his tongue and then pulls his bottom lip between his teeth.

Holy shit, I think he is.

He is going to kiss me.

He inches closer to me, his eyes flitting between my eyes and my mouth. My heart rate jumps the closer he gets. God, I can smell him, and it's taking all the control I have not to close my eyes and inhale him. He starts to open his mouth, like he's about to say something, when there's a knock on the door. Startled, as if he's coming out of a trance, he steps back.

"You win." He winks. "That'll be our food."

Oh my God, that was close.

Would he have gone through with it had the doorbell not rung?

Would I have let him?

Hell yes, I would have let him do just about anything.

We end our night with a binging of Stranger Things and gorging on tacos, chips, guacamole, and queso until we can barely breathe.

Kiss or no kiss, it's a perfect night in.

My first week or so here has gone incredibly smoothly thanks to Milo's kindness and hospitality. He's not home a good portion of the time as his schedule keeps him rather busy, be it practices, games, or promo obligations. It can get a bit lonely, but when he's not working, he's always here with me, and I've enjoyed hanging out with him more than I anticipated. He makes everything comfortable.

And safe.

I'm working on another round of book edits when the penthouse door swings open and Milo walks in. He tosses his duffel bag against the wall by the door as he always does and toes his shoes off.

"Hey, Goldilocks."

"Hey. How was practice?"

"Great. Hit the gym this morning and outran Colby. Watched

a few takes from our game the other night, then ran through a few new plays. Then I had to video conference with my agent for a bit and did a few interviews for Carissa."

"Who's Carissa?"

"She's our social media marketing guru. Always getting us involved in some sort of Instagram post or a wacky TikTok video."

"Ah, yes. Sounds like a busy day."

"Hey, speaking of Carissa, a bunch of us are hanging out at Colby and Carissa's tonight. When we have a short stretch like this, we get together and play video games or something ridiculous, but fun. Keeps us out of the public eye and out of trouble."

"Trouble?" I cock a brow. "Are your friends a group of rabble-rousers?"

"Well, I can't speak for all of us, because I'm all for a good book and a comfy chair, but there are some of us who prefer more of a party atmosphere. And when that happens, anything can go wrong, landing the team on the front page of the paper. And not for good reasons."

"Ah. I see."

"Yeah. So, Mario Kart or some equally obnoxious video game it is. But we usually have a good time."

"Okay. Have fun."

"No." He stops smiling. "Sorry, I should've made myself clearer. I was hoping you would come with me."

Is he serious right now?

He wants me to hang out with the team?

"You're inviting me to hang out with your friends?"

He cocks his head. "Of course. Why wouldn't I?"

"I..." I frown. "I guess I don't have an answer. But my eye..."

"They'll think it's badass, I promise. And it's nothing compared to the missing tooth Dex has going on right now. He took a fist to the face during our last game. He's lucky he didn't break his jaw."

"Who's Dex?"

Like I don't know who Dex is.

"Dex Foster. Teammate." He shakes his head. "Sorry. I forget sometimes you're not a huge hockey fan."

If you only knew.

"Oooh." I cringe. "That's like a strike two against me, eh? Your friends might not want me around."

"Are you kidding?" He laughs. "You're fresh meat. And you're coming. I'm going to change my shirt and I'll be down in a minute."

I peer down at what I have on, ripped jeans and a dark-green oversized sweater that hangs off my shoulder.

"Wait! What should I wear?"

"Nothing."

"Nothing?" I shout up at him with a laugh. He peers down from the steps, his eyes bulging.

"Shit. Did I say nothing? That's not what I meant. I meant nothing, as in, you don't need to change." He shakes his head, his hand smoothing down his face. "I'm so sorry. I should've said you look perfect just the way you are. Change nothing. That's what I meant. Change nothing. You look great. I'll only be a minute."

He takes a deep breath, his cheeks thirty shades of pink, and I giggle as I watch him take the steps two at a time up to his room. Though I feel bad for embarrassing him, he's cute when he's flustered. Grabbing my shoes by the door, I take a steadying breath and remind myself that a little social interaction is good for me. I can't stay holed up in this penthouse all day, every day.

But also, oh, my God!

I'm about to spend the evening with the Chicago Red Tails.

The hockey enthusiast in me wants to squeal in excitement because, from what Daveed and Jada have said in the past, these guys are a great group, and I've always wondered what it's like hanging out with players other than the Seattle Sea Brawlers. But the realist in me knows I'm the ex-girlfriend of a professional hockey player, currently sporting a healing shiner from his fist, and the last thing I want is to put myself in another one of those situations.

I trust Milo though. When push comes to shove, I know he

wouldn't let anything happen to me. He's back down the stairs in minutes, sporting a pair of dark jeans that hang off his waist perfectly and a long-sleeved black T-shirt that fits snugly around the boulders he calls biceps. And that's not even the best part.

Nope.

He just had to take things to the next level with his pièce de résistance.

His Red Tails hat sits backward on his head, and fuck me, he looks good.

And smells good.

Why?

Why right now?

Why this moment?

Is it because Jada put the thought into my head?

Is that why I'm suddenly looking at him like a piece of meat I could devour in one sitting?

Is she the reason my jaw is stuck in the open position? Why my eyes are wide?

Because watching him slip his shoes on and grab his coat, the way he moves his body, it's making me feel a way that I should not be feeling right now, and I have no idea what to do with that.

Except curse my best friend for planting the seed in my mind.

"You, okay?"

"Huh?"

Oh, sorry. I was wondering what your hands might feel like on my—

"Are you ready?"

"Yeah." I nod absentmindedly. "Ready."

Milo slips on his coat and opens the door to the penthouse, his hand on the small of my back as he follows behind me in the short walk to the elevators.

Shit.

This might be a long night.

CHAPTER 8

Milo

Me: Hey. I'm bringing Charlee with me tonight. That, okay?

Colby: Of course. Can't wait to meet her.

Dex: Hell yeah! Another chick to play with.

Me: Back off, Dex. She's not a toy.

Zeke: Was going to bring the girls, but Lori has a headache so she's going to stay home with the baby.

Colby: Hope she feels better, Zeke. Smalls will be here. Charlee won't be the only one.

Dex: Ugh. Rory wants to know if she can come hang? Her kindergarten booger brigade took a toll on her this week.

Hawken: Three chicks. That's an orgy right there.

Dex: We're not having an orgy with my fuckin' sister, you cum-bubble.

Hawken: Correction. YOU'RE not having an orgy with your sister. *smirk emoji*

Dex: Don't make me come after your dick with a hacksaw.

Hawken: Aww, you want to play with my dick, Dex?

Dex: *middle finger emoji* On second thought. I'll tell her not to come.

Colby: *GIF of Robert Downey Jr. rolling his eyes* Carissa says bring Rory with you. She loves her kid stories. I think she's got babies on the brain.

Hawken: *high five emoji* Tonsil hockey it is! *smirk emoji*

Dex: I swear to God I'm going to punch you.

Me: ANYWAYS...one thing about tonight. Charlee's shiner. It's been over a week so it's healing but the bruise almost makes it look worse. Please don't mention it. I don't want her to be uncomfortable.

Dex: Fair. But I might ask her bra size. Or her favorite sex position.

Me: Oddly enough I would expect nothing less from you, Dex. Quinton, you coming?

Quinton: Sorry. Ignoring all the sister fucking talk but yeah. I'll be there.

Colby: See y'all soon.

Everyone is down in Colby's entertainment room when we arrive, but Carissa greets us from the kitchen.

"Milo! Come on in!" she shouts over the running water of the sink. She walks out with a hand towel and greets me with a hug before turning to Charlee.

"It's Charlee, right?"

"Yeah. Great to meet you." Charlee smiles and offers her hand, but Carissa pulls her into a hug.

"Sorry, I'm a hugger. It's a pleasure to meet you, too. Any friend of Milo's is a friend of ours. Welcome."

"Thank you so much. Do you need help with anything in the kitchen?"

Carissa shakes her head. "Oh no. I'm sure Milo is chomping at the bit to introduce you to the guys." She brings her hand to her mouth like she's telling a secret. "Or maybe I should say the guys are a little excited to finally meet you."

"Uh-oh. Should I run?" Charlee jokes. Her ease with Carissa makes me smile.

One down. Several more to go.

"Nah. They all think they're badass guys, but there isn't a woman in their lives who doesn't already know they're nothing but a team of teddy bears."

"Hey. Who you callin' a teddy bear?" Colby comes up behind Carissa, wrapping his arms around her waist and kissing her neck. "I'm at least a grizzly bear, Smalls. Give me that much."

"I don't know." Charlee cocks her head, studying Colby and Carissa with a glint in her eye. "Holding on to her like that, you kind of look like a koala."

"Ooh, touché." Colby chuckles. "All right, I can accept that. Koalas are fuckin' cuddly, right, babe?"

She gives her husband a playful peck. "Totally."

"So, you must be Charlee Mags. I'm Colby."

He offers his hand to Charlee, and she shakes it confidently. "Pleasure to meet you. Your home is lovely."

"Well, our home is your home, so please make yourself comfortable." He smiles at her and then winks at me. "The guys are waiting for you in the basement."

Charlee glances between me and Colby. "What's in the basement?"

"My playroom," Colby answers.

Her eyes meet mine, and I know what she's thinking.

You don't say playroom to romance book readers.

It takes on a whole new meaning.

I hope Colby knows what he's doing though, because this chick doesn't back down.

"Playroom, huh?"

He nods. "Yep. Big room. Lots of toys."

Charlee nods as well, slowly, like she's solving a mystery. Even slides her finger and thumb over her chin. "You got plugs?"

"Oh yeah." Colby smiles. "Lots of 'em. In several different sizes."

Oh Lord.

Here we go.

"Do your toys vibrate?"

He chuckles. "They do if you push certain buttons."

Well, he's not wrong there.

"Swivel action?"

Carissa's eyes roll back in her head as she plays along. "Oh God, the swivel action!"

Colby kisses her cheek. "There is definitely swivel action down there."

"How about speed variations?"

He winks. "However you like it, Charlee Mags."

"Great." Charlee claps her hands together. "I want to be Toad."

"What the fuck? Why Toad?"

She gives him a pitying look. "Let me guess, you're always Bowser?"

"Damn right. He's the biggest and strongest."

Charlee chuckles softly. "But he's not the fastest."

"And you think Toad is the fastest?"

"Guess you'll find out when I kick your Bowser-loving ass. Let's do this."

Carissa and I both laugh as Colby gives Charlee a high five and wraps an arm over her shoulder, leading her toward the basement stairs. "Let's fuckin' do this."

Before Carissa and I follow them down the stairs, she tugs on my arm, stopping me so she can whisper, "She seems great."

"Yeah. She is."

"I'm glad you brought her tonight."

"Me too. She deserves a night of nonjudgmental fun."

Carissa giggles. "Not sure I can guarantee nonjudgmental. Have you met Dex?"

"Truer words were never spoken."

The two of us make it down the steps to the basement to find Dex shaking Charlee's hand. "Whoa, that's an impressive shiner."

Fucking Dex!

"Ass face!" Rory, Dex's younger sister, slaps his arm. "I swear to God, you listen worse than my kindergarteners. You weren't supposed to bring that up."

"I know," he says with an easy shrug. "But the elephant is literally in the middle of the room, so..."

Charlee takes it all in stride and shakes Dex's hand. "You should've seen the other guy."

Dex laughs. "No doubt! That's badass. I'm Dex."

"Charlee Mags."

"Nice to meet you, Mags."

"Likewise. I've heard a lot about you, Dex."

He gives me a sly grin to which I roll my eyes in response. "Is that so?"

Ignoring Dex's rascally personality, I introduce Charlee to Hawken, Zeke, Quinton, and Rory before Colby announces, "Charlee's in this round, and she wants to be Toad."

After six rounds of watching Charlee become the ultimate Mario Kart champion, kicking the asses of every one of us, we take a well-deserved pizza break.

"So, Milo says you're a book editor?" Rory asks Charlee.

"Yeah. For about six years or so now. I work as a contractor for Enchantment Publishing."

"Ooh. Romance books, right?"

"Yep. It's a huge industry. Keeps me pretty busy."

"Romance books, huh?" Dex says, stuffing his face. "Is it like, that porn that Milo reads?"

"It's not porn, Dex." I roll my eyes for the hundredth time.

Dex's brow shoots up. "Is there dick in those books, Mags?"

She grins and wags her brows. "Uh, yeah. Sometimes a lot of

dick."

"See? It's porn."

Charlee is about to argue with him, but I lay a hand on her shoulder. "Best not to engage."

"But he has no idea what he's missing."

"Missing?" He chuckles. "Why do I need to read about dick when I have one of my own?"

Charlee smirks. "Because romance books are like road maps to a woman's libido. You want to know how women think? What they think about? What they really want out of a guy? Read a good romance book."

"Yeah, but what's that got to do with libido?" Dex asks, stuffing his face with another piece of pizza.

"Oh, that's easy. The sex scenes alone in a well-written romance book will tell you all you need to know about how to make women happy."

I nod. "And that's exactly what my mother and sister told me when I was twenty-one."

"Wait, wait, wait." Rory waves her hand, giggling. "Your mother told you to read romance books?"

"Yep. I was probably being a cocky-ass bastard one night, bragging about how hot I was with the ladies or something ridiculous like that. Anyway, I had broken up with an old girlfriend, and my mom told me if I really wanted to learn what women want, I should pick up one of my sister's romance books. So, one night when she wasn't home, I did."

Rory rests her chin on her hand. "And has it helped?"

I nearly choke on my bite, coughing several times, my cheeks reddening. "Let's just say some of those books are very informative, and suddenly I had a lot of socks in the laundry. I'll leave it at that."

Charlee stifles a laugh, her finger pressing on her lips.

Quinton clears his throat. "But aren't they a bunch of unrealistic expectations for guys?"

"That's very pessimistic of you, Quinton," Hawken teases.

He lifts a shoulder. "I don't care much for all the lovey-dovey bullshit women want. But I like to fuck."

"To each their own, I guess. If you want to see it that way," Charlee answers. "Most of the guys in the books I edit and read are pretty relatable, though. What makes them so swoon-worthy is not just the way they feel about the women they pine for, or the inside look we get as readers, but the way the guy shows his feelings. Whether it's protecting her at all costs, supporting her through a change, getting the insecure woman to see how beautiful and lovable she is, saving the damsel in distress, or whatever the storyline is—women fall for the guy who knows his heart. The guy who isn't afraid to share his feelings. The guy who pays attention to the woman in his life."

"Fuck it," Dex announces, his hand slapping the counter. "I'm sold. Give me your best recommendation."

Charlee beams and gives me a high five. "Whoa! Two pro hockey players reading romance books? We could start a movement!"

I would definitely like to start something. That's for sure.

"Fuck, they got it loose!"

"Yes! Go, go, go!"

"What the hell is he doing?"

"Scrambling! They have to get Michlen away from the puck."

"La Roi's got it! He's got it! It's going in!"

"Shoot it!"

"Score!" Colby shouts at the television as we all celebrate Milwaukee's third goal.

"With two minutes left, Detroit doesn't stand a chance," Quinton says.

I shake my head. "You know damn well two minutes is a lifetime."

Colby nudges me. "How awesome would it be to play Milwaukee in the playoffs?"

"Hell yeah! Final Cup game. Can you imagine?"

I lean over toward Charlee and explain, "Colby and I have been Milwaukee fans since we both played in their minor league before being drafted to our first major league team. A little piece of home and a team we've always had massive respect for."

"Ah, I see. So, you guys have known each other a long time then?"

"Since childhood, yeah. His brother is one of my best friends as well. They're like brothers to me."

Colby swigs his beer and then points to me. "My parents would shit themselves to be at the game if it happens to work out that way."

"I know, man. I'm praying for it."

The last two minutes of the game are intense as Detroit scores a goal and looks to be digging in. We're all on the edge of our seats, literally.

"No fuckin' way," Quinton shouts as Detroit flings the puck down the ice.

Hawken joins him. "Icing, ref! That's icing!"

"Mackley better fix his defense."

"He's badass. They've got this."

Zeke shouts, "He needs to pass to La Roi!"

"One minute to go!"

The puck banks off the side and flies toward the center, where it's picked up by Detroit and shot down the ice.

"Shit!"

"Banking off the net!" Zeke throws his arms out to his sides. "Safe!"

Charlee shoots up from her seat, gesticulating toward the television. "Brewster, fix your goddamn five-hole! It stinks like the south end of a skunk!"

She plops down, and everyone stops.

All movement in the room halts.

Any sounds die away, except for the commentary on the TV.

All heads turn toward Charlee Mags.

"What?" she asks, noticing all the attention now on her. "His save average is usually off the charts. There's no excuse for looking like that tonight. If Milwaukee loses, it's on him."

"Wait a minute...how..." I shake my head, confused. "How do you know what a five-hole is?"

"And how do you know Brewster's stats?" Quinton adds.

My eyes grow in hesitant excitement. "I thought you said you didn't follow hockey."

Zeke scoffs. "There's no way she doesn't follow hockey if she knows Garin Brewster's stats."

A bubble of excitement grows in my chest.

Holy shit!

She knows hockey?

She's a fan?

She edits books, she's gorgeous, and she knows hockey?

Can she be any more fucking perfect?

How is this woman even in my life right now?

I want to sweep her up in my arms, tell her how attractive I think she is, and celebrate this newfound revelation about Charlee Mags, but I can't. Because if there's one person in this room not giving off an excited vibe, it's her.

Her head bowed, she chews on the inside of her cheek as she picks at her fingernails. I watch her battle numerous emotions at one time. Indifference, nervousness, fear, anger? Sadness?

Why the sudden retreat?

What's going on?

"Hey." I lower myself from the couch and kneel in front of her, taking her hand in mine. Her knee shakes, and I hold her hand as she breathes.

"I'm sorry," she whispers to me, shaking her head.

I speak softly. "Charlee, you have nothing to be sorry for."

She lifts her head and glances at each of us, and I squeeze her hand so she knows she's not alone.

"I lied to you, Milo. When I told you I don't follow hockey."

"Okay. I didn't mean to upset you by asking. I was surprised is all." I start to shake my head, dismissing her little white lie, but she stops me.

"It's not okay. I don't know what I was thinking except that..." She takes in a shuddering breath. "I knew I needed to get out of Seattle and away from him. I wasn't thinking about the fact I would be living with another hockey player when Jada told me about—"

"Wait." My empty hand takes her other hand. "Charlee, are you saying that before coming here, you lived with another player? A Sea Brawler?"

She nods silently.

My lips separate as another revelation hits me. "That means..."

I don't even have to finish my sentence. Her sorrowful eyes meet mine, and she nods again.

Oh my God, we've played Seattle numerous times.

I know many of them well.

And one of them hurt Charlee.

My earlier excitement has vanished, replaced with rage and hatred for whoever hurt her. Whoever it was that marked her face. I have to know what pathetic fucking asshole hurt her.

"Who was it, Charlee?"

Hawken watches her with narrowed eyes and murmurs, "McClacken."

She meets Hawken's stare like a deer in headlights, seemingly unable to comprehend how he knows.

My gaze shoots between them.

"McClacken? Jared McClacken? How do you know that?"

He shakes his head, his eyes never leaving Charlee, who sits quietly, her eyes now squeezed closed.

"I don't. It was a wild guess. Remember a couple of seasons ago, after that loss against Seattle, when we were all wondering what was up with McClacken? And I recalled hearing about him in the tabloids. For—"

"Threatening his..." I glance at Charlee and see a tear roll down her cheek. "Fuck. That was you?"

"I'm sorry, Milo," she says. "I didn't want to create drama for you. I don't want to mess with your season." She stands, lifting her chin. "I should go. I'll find a new place to stay."

"Whoa, whoa, whoa." I grab her hand. "What the hell? What's going on, Charlee?"

"You guys have a real chance this year, and if Jared finds me," she cries, shaking her head. "Especially if word gets out that I'm staying with y—"

"Hey, hey, hey." I pull her a little closer to me and wipe her tears gently with the pads of my thumbs, holding her face in my hands. "You don't need to go anywhere. It's okay. These guys here? In this room? They're a fortress when it comes to whatever any one of us needs. A fucking fortress, Charlee, all right? You're safe here, I promise you. That fucking prick of a man will know you're here over my dead body."

"And mine." Colby lays a hand on her shoulder.

"And mine," Hawken adds

"He'll have to get through all of us," Zeke tells her.

Fuck!

Is she really that frightened?

I want to promise her the goddamn moon right now.

I want to promise her she'll never have to endure a moment with that asshole ever again.

She'll never have to live a life like that.

I'll do anything to make her happy.

Anything to not see her in pain.

Worried about the ramifications of her situation.

Frightened for a team of players she barely even knows.

"Ugh, I'm sorry, you guys." She furiously wipes at her tears. "I'm not a good liar, and I'm not a crier by nature, so I'm really frustrated with myself right now."

"Nobody is judging you, Mags," Colby tells her.

"Damn right." Carissa smiles and offers Charlee her hand. "I, for one, am pumped you're a hockey fan because now I'll have someone fun to sit with to watch these clowns play."

She wraps an arm around Charlee's shoulder. "Now, how

about you, me, and Rory head upstairs for some non-hockey-related girl talk?"

"What?" Hawken whines. "Why can't we join the girl talk?"

Rory shoots up from her seat, beer in hand, and smirks at Hawken. "You can come if you want, but we're going to talk about tampon insertion, yeast infections, and how many penises have been in us in the past year."

"Hey, Smalls!" Colby calls after Carissa as they head up the stairs. "That number had better be fucking one! One penis!"

She cackles. "Don't worry, babe. You have the most colossal penis in the universe."

"Fuckin' right, I do," he mumbles as the door at the top of the stairs closes.

Dex chuckles. "That's just because she hasn't seen mine."

"Fuck you, Dexter."

"You all right, Milo?" Zeke asks, watching me from across the room as I pace back and forth, rage simmering inside me.

I shake my head and, with as little sound as possible, whisper-shout, "Fuck! Fuck! Fucking fuck!"

"Milo, it's—"

"Nah-ah-ah-ah." Colby blocks Quinton from stepping toward me. "Let him get it out."

"How the fuck could he do that to her? Jesus fucking ripe cunt bastard!"

"I swear to God, the next chance I get, that asshole is getting full-body checked so hard every bone in his body will break," Dex mumbles. "Who the fuck does he think he is?"

"Oh, he'll be fucking lucky if he can even walk out of the arena when I'm done with him. He sure as fuck won't have any goddamn teeth left."

The anger in me is overwhelming.

If looks could kill, Jared McClacken would be dead ten times over by now.

"All right." Colby finally steps in. "Listen, none of us are going to do a goddamn thing, because what we don't need is a PR nightmare, however valiant it may be. We're better than that rat bastard." He turns to me. "But now that we know what we know, maybe we can engage Daveed in a conversation about the feel of the team in Seattle. He'll tell us that much. He clearly cares for Charlee."

I plop down on the couch, my elbows resting on my knees and my hands shoving through my hair. "He had to have hit her fucking hard to have caused a bruise like that." I squeeze my eyes closed. "God, I can't unsee her face. Her tears. Her shame. Fuck!"

"She has nothing to be ashamed of as far as any of us are concerned," Quinton says. "You know that, Milo."

"Of course I do. She's one of the strongest women I've ever met. And I've told her as much."

Colby studies me. "You really like her."

I can't even deny it anymore.

"Watching her tonight, listening to her...it broke my heart, Colb. Her hand was shaking in mine. I don't ever want her to feel that kind of pain or fear again for as long as I live. And the longer I was holding her hand, the more I realized I would do anything to make her happy. Anything to make her feel safe, protected. Loved."

Dex smirks. "I think that's a yes, Nelson."

Colby nods with a gentle smile. "I think you might be right about that, Dex." He claps my shoulder and looks me in the eye. "And if that's how you truly feel, then I have no doubt Charlee Mags will be well protected and will want for nothing."

Zeke leans over to whisper in my ear. "And she now has an entire hockey team of new friends and bodyguards. Whatever you need, Milo. Always."

I need Charlee.

I want Charlee.

"I appreciate the gesture, guys. I do. But this is going to be the biggest fucking challenge of my life—trying to play it cool while she figures herself out. I won't barge into her safe space. Not until she's ready."

"You don't have to barge in, Milo." Hawken shrugs. "But you

can expand her safe space. Enhance it with personal touches she's probably never experienced before, given her history."

Colby nods. "He's right. Be the teddy bear version of Milo Landric that every woman loves."

Teddy bear.

Goldilocks and her bear.

This, I can do.

CHAPTER 9

Charlee

"How about a few shots, huh?" Carissa asks, reaching into their liquor cabinet. "Maybe a little vodka to calm the nerves a bit?"

"Anything stronger? I kind of feel like I jumped off a moving train."

"Sure. Tequila all right?"

"Perfect."

Carissa pours us each a shot and we clink our glasses with Rory and drink them in tandem.

"For what it's worth," Carissa says with a frown. "I'm really sorry for what you've gone through."

I almost start making excuses for Jared, but remember where I am, Jada's words floating through my mind from our last conversation.

"...let's not forget how long he'd been an asshole to you before that hit happened."

"He's a mega-douche, I won't deny it, but he only got one hit."
One very hard hit.

Rory pats my hand where it rests on the counter. "Good for you for getting out, girl. We're glad to have you here. God knows I could use friends who aren't plastering apples all over their classrooms in primary colors and wearing T-shirts that say things like 'Kind people are my kind of people.'" She rolls her eyes. "Seriously. Just once I want to walk into my kindergarten classroom with a shirt that says, 'Don't fuckin' touch me with your germ-infested fingers,' or maybe 'This teacher doesn't like apples. She prefers dick.'"

Carissa and I laugh, and I have to hold back a snort. "Oh my God, you teach kindergarten?"

"She's the best kindergarten teacher in the world."

"With that personality?" I chuckle. "I have no doubt."

"Don't get me wrong," Rory says, motioning for Carissa to fill her shot glass again, "I love my little booger brigade, but shit, sometimes I wish fuck wasn't a bad word. It's hard being filtered all day."

Carissa nods. "That is definitely something I don't have to worry about working around the guys. They have dirtier mouths than I could ever dream of having."

Rory narrows her eyes and leans in toward Carissa. "Okay, I've always wanted to ask this because I just need to know. Is Colby a dirty talker in bed? Because there's something about him that screams dirty talker."

She shakes her head. "I imagine Charlee here has read dirtier, but he has his moments when he shocks me with something he says."

"What about Milo? Do you think he's got a dirty mouth?"

Carissa and Rory both turn to me, my brows shooting up. "How the hell should I know? I've only lived with the guy for a roughly a week."

"Damn," Rory laughs. "I was hoping maybe you two had gotten together."

Because that's what I need.

I mean, I do need it.

God, do I need a stellar screamer of an orgasm.

And if I had to guess, Milo knows how to satisfy.

But I cannot be thinking that way right now.

"Uh...no. In case you missed it, I still have a black eye from the last guy I was with. Though...if I'm being honest, it's not like we've been, you know, together, in quite some time."

"Well, when you two do get together one of these days, you

must report back on Milo's bedside manner. Inquiring minds are dying to know."

I shake my head. "Sorry to disappoint you guys, but I really don't see that happening."

"What? Why?" Rory steps back. "He's totally smitten with you."

"I don't think so."

"Rissa, tell this woman she's crazy with a side of naïve."

Carissa bites her lower lip and cringes in my direction. "It was kind of hard to miss it down there, Charlee. He's protective of you."

"Protective, yes. But I think it's more because he knows where I came from. That's all. Well, he knows a lot more now but, you know what I mean."

"I don't think that's all," Rory reports. "Here's the thing you have to know about Milo. He doesn't date around. Since I've been around the team, to my knowledge, he's not had his eye on anyone."

Carissa nods. "I can vouch for that and say the same. I've been with Colby over two years now, and not once has Milo had a relationship with anyone."

"Right, but then you came along..." Rory smiles and cocks her head.

"Colby did say he talked about you in the gym the other day."

What?

He did?

My eyes grow large. "What did he say?"

"It was right after you got there. He thinks you're gorgeous." She smiles. "So, there's that."

"And hello!" Rory laughs. "The guy reads romance books! You edit romance books! You're a freaking match made in fairytale heaven, and there's something about him that's so...I don't know." She shrugs. "Teddy bear-like around you. It's kind of stupid cute."

Milo would certainly make a cuddly teddy bear.

"I'm sure he'll make someone very happy when the time

comes."

Rory throws back a third shot of tequila. "You mean he'll make you very happy...when you come."

Good Lord, how do I get out of this one?

Our ride home from Colby's may very well have been one of the most awkward rides of my life. Milo didn't have much to say, and as much as I wanted to know what he was thinking, all I had going through my mind were snippets of what the ladies had told me tonight.

"He's smitten with you."

"He thinks you're gorgeous."

"Do you think Milo is a dirty talker?"

"You're a freaking match made in fairytale heaven."

Then all I could do was sit there and imagine what being with a guy like Milo might be like. Is he a freak in the sheets or a gentle lover? What would it feel like having him whisper dirty thoughts in my ear? Does he even do that? Rory's right. He does come across more like a teddy bear kind of guy. From what I've seen of his body, the man is perfection, and I imagine he knows how to use it.

I can already tell he's a far cry from Jared who lives in the spotlight. He's not happy unless the world knows how famous he thinks he is. But Milo... Milo is different. He keeps to himself. Seems to have a steady head on his shoulders. He has bigger priorities in life than just hockey. The same priorities and dreams I also had at one time.

But now...

Now I'm not sure those dreams will ever come true for me.

Emotionally drained after an evening I didn't quite expect, I stand quietly behind Milo as he unlocks the door to the penthouse. He stands back to let me in first and then stomps in, tossing his keys on the counter and immediately reaching for a glass and a bottle of whiskey. I watch him pour a small amount and toss it down his throat.

He may as well chug from the bottle.

He pours another and shoots it back as well, still not saying a word.

And even though I'm drained mentally and physically, I can't help but feel his downward mood is all my fault.

"Milo, I'm really sorry about what happened tonight."

He shakes his head, capping his whiskey bottle and placing it back with the others. "You don't have anything to be sorry about, Charlee."

"Okay, but you haven't said two words since we left, and I—"

"I'm processing, all right?" His words are clipped short, he holds onto the edge of the counter, bowing his head. "I'm... really fucking pissed at McClacken right now." He pushes off the counter, shoving his hands through his hair. "Not that I loved the guy, because I never have. Everything about him oozes douche, but now..."

He paces back and forth in his kitchen, mumbling and ranting. Words like "Poor excuse for a hockey player" and "Terrible excuse for a man" fall from his mouth. I don't know what I could possibly say to make Milo feel better, so I simply remain silent. Everybody processes things differently. Perhaps this is how Milo deals with new information.

"The guy's a piece of shit, Charlee, and it's going to be really hard not to knock every single one of his fucking teeth out of his damn mouth next time we face-off."

My shoulders fall.

Part of me wishes I could crawl into some cozy, quiet hole somewhere and stay there.

So I'm out of everyone's way.

So I'm not upsetting anyone.

So I can deal with my life in solitude.

"This is why I didn't want to say anything," I mutter to myself, smoothing my hand across my forehead. "This is why I didn't want anyone to know."

"Why, wh...why, why, Charlee? Why did he do this? Were you fighting? What set him off? Did he just come at you? Because I can't understand what would drive a man to pull back his fist and hurt someone. And fuck, to hurt a woman." He holds his head in his hands, bewildered, and I rear my head back, flabbergasted by his line of questions.

"What the fuck difference does it make why he hit me, Milo?" My voice quivers, and he hears it. His head snapping up.

Shit.

Do NOT angry cry right now.

Just don't.

This is not the time for angry crying.

Get yourself together, Charlee.

"Are you seriously asking me why a grown-ass man punched me in the face?"

He shakes his head. "No, I—"

"Do you... did you..." Squeezing my eyes closed for a moment, I shake my head, completely befuddled. "Do you think I asked for it? Is that what you want to know? Did I do something to make him want to hit me? Huh? What, did I say the wrong thing? Wear the wrong thing? Did I not put out enough for his liking? Do you think I didn't ask myself those same questions?"

"Charlee..."

"No, Milo." Fuck. Here come the damn tears. I hate crying when I'm frustrated. "You know what? Tonight was exhausting. I mean, it was great. Your friends, your teammates, they're wonderful, and I appreciated the way they all treated me more than you know, but tonight was a lot, Milo. And I am tired and emotionally drained and...and you were so sweet about everything, and all I wanted to do was come home and know that I could relax around you even with some of my truth finally out there. But now, here we are."

"Charlee—"

"He hit me, Milo. He fucking punched me. One time. He

rammed his fist into my face and knocked me into a wall." I shake my head and turn toward the stairs, angrily swiping away my tears. "It doesn't fucking matter why."

"Charlee, I'm—"

"Good night, Milo."

He doesn't say another word to me as I climb the stairs to my room, but before I close my door, I hear him sigh loudly and say, "Fuck!"

Too tired to care about showering tonight, I slip out of my jeans and sweater and into a pair of sleep shorts and a ratty T-shirt. The conversation, or lack thereof, I had with Milo plays on repeat in my brain.

"What the hell difference does it make why he hit me? Ugh. Why would he even ask me that?" I grab a makeup removing wipe from its packet and start scrubbing at my face, catching the tears flowing down my cheeks. Insubordinate little bitches. Staring at myself in the bathroom mirror, I toss the used cloth angrily into the trash and grip the edge of the sink, poised much like Milo had been in the kitchen downstairs, as I try to regain my composure.

"He hit me because he's an asshole. That's why." I swipe away a few more tears, frustrated that I'm crying. Especially over someone like Jared, but I can never seem to control it. Why can't I be mad for a minute like a normal person?

"He's not worth crying about."

"You stupid, useless bitch!"

"I'm not going through another PR nightmare right now."

"I'm at the top of my game."

Could I have told Milo exactly why Jared hit me? Yes.

Would it have helped his mood even a tiny bit? Hell no.

It would have made things worse.

Not to mention, it would only make me feel worse than I already do. As grateful as I am for having met Milo's teammates and for the new friends I made this evening, the emotions I've managed to push away for the past week coupled with the years of his verbally abusive behavior are starting to catch up to me. I'm not sure I can keep the dam from breaking much longer, but at least I'm finally in my safe space where I can let go and not disturb anyone.

Flicking off the bathroom light, I fall onto my bed, clutching one of my pillows and allowing myself to succumb to my heady feelings.

Sad to have left my best friend behind in Seattle.

Homesick for my old life.

Scared to be doing this new life on my own in a huge city where I don't know many people.

Anxious about what will happen—not if, but when—Jared figures out where I am and who I'm with.

Eager to not be anybody's burden, but apprehensive to live on my own.

Nervous about what someone like Jared is capable of when he's mad.

Frightened of what he'll do to Milo or the guys on the team when they play each other.

Hurt that Milo doesn't understand.

Nobody understands.

I give myself a few minutes to cry out my anger, my frustration, my sadness, and my hurt, and then roll out of bed. Now that Milo has had time to go to his bedroom, I can sneak downstairs for a glass of water.

Or maybe something harder.

Turning on my bedside lamp, I tiptoe to my door, turn the handle, and nearly collide with a shirtless Milo Landric standing outside, a glass of water in hand.

His face contorts and his chest caves, and he lets out a choked whimper when he sees I've been crying. "Oh, God, Charlee, I'm so fucking sorry. I didn't mean it that way. Please forgive me, I didn't mean to make you..." His voice weakens, and his eyes soften as I cry at the sight of him. "I thought you might want some water."

I nod, wiping a now steady stream of tears. "That's very kind of you, Milo."

God, why is he so fucking nice?

"Charlee." My name is a pained whisper on his lips. "What can I do? Please, I was an asshole, and I didn't mean it. Please let me do something."

"It's okay," I sob. "I was just..."

Wait.

I lift my head up to meet his devastated expression. "Did you really bring that water up here...for me?"

He tilts his head, his lips trying to form a half-smile, but not quite making it. "Of course."

I step to the side, allowing him in my room, and watch as he sets the glass on my bedstand. Still a sobbing, wet mess by the door, he walks back to where I'm standing and reaches his hands out, apprehensive, but wanting. "Can I touch you, Charlee? Hug you?"

"I cry when I'm angry!"

I don't know what I'm doing, but the words just burst out of my mouth, so I guess this is happening.

He cringes a bit. "Oh. Okay. So, you're angry."

"No."

"Umm. Okay. You're not angry."

"I was so angry."

"You were."

"I was."

"Right."

"And then you showed up here with water."

I'm sounding all sorts of crazy, I know.

"Water for you."

"And now I'm a hot, sobbing mess because even after a little over a week, you give a damn, and he never gave a damn, Milo." I sniffle, "He never fucking gave a damn."

I watch as he realizes what and who I'm talking about, and he no longer waits for permission. He wraps an arm around me and pulls me tightly against him in a warm, strong, comforting embrace. One hand on my lower back, and the other on the back of my head, his fingers softly sifting through my hair. Whoa, I haven't cried like this in a long time, but somewhere deep inside, my emotions decided today is the day to let loose, and there is nothing I can do to stop them. So here I stand, a blubbery mess. But a blubbery mess in the arms of a man who gives a damn.

He brought me water.

"Of course I give a damn, Charlee. Don't ever doubt that."

I don't know what it is about this embrace. Maybe it's his strong arms holding me to him. Maybe it's his sculpted, but somehow comfortably soft bare chest, or the fact I can hear his heartbeat. Maybe it's the lingering scent of his cologne. Maybe it's his face resting on the top of my head and his fingers moving through my hair. I don't know, but what I do know is nobody has ever hugged me like this before.

Held me.

Comforted me.

Allowed me to be in my feelings.

"I'm sorry too, Milo. I'm just mad at Jared. This isn't your fault. I'm so sorry."

"Shhh. It's okay. Everything's going to be okay."

"What if it isn't?" I hiccup through my sniffles.

"I won't allow it to not be."

Gently, he lowers his arm behind my thighs and lifts me into his arms. I expect him to put me down on my bed, but he doesn't. Instead, he turns and carries me into the hall toward his room.

"Where are we going?" I sniffle.

"My room."

"Wh-why?" I sniffle again.

He gives me a sympathetic grin. "Because I have the bigger bed, and you like it."

"Milo..."

"Shhh. Trust me, Goldilocks."

He carries me into his room and lowers himself onto his bed, never once letting go of me, and then pulls the same throw blanket over us he had covered me with once before.

"Comfortable?" he murmurs.

"Mmm-hmm." I sigh.

I really am. Leaning against Milo's chest is way more comfortable than I should admit.

"Warm enough?"

"Mmm-hmm."

"Good. Feel free to close your eyes and relax while I read you a story."

I raise my head from his chest. "You're...what?"

My puffy eyes stare at him, mesmerized by his compassionate demeanor and noting the simple comfort reflected in his gaze. "I'm going to read to you. That okay?"

Somewhere underneath all the emotions of the evening, my insides melt into a puddle of swoon, if that's even possible.

He's going to read to me?

This man has me cocooned against his body, in his bed, and wants to read to me.

His idea of solace was one I wouldn't have thought of in a million years.

But so fitting for who he seems to be.

He really is a human teddy bear.

"Yeah, Milo," I mumble, trying not to cry over his tenderness. "I would love that."

He reaches for his kindle and opens it to a book I'm very familiar with. Another one from the series I edited.

"This one is my favorite of the three," he murmurs.

"Why?"

He's contemplative for a moment as he makes himself comfortable, then quietly explains, "Grayson's the nice guy. The golden retriever. He gets me. Also, I know this could sound slightly ironic, but I swear to God this is where I left off."

He doesn't say anything more. He leans back against the many fluffy pillows, his arms holding me, and begins to read.

"I grab Hannah a glass of water and the bottle of ibuprofen and then turn out the lights in the rest of the house, except for the light over the kitchen sink, assuming she'll probably just fall asleep when I see myself out. When I walk back to her room, she's curled up in a fetal position on her bed. I set the water and pills on the bedstand next to her, which she takes immediately.

'Thank you, Grayson.'

'Sure. You sure you're okay? What else can I do for you?'

'I'll be fine. I just have to get through the next twenty-four hours and the rest will be easy.'

'All right. Well, I should go and let you sleep.'

'Gray?'

'Yeah?'

'This is going to sound all sorts of...I don't know...weird and maybe even awkward, but it's been a shit day until you got here, and I would love nothing more than to just curl up and watch TV for a while, but...'

She doesn't want to be alone.

She's cute as fuck curled up in her llama pajamas. 'Do you need a snuggle buddy, Hann?'

She nods and it's cute as hell. 'Would that be okay? I mean, you're totally allowed to say no.'

Like I would ever say no to her..."

Milo's voice is thick with emotion. Velvety and warm. He continues to read and as he does, my thoughts jumble in my mind until they're one big knot of confusion.

Why is he doing this for me?

I don't deserve this kindness.

I wonder how he really feels about my knowledge of hockey.

His beautiful voice is lulling me to sleep.

I probably shouldn't fall asleep here.

I don't want things to be awkward between us.

But I'm comfortable here.

And I'm not alone.

"She curls herself around me and lays her head on my chest, snuggling in close to me, and it's the best fucking thing in the world. All these years I've dreamed of this. Of holding Hannah in my arms just like this. Sure, maybe I also dreamed that I would one day have her naked underneath me, thrusting into her over and over again as she screams my name, but I can settle for baby steps. I can be the man that Stone couldn't be for her. And if snuggling is all I get for now, I'll take it with zero complaint. I lean my head down and kiss the top of her head.

'What are we watching?'

She turns the TV on with the remote in her hand. 'How about...'"

Spoons.

That's what I'm dreaming about right before I finally open my eyes in the morning and find that I am currently the small spoon to Milo's big spoon. It takes me a minute to realize I'm still in Milo's bed and that I must've fallen asleep to him reading to me last night. Was I really dreaming about spoons being used as hockey sticks because I'm being spooned by Milo in his bed?

Weird.

The dream, I mean.

Not Milo.

The spooning is, well, it's really nice.

More than nice, if I'm being honest. He's pulled me against his chest, both of his arms wrapped around me. In my sleep, my T-shirt has ridden up, and Milo's left hand rests on my bare stomach. His even breathing and soft snores tell me he's still asleep, so I lie here for a few moments, and imagine where his hand might wander if he were awake.

Would he slide up my shirt?

Tease my breast?

Or maybe push below the waistband of my pajama shorts.

My body warms thinking about it.

I wonder if he has morning wood.

My ass isn't quite against him, but he's not so far away that I couldn't back myself up and find out. I could even pretend to still be sleeping. He would never know.

Don't do it, Charlee.

He's been so nice to you.

Totally do it.

You know you want to know.

It has to be massive, right?

There's no way his cock isn't massive.

Just a little feel.

I give in to my inner devil because hell, this could be the only chance I'll ever get to know. Closing my eyes, I pretend to be sleeping, just in case, and slowly stretch myself back until I'm right up against his... Holy shit.

Yeah.

Yep.

It's big.

As I move, Milo also moves, tightening his hold on me and squeezing me tighter against him, pulling his knees up and tightening his big spoon. If he does it anymore, he may steamroll right over me.

I mean, would that be so bad?

No.

Nope.

Not at all.

As he moves, his hand trails up my abdomen and comes to a rest under my breast and oh my God, he's almost touching my breast! My heart rate is accelerating and I'm trying everything I can to steady my breathing, but fuck, if he could slide his hand up a little bit more... my nipples are hard as stone thinking about it.

Dammit, I should not be doing this.

Milo and I are not a couple.

He brought me in here last night as a gesture of comfort and compassion.

I can't take advantage of that.

No matter how much his proximity is turning me on.

I lie here a couple extra minutes, enjoying this safe haven with my eyes closed when he stirs. All but certain he's awake, and unsure of how he'll react with us in this position, I pretend to be asleep so as not to embarrass him, just in case. He inhales deeply as his body stretches. His fingers move against my stomach, and I can tell the moment he realizes where his hands are and where my ass is. I can tell because I feel him harden against me instantly.

Oh my God, it's even bigger than I imagined!

I'm not entirely certain, but I swear I hear him whisper, "Fuck," before he carefully slides his hand out of my shirt and delicately releases my body. Not wanting him to feel like he did anything wrong, I lie here, still, as though I'm dreaming away as he rolls out of bed and until I know he's left the room.

And then I open my eyes and sigh in disappointment.

Because had this been real, if we were a real couple, this

morning would've gone entirely differently.

CHAPTER 10

Milo

"I don't know about this one, Goldilocks. I'm not feeling it."

Four and a half weeks.

That's how long I was able to stall before Charlee guilted me into accompanying her to check out a few apartments for rent.

"Come on, Milo. You promised me whatever I needed, and I need a man's opinion. I want to make sure I'm safe."

She's right. I did promise her, but she's safe with me, so why does she feel the need to leave the penthouse and get her own place? She already spends several nights a week in my bed—a monster I created by reading to her. So why leave, and have to sleep alone? I have zero regrets about bringing her into my bed that night. I wanted her to feel comfortable, and if I'm being real with myself I needed to be next to her, so I knew she wasn't hating me for hurting her. Now she asks me to read to her two or three times per week, and although it's been the thing between us I've loved the most, it's been torturous as hell sleeping next to her at night and not making some sort of move. I've almost broken down and tried a boob graze just to see what her reaction might be.

Ugh.

But I'm not that guy.

So instead, because I've ignored every opportunity to talk about my feelings and let her know how much I'm crushing on her, here I am in an empty apartment no less than thirty minutes away from mine, trying to come up with all the reasons the place isn't good enough for her.

Number one. It's thirty fucking minutes from mine on a good day.

Number two. It's not my penthouse next to me in my bed.

Number three. I don't want her to leave.

There. I admit it.

"Really? I think it has character. What don't you like?"

"Uhh, the bathroom." I shake my head and give her a doubtful look. "I mean, check out the lack of counter space. You won't have much room in here for all your stuff."

"My stuff?"

"Yeah." I tick off the list with my fingers. "Your hair stuff, your makeup, your makeup removers, your lotions—and then where do you even put the soap? There's not a lot of storage."

She peeks into the bathroom again and even though I suppose she could make it work, I fold my arms over my chest and stand my ground. "A woman needs storage, Charlee."

Her head bobs. "I suppose you're right. It could definitely use more storage." She looks up at the worn sconce on the wall. "And the lighting could be better."

"That's right." I nearly raise my finger like I'm damn Sherlock Holmes screaming Eureka! "Girls need their lighting. Plus, the living room area is kind of small. Not a lot of room for yoga. I think we should keep looking."

"What about this one?" she asks after we've walked through the second listing of the day. Already I'm shaking my head.

"No way. First of all, look at the view outside. Nothing but dark back alleys. You know what that means?"

Just as I say that, we hear cats scream outside.

How apropos.

"What?"

"It means drugs. Gangs. Prostitutes. All the bad shit I don't want you living around."

"But the price is—"

"Fuck the price, Charlee. You get what you pay for here. We can do better than this. We'll keep looking when I'm back from traveling."

"All right." She resigns, her shoulders dropping in a bit of disappointment.

I wrap an arm casually around her shoulders. "I don't need you dying on me, Mags, all right? I promise we'll find you the perfect place."

Perfect place being my penthouse with me.

"Thanks for doing this with me, Milo."

I would do anything for you, Charlee.

"Don't mention it. It's my pleasure."

The team is on the road for the next five games, which means I'll be away from Charlee for over a week. I knew this time was coming, but now that she's growing comfortable with me, it sucks that I'm leaving. It's like taking the wind out of my slow-moving sails.

"Are you sure you're going to be okay while I'm away? I can get you a family travel pass if you want to work on the road with the team."

She shakes her head, much to my misfortune. "My place isn't with the team, and I don't want someone to feel like they have to be responsible for me. It's all right. I have two books I need to get edited this week, and I have a couple staff meetings I can actually go to since I'm in town, so I'll have plenty to do to keep me busy."

How do I tell her I'll miss her when we're not really a thing?

"I'll be sure to text you. Check in. That kind of thing."

She smiles and nudges me with her shoulder. "Aww, I'll miss you too, Milo."

Yep. Time to look away before the redness of my cheeks gives me away.

"Come on, let's go get food. I'm starving."

> **Charlee: HOLY SHIT!!! That was a helluva hat trick!! I know you're not going to get this right away because you're still on the ice, but I'm so proud of you, Milo! Congratulations! Also, your neighbors downstairs might not like me very much with all the jumping up and down I've been doing.**

Seeing a text message on my phone the minute I open my locker brings a huge smile to my face.

"What are you cheesin' about over there, Landric?" Colby asks as he unlaces his skates.

"Just a text message."

Zeke scoffs. "Just a text message my ass. It's from her, isn't it? Charlee?"

I beam because I can't fucking help it. "Yep. Congratulating me on my hat trick. Now I fuckin' wish she was here so I could take her out to celebrate."

"So, take her out the minute you get home," Hawken says. "It's never too late to celebrate."

Colby nods. "He's right."

"You kiss her yet?" Dex asks, throwing off his jersey.

"Only about a thousand times in my mind, Dex."

"Dude, it's time to get some action. Time to make a move."

Quinton steps up next to me. "What's it been, like six weeks?"

"Five weeks, four days, and about four hours."

"That's oddly specific."

I laugh. "Fuck it, though, right? I'm keepin' track."

"So, let's round up to six weeks. That's long enough. She hasn't moved out yet, so that's something."

"She hasn't moved out because I've come up with one reason or another as to why she shouldn't take any of the places we've looked at. Eventually she's going to catch on to my game."

Quinton claps my shoulder. "Well, you got pushed into an unfair game, if you ask me. Taking in a beautiful female roommate and then crushing on her without being able to do anything about it."

"Let's ask Smallson," Dex says as Carissa pushes through the door.

"Great game, gentlemen! Ask me what?"

"Mags has lived with Milo for about six weeks now. That enough time to wait before he starts making a move?"

"Six weeks," she asks with narrowed eyes. "Hell yeah, that's long enough. She's been away from Meathead McClacken for at least a solid month, which is good." She winks at me. "And that also means her juice box is desperate for attention."

I cock my brow. "Her juice box?"

She nods slowly and speaks like I'm trying to understand a foreign language. "Yeah, Landric. Time to stick your straw in her juice box. Comprende?"

The snorts and cackles that follow from the guys make me laugh and blush all at the same time. It's not like I've never had sex before, but damn. Having Carissa explain it to me like I'm a goddamn teenage virgin is funny as hell.

"Yeah. I get you."

She pats my chest, right above my heart. "Good. Now go get a shower. You're a sweaty mess and you all smell like ass."

Me: Hey! Thanks for the text! Finally in for the night! What a game, huh?

Charlee: OMG Milo!! I'm still flying high for you!

Me: LOL me too. I don't know how I'm going to sleep tonight. It was a great first game out.

Charlee: I'm kinda jealous I wasn't there.

Me: Would've been great to have you here.

Charlee: I'll make it up to you, I promise! I'll be at the next home game.

Me: Deal! Everything okay at home?

Charlee: Yep. A quiet night with my book characters.

Me: Oh yeah? Editing tonight?

Charlee: Little bits at a time.

Me: Tell me about them.

Charlee: She's heading out on a cruise with college friends and her male companion bailed on her, so she needs to find a replacement. He lied to his family about being in a relationship so he's looking for a fake partner. They meet when she drops her bag in an airport and her dildo flies out of it.

Me: Oh...?

Charlee: And HE picks it up! LOL.

Me: That's a hell of a meet cute.

Charlee: Right? That's what I said!

Me: So, do they hit it off?

Charlee: What's that? Can't hear you. Going through a tunnel.

Me: LOL all right I get it. You can't tell me everything. I'll get it out of you eventually.

Charlee: You should get some shut-eye.

Me: Yeah, I suppose you're right. Travel is early tomorrow.

Charlee: G'night, Milo.

Me: Night Goldilocks

Charlee: That's a lot of blood.
Hope Dex is okay.

Me: HA! Yeah, he's good.
Foreheads bleed a lot. Few
stitches and he's like new. Wanted
to rip Sveltski's nuts off though.

Charlee: I wanted to do it for him.
That was a hell of a check.

Me: All in the job. Sending him
to the sin bin was good for us
though.

Charlee: Yep. Power play goal is
still a goal! Great win!

Me: We'll take 'em any way we
can get 'em. What are you up to
tonight?

Charlee: Had dinner with Rory.
She's a hoot! I really like her. She's
great at girl talk.

Me: Oh yeah? Girl talk, huh? You two swapping smut stories or what?

Charlee: Something like that...

Me: Uuuhhhh I see those drama dots Goldilocks. Now I'm intrigued.

Charlee: She may have talked about one of your teammates more than she probably realized.

Me: No shit! Rory has a crush on one of us? Who is it? Is it me?

Charlee: Do you want it to be you?

Me: That's a big no from me. Rory's great but she's not my type.

Charlee: Oh yeah? And what's your type?

Fuck me. How do I answer a text like that without simply saying "You're my type"?

Me: Mila Kunis, remember? Mila Kunis, but real. Imperfect.

Charlee: Aaaaand??

Me: Someone who is down to earth. Confident but vulnerable. Confidence can be sexy as fuck on a woman, but what I like the most is someone who isn't afraid to be vulnerable and show me the parts of her she doesn't want others to see. Because she trusts me.

Charlee: Well, for what it's worth, it's easy to be vulnerable around you. You have this...I don't know, soothing aura about you.

Me: I'm glad I make you comfortable.

Charlee: It's more than comfortable Milo. You make me feel safe.

Me: Confession time?

Charlee: Okay...?

Me: I wouldn't wish what you've been through on anyone, but for what it's worth, I'm glad Jada brought you to me.

Charlee: Honest truth?

Me: Always.

> **Charlee: I wish I had met you three years ago instead of him.**

"Holy shit!"

"Did she just...?"

I spring up in my bed, staring at my phone. Reading her last line over and over and over again, wondering if her words are going to disappear—if this is all a dream.

Do I text her back?

What the hell do I say?

Do I tell her how I feel?

Is she ready to hear it?

Is that what she's telling me?

Maybe I should go wake up Colby and ask him.

No way, dipshit. He's balls deep inside Smalls right now.

Maybe Dex.

Nah. He's balls deep in some bunny no doubt.

Ugh. Where are my guys when I need them?

Before I decide what to do next, those little moving dots appear on the screen again and I watch them for several long seconds as she types out her text. Finally, the bubble appears.

> **Charlee: G'night, Milo. *heart emoji***

Oh fuck.

She used a heart emoji!

Do I use one too?

Is that too forward of me?

If she can do it, I can do it, right?

Yeah. Totally. I can do this.

Okay, okay. Here goes...

> **Me: G'night, Goldilocks. *heart emoji***

I lay back down and continue to stare at Charlee's words until my eyes are too tired to stay open. And my night is filled with an abundance of sweet dreams.

> **Charlee: Friggs deserves a stick up his ass after that kind of behavior on the ice.**

> **Me: I've never wanted to rip a man's dick off and shove it down his throat more than I did tonight. Friggs is nothing but a droopy pussy.**

> **Charlee: LOL a droopy pussy? Man, that's sad. Are you speaking with experience here? Have you actually seen a droopy pussy?**

> **Me: Yeah. His name is Friggs and he plays for Miami and I swear to God he flaps around the ice like a pair of droopy pussy lips.**

> **Charlee: LOL Droopy Pussy Lips would make a great band name.**

Me: LOL thanks for making me laugh. I needed that. I got him good though after the game.

Charlee: Oh yeah?

Me: Yep. Gifted my stick to his son who was waiting outside the press room. Even took a picture with him. Friggs can suck my dick.

Charlee: Always the nice guy, Landric. Well done.

Me: What are you up to?

Charlee: Uh…if you must know, I'm taking a bath.

Me: Shit. You're naked and texting me right now??

Charlee: *GIF of John C. Reilly saying "yep"*

Me: ......fuuuuck.

Charlee: You, okay?

Charlee: What's going on? Milo?

Me: Shhhh I'm trying to get a visual of you in the bathtub.

Charlee: OMG! LOL! It's no big deal. It's just a bath.

Me: Uh, correction. It is not just a bath. It is a woman who resembles Mila Kunis naked in my bathtub. And I'm not there to witness it. Yeah. No big deal. *eye roll emoji* *wink emoji*

Charlee: I'm sure you've had plenty of naked women in your bathtub before me. *eye roll emoji*

Me: Negative.

Charlee: What?

Me: There has never been another woman aside from my sister, my mother, Zeke's wife, Lori, and Carissa even in my penthouse before you, let alone naked in my bathtub.

Charlee: *looks around the bathroom for secret cameras*

Me: LOL You're safe. I promise. No cameras in my house. Well, except for that one.

Charlee: WHAT?? WHERE??

Me: Those were nice panties by the way. And that yoga pose... MMMMM!

Charlee: MILO!!

Me: LOL Kidding. I'm kidding. I swear. Just teasing you. But after that reaction... If you're doing yoga in your panties and I'm not there to witness that either, we're going to have a serious conversation when I get back.

Charlee: What you don't know won't kill you. *wink emoji*

Me: You're killing me, Mags. One more game and I'm home.

Charlee: Hey! Hopefully you read this before you're in the arena for the night. Good luck by the way! Is it okay with you if Rory hangs out here with me tonight? We wanted to watch your game together.

Me: Of course. My place is your place. You know that.

> **Charlee: Great! Because what I meant to say instead of Rory was RAGER. I'm going to have a rager here during your last game. I'll save you a beer and a slice of pizza *wink emoji***

> **Me: LOL how kind of you. Thanks for thinking of me.**

> **Charlee: Always! *Smiley face***

"Ten minutes till we hit the ice!" Coach announces after his last pep talk of the week. We're undefeated going into our eighth game in a row and the energy is high in the locker room tonight. We're ready to take this last win home to our own turf for the last few games before the playoffs start. I finish lacing up my skate as my phone dings with an incoming message. It's not a number I recognize but when I see what comes through, I don't give a rat's ass whose number it is.

Though I'm pretty certain it's Rory's.

The message accompanying a picture and video says, "Yes, we've been drinking. Yes, she went through your closet because she misses you Shhh! Don't tell her I told you. So I thought you might want to see this with your own eyes. Good luck tonight, Milo! She's rooting for you." *wink emoji*

My jaw drops when I open a picture of Charlee. She's wearing one of my jerseys and a pair of my socks that go up to her knees like leg warmers. Her dark brown waves are piled high on her head in a knot, and she does not appear to be wearing pants. She's sitting in the corner of the couch with her legs propped up in front of her.

My jersey is pulled up under her nose, and her eyes are closed.

She's sniffing my jersey.

She's sniffing me.

I've never seen a more gorgeous picture.

"Fuck me." My heart flips, my jaw drops, and my legs go weak, causing my entire body to drop to the bench behind me. The only part of me that can move right now is my dick, and it's doing enough to make things awkward while wearing a jockstrap.

"Milo?" Colby notices my movement, his brows furrowing. "What's going on?"

I clear my throat and swipe my thumb over my phone opening the video Rory sent me along with the picture. The video is shaky as I can only assume Rory is dancing with her, but there in the middle of my kitchen, wearing the same outfit, is Charlee with a beer in hand, dancing and singing her heart out to some song about trust falls, with the most magnificent smile on her face.

She's gorgeous.

Sexy.

Alluring.

And I'm speechless.

I wipe my hand down my face, unable to hide my smile.

"Dude, what the fuck are you grinning about?"

She likes me.

Before I can answer him, Carissa runs into the locker room, her eyes bulging and sporting her own huge smile. She comes right up to me with her phone in hand.

"Tell me you got the same video I did!"

"And more." I nod with a lovesick grin.

She squeals and does this little happy jig that makes me laugh, even though I'm finding it very hard to keep my attention on her when all I want to do is look at my phone.

"I told you, Landric! Juicebox!"

"Would one of you two tell me what the fuck is happening?" Colby asks, annoyed he's not privy to our conversation.

"Sorry, babe." Carissa pecks him on the cheek. "Rory and

Charlee are hanging out tonight, and she snapped a few goodies for Milo."

"What?" Dex's brows pop up. "Show and tell, man!"

"Wait," Hawken mumbles, looking confused and a little irritated. "Milo and Rory? You guys are a thing?"

"No, bro," Dex says, shaking his head. "He knows better than to hit on my sister. She's talking about Charlee."

"Show and tell, man. Is this a naughty pic that we can't see?"

"I mean, if Carissa got to see it..." Quinton smirks.

"All right, all right. It's a picture of Charlee...in my jersey."

I turn my phone around and let the guys see it.

"Fuck! That's a great picture."

"She's hot."

"That's hot."

"Hell yeah."

"Lucky man, Milo."

"Did you give her that jersey?" Colby asks.

I shake my head. "Nope. Rory said they've been drinking, and she went through my closet."

"A hundred bucks says Rory told her to do it." Dex rolls his eyes. "She's picked through my closet since high school and still does it."

"Well, if that isn't a good omen for tonight, I don't know what is." Colby claps my shoulder. "Let's go win this one so our boy here can get home to his girl."

My girl.

That sounds nice.

And for the first time it actually feels...right.

She's all I can think about now.

She's all the adrenaline I need.

She's all I picture as we circle up in the tunnel before taking the ice.

I'll win this one for her.

Our gloved hands connect in the middle of our circle as we shout the same mantra before every game. "Hustle, hit, and never quit!"

And then, we play.

CHAPTER 11

Charlee

Me: Miloooooooo!

Milo: Charleeeeeeeee!

Me: LOL!

Milo: Having fun over there?

Me: When is hanging out with Rorky not a good time?

Me: Rorpy.

Me: Rorfu.

Me: Rorgy.

Me: Fuck.

Me: RORY

Milo: *thinking emoji* Someone's had a drink or two tonight.

Me: haha yep. Sorrybutnotsorry. That was a great game.

Milo: It felt great.

Me: I'm wearing your jersey. Stole it from your closet. Hope it's okay.

Milo: Well, you'll have to pay the fee.

Me: LOL. A fee? Ok how much?

Milo: Show me. I want to see how you look.

Grinning at his request, I hold my phone up and snap a selfie.

"What are you doing?" Rory giggles.

"Milo asked for a picture of me wearing his jersey."

"Oh, here, let me." Rory grabs my phone and turns it around to take a few shots of me. "Give him a good sexy pose."

"Like what?"

"I don't know. Ummm, oh, I've got it." She grabs one of the chairs from the dining area and pulls it away from the table. "Here. Straddle this chair. That way he can see his name across your back."

She snaps the shot and then has me stand at the counter with my beer so she can take a full-body shot. "This is great. He'll totally think you're not wearing pants. So scandalous, Charlee!"

"Eat your heart out, Milo!" I laugh as she takes another picture. "Or eat me out. Whichever comes first."

Rory shrieks with laughter. "Oh my God if he were here right now to hear you say that! Girl, I'm pretty sure you would be wide open on this kitchen counter right now because he would not be able to resist you."

She hands me back my phone. "Here. Send him these."

I tap on the pictures in my album and send them to Milo who writes back immediately.

Milo: Shit.

Me: What? You don't like it?

My stomach drops a tiny bit at his response. I really thought he wouldn't mind.

Milo: No. I don't like them.

Milo: I LOVE THEM. You look fucking HOT, Goldilocks.

Me: I promise I'll wish it tomorrow.

Me: Wssh.

Me: Ugh. WASH.

Milo: You will do NO such thing. You can sleep in it for all care. Live in it. Wear it 24/7. As long as you'll let me gawk at you.

Me: *wink emoji*

Milo: On second thought. I might struggle to keep my hands off you when you look like that. Maybe you should take it off.

Me: Buuut if I take it off, I won't have anything to wear. *sad face*

Milo: Even better!

Me: LOL!

Milo: Do me a favor and fulfill a man's dream and tell me you're not wearing pants right now.

Me: I won't be wearing pants in about an hour when I'm in bed.

Milo: My bed. Will you sleep in my bed tonight, Goldilocks?

Me: I'll have to change the sheets again.

Milo: NO, you fucking will NOT. Leave the sheets. You make my bed smell nice.

Me: I do? What does it smell like?

Milo: It smells like you. And I like it. Helps me sleep.

Me: Confession time...

Milo: Okay...

Me: The first night you brought me to your bed and I fell asleep, you held on to me all night long. And when I woke up, your hand was pressed against my stomach. Under my shirt. But I pretended to be asleep.

Milo: I'm sorry, Charlee. I swear it wasn't on purpose. I wasn't trying to cop a feel.

Me: I really liked it.

Milo: Oh. You did?

Me: I was dying for you to move your hand up or down. I felt you behind me and I was so turned on by you.

Milo: Fuuuuuuck, Charlee. You have no idea what you're doing to me right now. Why are you telling me this?

Me: Alcohol makes me brave. *Smiley face* Will I see you tomorrow?

Milo: Fuck, do I wish, but probably not before the game. By the time we get in we'll have a quick practice and then we'll have to be in the arena. But you're coming to the game, right?

Me: Wouldn't miss it! I'll be cheering for you!

Milo: Stick with Carissa when you meet up with her. She'll bring you downstairs to meet up with us after.

Me: G'night Milo. *heart emoji*

Milo: Sweet dreams, Goldilocks. *heart emoji*

"Oh my God, I cannot believe I sent those pictures to him!" I tell Rory and Carissa over dinner before the game. "I think I may have had way more to drink than I thought. Normal me would never have been that brave."

"And that's exactly why it's good you were a little off-kilter." Rory shrugs. "Sometimes we need to lower our inhibitions a bit to be brave enough to do scary things. You know...like send Milo a sexy pose of you in his jersey."

I bring my palm to my face. "What is he going to say when he has to see me in person now? Ugh. I don't know what I was thinking."

Carissa bites off the end of a French fry. "I don't know what you were thinking, but I can absolutely tell you what Milo was thinking."

"What? What do you mean?"

"I was there last night when he got them. We were all celebrating the win in the hotel bar. I was sitting right next to him." She leans across the table. "That backward chair pic? Fucking hot, Charlee! He about died and was all grins and smiles for the rest of the night."

"What is even going on, though? We haven't talked about this at all. We're not a thing, you know?"

"But you wouldn't mind being a thing, yes?" Rory asks, picking up her drink.

"I don't know."

"Bullshit, Charlee." She laughs, rolling her eyes. "You like Milo. It's okay to say it out loud. It's okay to want to be an item, because I'm pretty dang sure it's what he wants."

"It's definitely what he wants," Carissa reports, munching on another fry. "He's just been biding his time, letting you have space to get over the Seattle twat monster."

Her nickname for Jared makes me laugh, mainly because it's so fitting.

"It's been weeks. I'm way more comfortable here now than I was, obviously. Things seem to have settled pretty well, except for finding a new place."

"You'll find the right place. That's easy."

"Not when I take Milo." I chuckle. "He hasn't liked any of the places we've visited so far."

Carissa tilts her head. "And why do you think that is?"

Holding my burger in front of my mouth, I stop before taking a bite and stare at her across the table.

"Wait. Are you serious?"

She doesn't respond, but she doesn't have to. Her grin and cocked brow say enough.

"He's been finding something wrong with each place on

purpose?"

Carissa winks and lifts her shoulder. "Whatever keeps you at his place longer."

"Okay, that is epic!" Rory laughs. "I can't believe you didn't see through that!"

I laugh with them because it's all I can do. "Well, shit. I can't even be mad at him. If I read what he's doing in a romance book, I would swoon over the guy."

"Right?" Rory snickers. "Well played, Milo. I think it's cute. But if you're serious about moving into your own place, you might want to trust your gut. You know what you want."

"Do I know what I want though?"

"Girl, yes. You want the hot hockey player who is smitten with you beyond belief. You want some good, fresh dick and all the tongue action you can get. You want cozy mornings, and exciting nights watching the team play, and you want your happily ever after. It's a dream life. And Carissa and I are both here for it!"

Carissa smirks at Rory. "So, we need to set you up with one of the guys too. That way we can all do this life together."

"Mmm, yeah, I don't know," she says, scrunching her face. "I don't know many hot, sexy hockey players that are married to kindergarten teachers."

"Never say never, my friend."

"And then there's my brother to contend with."

Carissa snorts. "Truth. I can see that being a major hurdle."

Rory and I stick next to Carissa as she flits around the arena, snapping pictures and taking videos for the team's social media. Her personality is perfect for this type of job, and she so easily gets the fans engaged in her posts. The team is lucky to have her.

I'm lucky to know her.

"Okay, let's go see the team before they hit the ice, and then we'll take our seats."

Nervous butterflies erupt in my stomach.

I haven't seen Milo in eight long days. The only communication between us has been daily text messages. I haven't seen his face or heard his voice in a while.

I've missed him.

There's a serious part of me that wishes he would sweep me off my feet as soon as he sees me, shower me in kisses, and profess his infatuation with me. But I know from experience how important game day is. He'll need to be focused on his job. I get that. I certainly don't want to make an ass of myself in front of the whole team. After crying in front of them the last time we were together, I would much rather they see the happy, hockey-loving, supportive me.

As we near the locker room, loud music blasts from inside. Not just any loud music though. A baffled smile on my face, I turn to Carissa.

"Who the heck listens to Taylor Swift before a game?"

She looks over her shoulder with her hand on the door. "Take one guess."

When we step inside, my question is answered as Dex and Hawken are dancing to Swift's newest album, the rest of the team cheering them on. It brings a huge smile to my face because nothing like this ever happens in the Sea Brawlers locker room. Jared wouldn't have been caught dead dancing.

"Charlee!" Dex shouts "Come join... Wait." He stops and taps his phone to turn off the music. "Where's your jersey?"

"What jersey?"

He wags his brows. "The one you were wearing last night, hot stuff."

Oh my God, they all saw my picture?

My mouth opens to answer Dex, but then I lock eyes with Milo for the first time in over a week, and excitement blooms inside me. My smile grows, but my feet feel heavy, like lead weights. I can't get myself to move any closer to him. I wish I knew what he was thinking right now because his facial expression is giving me zero indication.

"Hey," Milo says, standing next to Colby and Zeke and two other people I've never met.

"Hey, yourself."

Damn.

Why am I suddenly so nervous?

It's just Milo.

The same Milo who told me he sleeps better with my scent in his bed. The same Milo I confessed to enjoy sleeping with last night. The same Milo who now knows how much I liked feeling his erection against me.

Yep. It's fine.

Everything is fine.

It's just Milo.

Milo and the entire Red Tails team.

He clears his throat. "Uh, Charlee, this is, Elias Nelson. Colby's brother, and my brother from another mother. Elias is one of the accountants for the team. And this is his wife, Whitney."

My feet finally move, and we shake hands all around, exchanging pleasantries. "Pleasure to meet you both. Do you live in the city as well? ?"

"Not anymore.." Elias shakes his head with a smile. "I used to work in the area, but we're actually in Bardstown, Kentucky, now."

"Wow," I say. "That's quite the commute for a game."

Elias nods. "Yeah but it's worth it. My colleague, Beckham Fox, who used to work with me in here in the city moved back to his hometown to marry Whitney's best friend and live closer to his brothers. He offered me the opportunity to partner with him and open our own firm in Bardstown and I couldn't pass that up, so I left the big city for the small town.

"Ah. I see," I try to make it to a few home games every year, and of course, each time the team plays in Louisville. Wouldn't miss cheering them on."

"That's really great."

As I chat with Elias and Whitney, I notice Milo studying me.

"What?"

"You're not wearing the jersey."

My shoulders fall, and I glance down quickly at my outfit. Black leggings and a long-sleeved Red Tails T-shirt, knotted at my side because it's so big.

"I didn't want to get anything on it. It's not mine."

"You need a jersey, Mags?" Dex asks. "I'll give you mine."

"Fuck off, Dex," Milo says to my surprise. He swiftly pulls off the jersey he's wearing, his heavily sculpted abs now on full display, and slips it over my head, growling in my ear, "If you're sleeping in my bed, you're wearing my name."

Taking the opportunity while it's right in front of me, I breathe him in, committing his scent to memory, and then whisper, "Yes, sir."

"Good girl."

Holy fuckballs.

His voice.

The velvety, sensual tones of his voice combined with his breath on my ear make me nearly come on the spot.

Good God!

If women experienced erections the way men experience erections, I would look like fucking Pinocchio right now. I've never orgasmed by listening to someone speak, but if he were to say those words in my ear one more time, I'm pretty damn sure I would lose all control. And now I'll spend the rest of the game with all kinds of dirty thoughts swirling around in my head.

"Thank you," I spit out, unable to say much more. My cheeks are a hot, red mess, my nether regions are growing wetter by the second, and when Milo steps back, our eyes lock, and we seem to have an entire conversation silently between us.

"What I really want to do is peel that off of you."

"And then what?"

"I don't think you understand how desperate I am to be between those beautiful, warm thighs.

"I would be lying if I said I haven't wondered how good it

would be."

"I want to make you come with my tongue while my name is wrapped around your back."

"Oh God, yes..."

"I want to feel your fingers in my hair, caressing my scalp as I slide my tongue through your pussy, and I want to hear you moan for me."

"Sweet little baby Jesus, I'm all wet just looking at you."

"So, we're going to go," Rory says, taking my hand, pulling me from my wild imagination, backing me away from my staring contest with Milo. "Good luck out there, guys! We'll be cheering for you!"

Milo's mouth turns up in the corner as he watches me get pulled toward the door. He lifts his chin and then winks, and I have to stop myself from blowing him a damn kiss.

Once we're outside the door, Rory huffs out a deep laugh. "What the fuck was that in there, Mags?"

"What? What was what?"

"What do you mean, what was what? Girl, I don't even smoke, but I suddenly crave a cigarette! You two were practically eye-fucking each other in there, and it was hot!"

"Is that what it looked like?"

She guffaws. "Uhh, yeah. Totally."

"Fuck it." I wince. "I think I'm falling for Milo."

She laughs and hooks her arm through mine. "Yeah, you are."

CHAPTER 12

Milo

I've never wholeheartedly enjoyed a game as much as this one in all my life. Flying freely up and down the ice, I shoot the puck with speed and precision maneuvering around our opponents, outsmarting them with every turn. We're up three goals to two in the second period, thanks to Dex, Quinton, and Hawk. We're a fucking tight team, kicking ass and taking names.

I located Charlee before my first faceoff. She's about eight rows behind me and is seated next to Rory. Some guy sits on her other side along with his buddy, and I noticed them all chatting when I was coming off the ice earlier.

Never have I ever wanted to sit in the stands during a game. I'm a bit jealous of the men sitting next to her, who get to chat with her all evening, but then I remind myself, I'm the one down here on fire. And I'm the one taking her home tonight.

I'm the one she'll end her night with and begin her day with tomorrow morning...however that might look.

So yeah, I'm glad she's here and I'm glad she's having fun. I am nothing but goddamn smiles tonight.

"Dude, your glee is showing," Colby mumbles beside me after our first shift of the period.

"What?" Instinctively, I glance down at my crotch even though, duh, it's my uniform. Colby laughs, nudging me with his elbow. "You're smiling, numbnuts. You've been smiling this entire game."

"So?" I pant, squeezing water from my sports bottle into my

mouth.

"So, you might look a little ridiculous next to almost everyone on the ice right now." He chuckles, his body shaking with laughter. "They've all got their Viking faces on, and you're out there smiling like a kid in a fuckin' candy store."

"I can't help it, man. She's wearing my jersey."

"I saw that. You know what else I saw?"

"What?"

"The eye-fucking going on between the two of you. What the hell was that about?"

"I don't know." I huff out a laugh, shaking my head in disbelief. "But fuck was I thinking things I should not have been thinking at that moment."

"Been there, bro. Makes for one hell of an uncomfortable jockstrap."

"It fucking does." I laugh.

"You gonna do something about those feelings tonight?"

"Maybe. I kind of want to let things play out and see what happens. Let her take the lead, you know? I don't want to force anything, but fuck do I want to kiss the hell out of her."

He cackles next to me. "Oh, I don't think you'll have to force anything, my friend."

The third period has us holding steady. Our defense is on point tonight, and our offense wants the win so bad they can taste it. When I'm back on the ice, Zeke blocks a San Diego shot and passes the puck my way. Dex almost gets checked by one of San Diego's players, but he slips away and takes possession behind the net. Quinton goes down after a hit from the side, and it's enough to distract their goalie. Dex swings around and takes the shot, his arms flying up in triumph when the puck sails into the back of the net.

"Let's fucking go!" I shout.

We all huddle around Dex to congratulate him on his goal, and the crowd rises to their feet, celebrating with us. We're now up four to two. This game is ours.

"Fuck, that felt good!" Dex shouts on the bench, lifting his helmet off his head and grabbing his water bottle.

"That was a fucking great play, Dexter." I slap his leg. "I think we'll keep you."

Up on the jumbotron, the cameras are filming the fans as each section of the arena goes wild, competing to see who can make the most noise. It's great to have so many fans cheering us on. The cup is within our reach this year. We might very well make it.

My attention is back on the ice when I suddenly hear a collective "aww" from the fans. The kiss cam goes through the crowd and stops first on an elderly couple.

What is it about old people smooching that is so cute?

The camera moves to a young couple on the opposite side of the rink, and if I had to guess based on how the dude is kissing his girl, I'm going to say he's a little sloshed.

"Fuck, that's gross." Dex laughs.

"Right? She doesn't need to be licked, man? Just kiss her and get on with it."

"Pretty sure if the camera doesn't move soon, this kiss is going to turn into something not suitable for work."

Finally, the camera moves and the crowd cheers, but when it stops, my stomach bottoms out. They zoom in on Charlee and the guy she's sitting next to.

"No, no, no, no, no."

Is she going to do it?

I don't want to watch.

But I need to know what she does.

He better not lay a hand on her or I'll be off this bench in two seconds.

Charlee shakes her head bashfully on the jumbotron as the crowd cheers them on.

"Thank Christ."

The camera doesn't leave them alone though, and it's really starting to piss me off. The crowd gets louder and starts chanting

"Kiss the girl! Kiss the girl! Kiss the girl!"

"Don't you fucking kiss that girl," I growl, starting to stand up, but Dex and Colby literally hold me down.

"Don't make a scene, man. It's nothing." I don't even get the chance to argue because the crowd erupts around us, as the guy she's sitting next to leans over and kisses her cheek.

Two seconds too long if you ask me.

"Fuck!" I shout as loud as I can, but even then, my voice is drowned out by the energy of the fans.

"Take it out on the game, man. Only a few minutes left, then you can give her the kiss she really deserves."

I'm a smart man. I really am. I'm fully aware that the kiss cam is a stupid ploy to get the fans engaged and loud during a game. It's all for fun and doesn't mean shit. I'm also fully aware that I'm fucking jealous of the cum-bubble sitting next to Charlee because he got to have his lips on her first.

I'm only human.

A human with a small crush.

Okay, maybe a big crush.

I'm so pent up with rage and frustration now, I'm like a wild dog the next time I hit the ice. I fly around the rink with eagle eyes on the puck and fucking nobody is getting in my way. I intercept a pass from our opponent and take the puck down the ice, but I'm hip-checked by Lefabre and knocked into the wall.

"Fucking prick!" I scream at him. "Do it again asshole and you'll choke on your own dick!"

I turn around and check Lefabre from behind, the referee's whistle blowing the instant it happens. It's the sin bin for me, but it's worth the penalty. The game is about to end anyway. I make my way to the penalty box, and when I sit down, I spot Charlee in the stands, clapping and screaming for the rest of the team.

San Diego scores during their power play, but even that one goal isn't enough to win the game, so I could give two shits. At the buzzer, the game ends. We all shake hands, and I'm off the ice in an instant.

"Dude, really?" Dex chuckles when we're in the tunnel. "You feel better now after checking Lefabre?"

"He deserved it."

He claps me on the shoulder. "He totally did. I feel you, bro. A hot shower will do you good."

A shower will not do me good. There's only one thing that will do me good, and I need to make it happen before anything else happens.

"Milo, you're wanted in the press room."

"Fuck the press, Quinton!"

Colby stops me in the hallway with a hand to my chest. "Hey. Ain't no way you want to be this hot when she comes down that hallway, so go do your press time so you can fuckin' cool off. It'll take them a few minutes to get down here anyway. Don't be a prick."

I give him a cold, hard stare, but he doesn't take my shit, and I wordlessly turn around and head into the press room for a quick interview.

"Milo, you had a solid game tonight, but then Lefabre took the wind out of your sails a bit. Why?"

Because he's a major dick, Tom.

"Uh, I don't know. I'm sure you can watch the replays like everyone else. He hip-checked me and it pissed me off, so I retaliated."

"Worth the last couple minutes in the sin bin?"

Trying not to smirk, I answer, "We won, didn't we? So, no harm, no foul."

"You've had an excellent set of games over the past eight or nine days. Even a hat trick last week against Miami. Can you attribute your successes to anything new in your routine?"

Yeah, I'm crushing on my roommate.

And she wore my jersey.

With no fucking pants.

"No, Tom. Just keeping up with practices and workouts. You know the drill."

"Thanks, Milo. Enjoy your next couple days off. You guys deserve it."

I don't say another word before I bolt out of the press room and march down the hall to the locker room.

Charlee.

Find Charlee.

"Milo!" Carissa squeals. "Congratulations! Great game!"

On any other day, I would beam back at Carissa and give her a gigantic Milo hug, but today is not any other day. Today is the day I watched another man put his lips on my girl.

There's only one person I want right now, and she's standing along the wall next to Rory, Whitney, and Elias. She locks eyes with me as I get closer to her, and once I'm in front of her, without stopping, I grab her hand and pull her along behind me.

She grunts a little and almost trips when I pluck her from the wall, but I make quick work of where I'm headed. I just need a goddamn minute alone with her. I silently swing open the door to the gym, pull her inside, and then slam the door.

"Milo what—"

"Not a word." That's all I can say before I press her against the same door I slammed shut, cradle her face and neck in my hands, and crash my lips to hers.

Fucking Christ, her lips are soft, as I knew they would be, and she tastes good. Like beer with a hint of whatever fruity lip gloss she's wearing. I tilt her head to the side a little more so I can deepen this kiss and then swipe my tongue against her mouth. She spreads her lips for me, and holy fucking shit this kiss is everything I needed it to be.

She moans, and I groan against her mouth. She grabs onto my jersey, pulling me to her, my cock hardening to uncomfortable proportions. I wish I wasn't wearing so many goddamn clothes right now so I could feel her body against mine, but I'll take this kiss however I can get it. I'll suffer through the jockstrap erection. I just want to get lost in her.

I dip my tongue into her mouth, swirling it inside her,

listening to her soft moans, aching to have her underneath me.

Christ, she's so fucking sweet.

Though parts of me are turned on and ready for more, having Charlee in my arms, kissing her, tasting her...calms me, and it's enough for now.

It's what I needed.

She brings me back to my senses.

When we finally separate, we're both breathless.

Her beautiful, doe-like eyes glance up at me, her cheeks heated as I stare down at her. I connect my forehead with hers and close my eyes, feeling us breathe in tandem.

"Jumbotron guy kissed you before I did, and I didn't like it," I whisper against her mouth.

She smiles and brings a soft hand to my cheek. "Aww, poor Milo. Why didn't you kiss me first?"

My shoulders drop. "I've wanted to longer than you know."

"I've wanted you to."

Fuck.

"Are you telling me this is okay then? I don't want to apologize for it, because it was a fucking good kiss, but if it's not what you want, if you're not—"

She presses her finger to my lips. "It was perfect, Milo. And I look forward to doing it again. And again. And again."

"Charlee, this isn't..." I release my breath. "This isn't just a sex thing for me, okay? I'm not that guy. I need you to understand that. I like you. I want to know you. All of you. And I want you to know me."

For a moment, she seems apprehensive, but then smiles and nods. "I like you too, Milo."

"I want you to be my girl, Charlee. I want to date you and kiss you and touch you."

"But—"

"No buts." I shake my head. "I want to give you everything you want because you deserve it. I want to read to you every night. Even the steamy scenes. Hell, I'll act them out with you. Whatever you want, I—"

"Milo, stop." She lays a finger against my lips.

Fuck.

Too fast, Milo.

I overstepped.

This isn't what she wants?

I thought...

"I want all those things too, Milo," she says. "But I think we should talk first."

I shake my head, slightly confused. "Look, if this is about Jared, it's okay. I ju—"

"It's not all Jared." She tries to smile for me, but her eyes aren't smiling, and that doesn't make me feel very optimistic. "There's a lot you don't know about me. Big things. Things that could... I don't know, change your mind. And I wouldn't blame you."

"Like what, Mags? Are you secretly a vegan because you said you liked meat and—"

She shakes her head, finally chuckling. "No. I'm not a vegan."

"Okay, umm, do you have a third nipple I don't know about? A fourth maybe? I mean, it's a little weird but all the more fun for—"

"Nope. No third nipple." God, I love it when she smiles.

I lower my voice to almost a whisper. "Are you into like, the super kinky shit? Seriously, don't be bashful. Whatever you want, I'm game."

"Enticing." She winks. "But no." She lays her hands on my chest and I cover them with my own. "I promise I'll tell you everything, okay?"

"Tonight? Can we talk tonight?"

"If that's what you want."

"I don't want to wait for you any longer than I have to, Goldilocks. Whatever it is, I'm all ears, and then I want to spend the rest of the night kissing you in my bed because I have fucking missed you."

She raises up on her tiptoes and kisses my cheek but then I

sift my fingers through her hair once more and pull her to my lips.

"Tonight then."

"Tonight...after we go to Pringle's." She winces. "Because I kind of said we would go when Elias and Whitney asked."

I huff out a soft chuckle. "Shit. I forgot they were out there."

Nice cock block, Elias.

"Now, get out of that uniform and get yourself to the showers." She taps my ass, making me grin. "I'm hungry."

I kiss her one more time and then open the door of the gym to find our friends still leaning along the wall outside the locker room waiting patiently. Elias cocks a brow my way and I nod to let him know I got what I needed. He knows we'll talk later. I guess we have some catching up to do.

"Jared McClacken?" Elias scowls as I explain the goings-on of the past couple months while the ladies are dancing. I've already asked Charlee if she's tired and ready to head out once, but she simply kissed me and told me how cute I was.

I'd be cuter half naked and alone with her in my bed.

"How'd she get mixed up with that douche?"

"Don't know, man. I don't know all the details."

Maybe I'll find out more tonight if we ever get out of here.

"Everybody knows that guy's a grade-A asshole."

"Yeah."

"She came to the right place at the right time though, eh, Milo?" Colby nudges my shoulder and takes a sip of beer. "He's been smitten with her since the day she arrived."

Elias's brows shoot up. "I would've been surprised if he wasn't. You sure do have a type there, my friend."

I nod, and we both laugh as we say "Mila Kunis" at the same time.

"So uh, what were you doing in the gym?" Elias asks. "Or do I even need to ask?"

Colby's head snaps toward me, his brows rising as he awaits an explanation.

"I had to kiss her, and I wasn't waiting another goddamn second." I chuckle, feeling only slightly embarrassed by my behavior. "I could've killed that jumbotron guy for putting his lips on her. I had to make it right."

Colby laughs. "I wondered where you were. So, how'd it go?"

I sit back in the booth, swirling the remnants of my Old Fashioned in its glass. "It was amazing, as I expected it would be."

"I'm happy for you." Elias nods. "You're a good man and she's lucky to have you."

Colby nods. "Agreed. So, you guys are officially a thing now?"

I shake my head. "Not exactly, no." I take a deep breath and tell them what's going on. "She wants to talk tonight. Says there's more to her that I don't know, and it could make me change my mind about her. Whatever that means."

"What, like a third nipple?"

I laugh at Colby's question. "That's exactly what I said. I don't know." Sliding my glass back onto the table, I lean forward. "I mean it can't be anything that huge, right? What could possibly make me not want her?"

"Does she have syphilis?" Colby asks.

"What? Why syphilis?"

"I don't know." He laughs. "It just popped in my mind."

"I can't imagine she has syphilis, no. But that wouldn't stop me from wanting her. That's what they make condoms for."

"She pregnant?" Elias murmurs.

Oh shit.

I didn't think of that one.

Staring at my best friend across the table, my face falls and I shake my head, lifting a shoulder. "You know, I never asked. But she's had plenty of alcohol in the last few weeks, so I would like to think that's not the case."

"You know I had to ask." He winks. Elias is a new father, thanks to a one-night stand he had at Colby and Carissa's wedding during Mardi Gras who ended up pregnant. Lucky for them, they actually knew each other and ended up falling in love.

"You totally did. I don't think there will be any more babies born in our locker room, Nelson. You can keep that trophy."

"Don't mind if I do." He beams. "But look, whatever it is, Charlee clearly feels like it's a big deal, so go into your conversation with an open mind. Remind her that her feelings are valid. Her fears are valid, but you care about her no matter what."

"Yeah. I do care about her no matter' what." I take one last swallow of my drink and then rest my glass on the table. "Hey, how's the baby?"

"Josie's great," Elias tells us. "She's a little spitfire, and I've already had her on the ice. She'll be a skating pro before we know it."

"Wow. They make skates that small?" I arch a brow knowing there's no way in hell a baby that young is actually skating.

Elias bobs his head. "Okay, semantics. I've carried her around on the ice, but trust me, she'll be a pro in no time."

"Especially if Uncle Colby has anything to say about it." Colby winks. "Who's watching her tonight anyway?"

Elias laughs. "Oh, she's surrounded by the entire Fox family for two days. I'm not sure who was more excited, Beckham's mother or Beckham's wife."

"Oh, good Lord, between the two of them she'll be spoiled rotten."

"Yep. That's the plan."

We're at Pringle's for at least another hour. Carissa, Whitney, Rory, and Charlee have been dancing almost nonstop. Are they sexy as hell to watch? Sure. But what I really want is to get Charlee home and into my bed so we can finally talk. Every time I've asked her if she's tired, she laughs and heads out for another dance.

I'm beginning to wonder if maybe she's stalling on purpose.

And I'm getting edgier with every passing minute.

Finally, after midnight, we say our goodbyes and head back to the penthouse.

A bit sweaty after a night of celebrating, Charlee retreats to her room to take a shower, and I'm forced, once again, to wait. She wasn't particularly talkative in the car on the way home, and that bothers me. I was hoping she would be more excited about whatever is going on between us.

I like you too, Milo.

She said the words.

I wasn't imagining it.

"Calm down, Milo," I mumble to myself in the kitchen. "Maybe she's nervous. Hell, maybe she's scared." I have to remind myself, though wanting to be with her is easy for me, it may not be as easy for her, coming from the last experience she had.

Fucking McClacken.

The water stops upstairs, and I wait another twenty minutes, hoping she'll come down, but there's still no sign of her.

Maybe she fell asleep?

I pad over to the front door, making sure the lock is secure, and then turn out the lights downstairs before making my way up to check on Charlee. When I reach her bedroom, her door is ajar, her bedside lamp providing a warm glow to the several stacks of folded clothes on her bed.

Is she doing laundry?

An odd time of night to be worrying about it, but okay.

Reorganizing?

I knock lightly on her door. "Charlee?"

She pops out of her open closet, wearing pajama bottoms and a pink tank top sans bra, the peaks of her nipples poking through the fabric, making my cock twitch in my pants. Finally, my eyes drop to what she's holding in her hand. My brows pinch, and I frown.

"What are you doing with a duffel bag?"

She stares at me, a deer-in-the-headlights expression on her face. "Packing."

"Packing?"

She nods silently.

Panic builds up inside my chest.

"Wha—why? Why are you packing, Charlee? What's going on?"

"Milo, I don't want to make this any harder—"

"No, no, no, no, no." I shake my head, stepping into her room, feeling the space get smaller around me with every step. Feeling her build a wall right in front of me. "Charlee, what is this about? Why aren't you talking to me?"

"Milo."

"You promised we would talk. I told you how I felt, Charlee." I gesture toward the door. "That kiss... We... You—"

"I know." She tilts her head and gives me a sympathetic glance. "But, Milo, you deserve someone who can be what you need."

"What the hell does that even mean? I don't want someone else, Charlee. I want you. You are what I need."

Is this really happening?

She's running?

What did I do?

She shakes her head, her eyes glistening, and my heart summersaults inside my chest.

"Shit, Charlee. Don't cry. It kills me to see you cry. Please, just talk to me. Let me be here for you. Why can't we sit and—"

"I had cancer, Milo."

CHAPTER 13

Charlee

He stares, dumbfounded, in front of me. His head tilts, and his eyes soften.

"What?"

"Cancer, Milo." I swallow the nervous lump in my throat. "Leukemia."

God, I can't believe I'm doing this.

I know he's hearing me but, he's slow to process and slow to respond. "Forgive me, but did you say have? You have Leukemia? Or you had leukemia?"

"Had."

I lift my arms in a defeated shrug.

"Or have. Might have. I don't know anymore."

"Whoa, whoa, wait. Hold on." He takes the duffel bag from my hand and walks it back into my closet, where he stores it up on the top shelf. When he comes back, he wraps his warm hand around mine and sits me down on the bed. Then he gathers my piles of clothes and puts them away in my closet. A few rebel tears slide down my cheek as I watch him, not out of self-pity, but because I know I'm going to hurt him with what I have to tell him, and I like him too much to want to do that. He's the perfect guy. The forever kind of guy.

But I'll never be able to fulfill his every wish.

I'm damaged goods.

I'm broken.

Once the bed is clear, he sits next to me, holding my hand

again.

"First of all, I promised to keep you safe, so whatever it is you thought you were doing, don't. I'm not letting you run away. Especially when I don't know what's going on. I want to know everything. Charlee, if you're sick, we need to get you to the right doctors, and I can help you with that."

I shake my head. "I'm not sick, Milo. At least not right now."

"What does that mean?"

Taking a deep breath, I close my eyes and say a quick prayer that I get through this without a massive breakdown.

Time to rip off the Band-Aid.

"I was diagnosed with acute myeloid leukemia when I was nineteen."

He winces slightly. "Can you explain what that is exactly?"

"It's blood cancer, basically. To put it in layman's terms, these little asshole white blood cells keep blasting and making more little asshole white blood cells, so there's no room for the nice blood cells—red, pink, purple, black, white, or otherwise."

"That's a creative way to put it. Okay, so you had leukemia when you were nineteen." He shakes his head. "But you don't now?"

"No. I went into remission after about a year and a half of treatment."

"That's great...right?"

"Sure. But it's not without its downsides. All magic comes at a price. I'm sure you've heard that saying before."

"What reader hasn't?" He squeezes my hand and gives me a half smile, but I can't bring myself to return the favor.

"Milo, the cancer can always come back."

"And...?" He shrugs.

"It could always come back as something worse than leukemia. Or maybe a stronger type of leukemia."

"All right. So, let's say it does. What are you going to do about it?"

"Uh, I'll have to fight it again."

"Fucking right, you will. And I'll be there holding your hand every goddamn step of the way."

I release a long sigh, my shoulders dropping. "Milo, I would never expect you to put your life on hold to help me through something like that."

"Well, you don't get to make that decision for me. What I do with my life isn't up to you, so suck it up, Goldilocks. I'm here for whatever life throws your way. Because I want to be here. And I want *you* to be here.

"But there's more bad news."

He takes my hand in his. "Charlee, so far I've heard you say you had cancer and beat it and you're healthy now, so as far as I'm concerned, I've only heard good news so far and that's—"

"Milo, I had to go through several rounds of chemotherapy while I was sick, and the chemo may very well have destroyed all my eggs rendering me infertile. I can't..." I choke on my words. "I know you're a family man. You said yourself you wanted to have kids, and I would love nothing more than to give them to you one day, but I...I can't have..." I bow my head to hide my tears from him, but it's no use. He doesn't hesitate to lift my chin with his finger and look deeply into my eyes.

There's no pain there.

No sadness.

No anger.

No pity.

Only confusion.

"Is that it?"

I scoff. "That's a pretty big *it*, Milo."

He cocks his head slowly. "Charlee Mags, have you honestly been telling yourself in that pretty little head of yours that if you can't have kids, I won't want you?"

"I—"

Cupping my face in his hands, he smooths away my tears and kisses my forehead.

"You had fucking cancer, and you beat it, Charlee. I don't

mean to belittle the price you paid, because you're right, it's a hefty price, but you are alive. There are lots of ways for people to become parents, so let's celebrate the fact you are living and breathing because you survived Hell. My God, you even survived... Wait..." His smile falters. "Wait..." He sits back, his eyes squeeze closed for second, and he shakes his head.

Now he's putting it all together.

"Is that what... Oh fuck, Charlee. Is that what Jared told you?" He grabs my hands again, smoothing his thumbs over my skin. "Is that why you're here? Good God, is that why he hit you?"

Through watery eyes, I shake my head and huff out a blubbery laugh. "Jared hit me because I forgot his protein powder when I ordered groceries."

"Jesus Christ."

"I believe the words 'worthless cunt' were thrown my way." I laugh again, not because I find any of this funny, but because it's so ridiculous to say out loud all I can do is laugh. "He was a relatively good man in the beginning, but when we discussed a future together, I told him about my cancer, and it's like a switch flipped inside him. We tried. I tried. I told him I froze some of my eggs before chemo started, but he didn't want to have 'test tube babies' he called them. So we tried the old fashioned way. We did all the things to try to conceive, but it wasn't happening. I was nothing but damaged goods to him. Useless. So, we started drifting apart."

"Charlee," he breathes my name, and I feel his pity even though I don't want it. I don't want to relive all this over and over again. I want to be done with it.

But it'll never be done.

It'll always be with me.

I can't change the past.

"He came home from a bad game, ranting about how the team let him down. How useless they all were. Him, him, him. It was always about him," I sniffle. He went to grab his protein powder to make a shake, and it wasn't there. When he asked me about it, I told him I must've forgotten to add it to the list, and he..." I shrug and sniffle again. "Snapped."

"Goddammit."

"He punched me two times in a row. The first time, he knocked me back against the wall, and then he hit me one more time. I don't know...for fun, I guess. And that's the moment I knew I had to get out. There was no way I was going to let him do it again. Jared left the next morning for their away game stretch, so I called Jada to help me get out while he was gone, and here I am."

He studies me for a moment and then says, "I...don't know what to say other than I'm so fucking proud of you, Charlee. And I'm sorry. I'm sorry for what you've been through all on your own."

"Listen, Milo, he may have been a major dick, but he has a point."

"The fuck he does. Nothing that man says is true."

"I'm damaged goods, Milo. It's a fact, and as much as I like the idea of being with you, I can't—"

"I'm going to stop you right there." He presses two fingers to my lips and leans so close to me I assume he's going to kiss me. But he doesn't.

"First of all, I don't ever want to hear you refer to yourself as damaged goods again. You're not damaged goods, Charlee. You're so fucking beautiful I can't think straight when I'm around you. You're perfect just the way you are. And secondly, as to whether or not your body can carry children, if you think I'm that narrow-minded, that egotistical, that...fucking selfish that I wouldn't want you because you personally can't bear my child, then you don't know me at all, and that hurts. It hurts because I've tried so damn hard to make sure you're comfortable and happy here because I fucking care about you. I've tried not to stare at you when you're all bendy with your yoga, and I've kept my hands to myself when you've slept in my bed, even though I've been dying to touch you, to fucking worship you, the way you deserve to be worshiped."

"Milo..."

"Jesus, Charlee." He springs from my bed and paces my room,

his hands pushing through his hair. Pain flickers through his eyes as he continues. "I spent all last week lying in bed with a hard-on every night, thinking about you. What you were doing. What you were wearing to bed. Whether or not you were in my bed. Whether or not you were thinking of me. Missing me as much as I was missing you. Fuck, I was driving myself crazy because I'm infatuated with you. You beguiled me the very day you walked into my apartment, and I lived with it because you needed time and space. You needed to heal, and I wanted you to get to know me. I wanted you to understand not all guys are monsters who hurt the women they care about. I'm not that guy, Charlee," he says, patting his chest.

"I do see you, Milo," I tell him. "I see you as the kind of man I could easily fall in love with. You're strong and independent, compassionate and helpful. You're a damn golden retriever. Total Boy Scout material. The whole damn package. You're a forever guy."

"That's right. I am a forever guy. And I'm a forever guy who has been falling for his roommate, and now I find out that this whole time, you've carried this extra burden on your shoulders, convincing yourself I don't want you and that doesn't sit well with me, Charlee."

I watch him, stunned by all he's said. Trying to process his words and remind myself to breathe at the same time.

"You're falling for me?"

His shoulders drop, and some of his tension melts away as he steps up to me and offers me his hand, pulling me up and into his arms. "Falling...fallen...however you want to look at it, yes, Goldilocks. I've had a crush on you for what feels like a very long time."

"You really want...me?"

"I want you more than I've ever wanted another human being in my life." He shakes his head. "Look, I know we're doing this a little backwards here. I should be asking you on a date and courting you the way society says we should, but fuck it. I want a relationship with you. And I don't want you to be worrying about how kids come into the mix because if and when we get to that point, there's more than one way to become a parent. And if and when that time comes, I'll journey through each of those ways with you."

Tears cascade down my cheek. "What the hell did I do to deserve you, Milo Landric? How the fuck are you this perfect?"

"I'm not perfect, Charlee. Definitely not perfect."

"I think you're wrong about that." I slip my hand up his cheek, feeling the warmth emanating from his body. "I think you might very well be perfect for me."

"I could say the same thing. Now, what can I do to dry these tears and convince you to stay with me? I'll burn all the duffel bags and suitcases if I have to, just...please don't leave."

I frustratingly wipe away my tears. For Pete's sake, I feel like I haven't cried this much in...well, I can't even remember how long.

"Thank you for not making me feel inferior, Milo."

He wraps his arms around me, squeezing me to him. "It's okay to feel inferior. But you're not damaged. You're not broken." He presses his lips to mine in a tender, heated kiss, like he's aching to breathe new life into me. "And if you'll allow me, I'll spend the entire night exploring every damn inch of you to prove it."

I lift my brows questioningly. "In your bed?"

"Goldilocks, I will honor you on any surface, in any room, in any way you want."

"That sounds...orgasmic."

He chuckles, and I feel it in his chest. "You have no idea."

"Then tell me."

He places his hands under my rear and lifts me up, my legs circling his waist. And then he leans me against the wall. "I have a couple days off now, and all I want to do is spend them buried deep inside you, memorizing your body, inch by fucking inch, inside and out."

Oh God, yes please.

"I want to gorge myself on what I'm certain is the sweetest

pussy I will ever eat."

A heartsick whimper escapes my lips.

"And I want to hear you say my name as I tip you over the edge more times than you could possibly count."

"Tell me more," I beg, my tears drying with his every word.

He kisses me softly and then smiles. "And when we're done, I want to hold you in my arms while we sleep, only to start all over again in the morning."

"No breakfast? I thought breakfast was the most important meal of the day?"

"You're wrong, Goldilocks."

"Oh?"

He kisses me again, this time loosening my lips with the swipe of his soft, warm tongue. He gently bites my bottom lip, pulling it into his mouth. Sucking.

"Pussy," he murmurs against me. "Pussy is the most important meal of the day. You wouldn't want to deny a star athlete his most important meal now, would you?"

I shake my head with a smirk and wipe away the rest of my tears. "Never. Take me to bed, Milo."

"As you wish." He kisses my forehead and then flips me in his arms so he's carrying me like a new bride to his bedroom. When he lays me down on the mattress, he hovers his body over me, his heated expression making me feel wanted, desired. He smooths my hair back from my face and kisses my forehead again, moving down to my temple, my cheeks, my chin, and then he finds my lips again.

He lies beside me, propping himself up on one arm so he can look at me. "You are so unbelievably beautiful. If I've never told you that, I'm an asshole."

"I think that's a little too self-deprecating for someone like you, Milo. I'm pretty sure you've told me numerous times. And if you haven't told me with words, I've received the message often in the way you look at me."

He smooths his thumb gently over my cheek, then slides his

hand down my neck to my chest, stopping between my breasts. Feeling my heartbeat. "I've been aching to touch you like this. Is this okay?"

God, he's too sweet.

Always taking care of me.

Always making sure I'm all right.

That I feel safe. Valued. Appreciated.

I can't believe I'm here.

In his bed.

In his arms.

"Yes, please, Milo. Touch me."

He leans down to kiss me, his lips laboriously slow, as he maneuvers his hand over my breast.

Hell...that's good.

Palming me in his hand, he lifts and squeezes, his fingers feathering over my nipple, causing it to harden under his touch. My back arches off the bed and he takes the lift as an opportunity to push my tank top up, exposing my naked breasts to him.

"Fucking gorgeous."

"Milo."

His name comes out as a whisper.

A plea.

And he's quick to respond.

He pulls his shirt over his head, depositing it on the floor, and then hovers over me, his sculpture-like abs on full display.

He's so beautiful.

He kisses my lips and then murmurs against me, "Let me take care of you, Charlee."

I don't have to say a word before Milo's helping me out of my tank top and lowering his mouth to my breast, dragging my nipple into his mouth, brushing it with his tongue in small, quick circles.

"Oh...God." It feels as if my body reacts to him on its own. My back arching further off the mattress, the nerves inside me burning for his touch. His mouth. His body.

He repeats his movements, palming my other breast, then

he continues south. Kissing my stomach, licking my navel, and gazing back up at me before he presses his fingers inside the waist band of my pajama pants and slowly pulls them down my legs along with my black satin panties.

"You'll tell me if anything is too much?"

"It's not too much, Milo," I moan. "God, it's been so long."

"How long?"

I don't even want to think about the last time Jared and I were intimate, but it was at least, "Six...seven...eight months? I don't know, but God it never felt like this."

"Tell me how it feels. Tell me everything. You know I'll give you anything you desire. I want to hear it.."

He peppers kisses across my abdomen from one side to the other, then comes back up, rolling his tongue across my nipples once more.

"Mother f... God, Milo. Yes. It's incredible."

"I can smell you, Charlee. You're intoxicating." Sliding his hand down my abdomen, he drags two fingers gingerly between my legs. "Fuck. Do you even know how wet you are?"

A loud moan escapes me in response.

"So wet for me, Goldilocks. So deliciously wet. I think it's time for my midnight snack."

He climbs off the bed and lowers himself to his knees, pulling my body to the edge of the bed. I'm already writhing, my breathing unsteady with every touch.

His gentle hands part my legs, and he kisses up my thighs until he reaches that warm, wet spot. With one long, languid stroke, he licks through my arousal, my mouth falling open as I gasp a huge breath at his contact.

"Oh my God! Milo." I grab at the sheets on both sides of me.

"Christ," he murmurs. "I've wanted to taste this pussy for so long, Goldilocks, and it does not fucking disappoint." He laps at me again with a long, lazy glide of his tongue only this time when he reaches my clit, he circles it and flicks it before starting all over again.

I moan.

He groans against me and the vibrations heighten my pleasure.

"Milo, you're going to make me come."

"Fuckin' right I am, Goldilocks. Give it to me. I want to take it all. Taste every last morsel of you. Please don't hold back."

He slowly pushes two fingers inside me, curling them against my G-spot.

"Oh fuck! Milo!" I scream unable to hold back. The way this man makes me feel. The way he's worshiping my body, so slowly, lazily, deliberately, is driving me insane.

His fingers move inside me as he continues his assault on my clit until I can't hold on any longer.

"Milo! I'm there! God, I'm..."

CHAPTER 14

Milo

Her gasp is deep before her legs start to shake against my head, and she lets out a long, intense moan.

Fuck, she's beautiful when she comes.

Her chest heaves as I continue to suck her clit and lap every drop she has like it's my last meal on this earth. If there's one thing I refuse to do before we sleep, it's leave her wanting in any way. Once I'm done, I gently lower her legs to the bed and watch her come down from her well-deserved high.

My dick is so hard right now. I wondered if I might come simply by listening to Charlee. I consider tearing my pants off and sinking myself inside her, but then I hear a sniffle, and my heart sinks.

"Charlee?" I spring up onto the bed and see her swiping at her tears. "Fuck, babe, what's wrong? Did I hurt you? You didn't tell me to stop. I—"

"I'm fine, Milo. Everything is..." She sniffles.

This is so not fine.

I've never had a woman cry after eating her out before.

"Talk to me, babe. You're scaring me. Please tell me what's going on. I'm sorry. I just thought—"

"You were magnificent, Milo." She cries, rolling toward me. "You're so fucking perfect, and I don't understand why I'm the lucky one right now."

She sniffles again and my heart melts. "I think you have that wrong, Goldilocks. I'm the lucky one."

"I forgot what it felt like," she tells me, still trying to catch her breath. "I forgot what it felt like to be...desired. Wanted. Cherished."

"Then I'll spend the rest of my days reminding you, because you deserve to be loved and cared for and worshiped."

"I want to feel you, Milo."

Fucking hell.

"I want to feel you inside me. I can't get pregnant, so you don't have to worry."

Worry?

I wrap my arms around her and roll us until she's on top of me, my hands rubbing up and down her thighs.

"Let's get one thing straight, Goldilocks," I tell her, locking eyes with her. "Right here, with you, in this room, I have zero worries. I want to give you everything you want. If you want to feel me, feel me."

I lift my pelvis a bit so she understands how hard I am for her. "Feel that? That's what you do to me."

Her eyes close momentarily, and when they open again, she's hungry, needy, heated.

"I need more."

"Tell me."

"You're wearing too many clothes."

"Well, maybe you can help me with that." I put my hands behind my head and lie back, giving her full control over my body. She now decides what happens next. I want this experience to be at her pace.

She glances down to undo my jeans and tugs on the zipper, my cock stirring under my black boxer briefs.

"You're stunning like this, you know." I can't believe I seriously have this woman straddling my cock right now. Her body is on full display for my viewing pleasure. Fuck, I am one lucky man. "If you want to sit right here all night so I can stare at you, I will not complain."

She grins, her cheeks pink. "I might consider it once I have these pants off you." She tugs at my jeans and briefs, pulling them down my legs and tossing them on the floor. Then her jaw drops, and her eyes widen.

"Ho-ly shit."

That's right, babe.

And it's all for you.

"Big dick energy," she whispers, staring at me in amazement. I nearly snort because she's so damn cute.

"Think you can handle it, Goldilocks?"

She nods. "If I can't, I'll gladly die trying." And with that, she wraps her hands around my hardened shaft and lowers her mouth over me, sucking me in inch by inch.

"Mother fucker." I want to squeeze my eyes closed and focus on how amazing she feels with her lips wrapped around my cock, but with a breathtaking view of her mouth taking me in, I can't hold back in my desire to keep my eyes wide open in order to watch her every move.

"Charlee, fuck," I groan.

She swirls her tongue around the tip and grips the bottom of my shaft, pumping her hand up to her mouth and back.

"Jesus Christ." My head falls back, and I squeeze my eyes closed, relishing that warm tight pressure. With every murmur of encouragement, she takes me further, deeper into her mouth, until I'm touching the back of her throat, and then she pulls all the way out. Whatever sound comes out of me next is unintelligible.

Slipping my hand into her hair, I push it back from her face so I can have a clear view of this gorgeous woman with my stiff cock in her mouth. It's all I can do not to get lost in the feeling of her, the sight of her.

She's mesmerizing.

I smooth my thumb over her cheek as she pulls back again, this time dragging her teeth ever so gently over my sensitive shaft.

"Fuck, yes, baby. Just like that. God, you're amazing."

She moans against my skin, and I swear I grow another inch. Everything tightens. She squeezes harder, and I suck in a deep breath. She cradles my balls in her other hand, rolling them gently in her palm, and I'm nearly a goner.

"Babe... Charlee. Fuck."

She doesn't relent.

She sucks faster.

Squeezes harder.

Flicks her tongue.

"Hell, Charlee, if you're not careful, I'm going to... Shit."

Breathe Milo.

Breathe.

Steady.

Not like this.

Knowing I'll never last if she continues this onslaught, I pull her up and wrap my arms around her, my tongue swirling inside her mouth as I roll us over, and she's under me once again. "I don't want to know where you learned to blow a cock, but goddamn, Charlee. I would've lost myself if I didn't make you stop."

She gives me a smile. "I would've gladly kept going."

"I know, but I don't want to end that way. Not tonight."

"Me either."

"Tell me what you want."

"You know what I want," she whispers.

"Not good enough." I shake my head. "I need you to tell me, Charlee. I'm not crossing a boundary with you without your permission. I need your permission."

She brings a palm to my cheek, and I lean into it. "I want you, Milo. I want to feel you inside me. Please."

I lift her legs up and roll them to the side, bending them at her knees and curling them up. This angle gives me the perfect view of her glistening pussy, her rounded tits, and her stunning brown eyes that I can't look away from. I line my cock up with her entrance and tease her, her mouth falling open.

"Yes, please, Milo. Please."

Squeezing the base of my cock, I push my tip inside her, my head falling back at the tight sensation.

"Fucking hell..." It's perfect like this. She's perfect like this. I can see all of her at this angle, and the tightness has me wanting to accelerate for more friction as my need to chase an impending orgasm heightens. I thrust harder inside her, and she gasps.

"Milo! Oh my God!"

I hover above her, reveling in the way her body grasps mine from the inside out. "Is this okay? Are you okay?"

"Yes." She nods emphatically. "I'm perfect, Milo. More. Please. I need more."

At her encouragement, I quicken my pace, pulsing in and out of her, coated in her slick arousal.

Sex has never felt so goddamn good in my life.

"You're so wet for me, Charlee."

She groans louder, her breaths quickening.

"You make me this way."

I moan as my balls tighten when they slap her skin.

Leaning down, I pull her nipple into my mouth as I thrust inside her and she screams like I've never heard her before. Fuck, that is a sound I want to hear again, and again, and again. Her hands grab at my back, her nails digging into my flesh as her hips move as much as they can in this position.

"Milo! Fuck, Milo."

"I know, babe. Your body, Charlee. Fuck, it's so damn good."

"Too good. I'm going... shit. I'm going to come, Milo."

"Yes, baby. Let it out. Come on my cock. I want to feel you pulse around me."

I swirl my tongue a few more times around her nipple and then tug on it with my teeth, and suddenly her body shakes, her mouth falls open, and she groans powerfully as a second orgasm rips through her.

Feeling her body throb against my cock, milking me, I race the tingle at the base of my spine, thrusting into her hard and fast, listening to our bodies slap against each other until white-hot heat zips through my body, and I'm exploding inside her.

"Fuck, yes."

My body spasms as I empty all of my pent-up emotion, frustration, and need inside her and then I still, hovering above her. I sink down behind her as our breathing evens out, and we quietly recover. I kiss the back of her head, her shoulder, between her shoulder blades, and then trail my hands lightly up and down her back. She barely moves, and I suddenly feel like the weight of her world is on my shoulders.

"Charlee, are you okay? Did I hurt you?"

Dear God, the last thing I would ever want to do is hurt her. I would never forgive myself.

Finally, she rolls toward me with a sleepy smile on her beautiful face. "I'm perfect, Milo. That was...perfect."

I kiss her forehead and then her sweet lips. "Good. You would tell me if it were ever too much, right?"

She lifts up on her forearms. "I want to tell you to stop worrying, that I'm not a doll you can break, but..."

"But what?"

"But you're you," she says. "And what we just did was unlike anything I've ever experienced in my life."

"For me too."

"You make me feel like the most important person in the room."

"Because you are, Charlee. You're the most important to me."

She lays a hand on my cheek. "Thank you for showing me what real intimacy can feel like, Milo."

Wow. I don't even know what to say to that, so I bring a hand behind her head and pull her to me, kissing her with all the energy I have left in me. When she pulls back, she excuses herself to clean up in the restroom, and then I do the same.

And then we sleep.

Together.

My body wrapped around hers. The security blanket she's always wished for.

And within my arms, the soulmate I never knew I was searching for.

"Nope. No good."

"What?" She juts her hip out and rolls her eyes. "What do you mean, no good? What's wrong with it? We haven't even gone inside."

"It's too far away from my place."

"Oh, my goodness, it's like twenty minutes on the train." She opens her door and hops out before I can argue. When her door shuts, I sigh loudly and then step out onto the street. Making my way around the car, I gather her in my arms and pull her snug against me.

"That's too far, babe." I kiss the tip of her nose. "What if I come home from a game and want a midnight feast between your legs?"

"Oh my God." She chuckles, swatting my arm. "You're incorrigible."

"And you're delectable. I can't help it, now that I've had a taste, I can't get enough." I grab her ass and kiss her hard. "Why don't you let me get you a place in my building?"

She backs away from me, and I already feel lonely. "Because you know damn well if you do that, I'll end up spending every night in your bed. And then what's the point of having my own place?"

"Glad we cleared that up," I smirk and open the passenger side door for her to get in.

She laughs. "Milo, I'm serious. I need to be able to do this living thing on my own."

"I'll give you ten orgasms in the car right now if you'll reconsider."

She tugs on my arm. "Come on. Let's at least go have a look."

"Stick it in! Stick it in! *Stick. It. In!*" Charlee shouts at the top of her lungs. I nearly spit out my beer, laughing at how cutthroat but adorable she is. The hockey player she's rooting for sinks the puck into the net, and she hops off the couch, her fist pumping in victory.

"Atta boy Magallan!" She does a little dance in front of the living room window, and I can't help but watch her with the most endearing smile. Her excitement and knowledge of the game of hockey matches that of my own, so she's a lot of fun to watch games with. She happened upon a televised game of Anaheim versus St. Louis, and we've been snuggled on the couch together watching it ever since. She's gone through stats for more of the Anaheim players than I can keep track of, and I'm thoroughly impressed.

"How the hell do you know all this? Tell me you didn't work for their team."

She cocks a brow and snorts. "What, editing romance books for the Anaheim players? Now wouldn't that be something." She shrugs. "I don't know, I just... they're my favorite team."

Now my brows raise. "Excuse me?"

She smirks. "I said what I said."

"I think you might want to edit and rephrase that statement." I stand slowly, like a tiger watching its prey.

She giggles. "Okay, how about...the Anaheim Stars are my favorite team?"

I shake my head and take another step closer to her. "Nah uh. I don't think so. Try again."

"Umm, I like the Anaheim Stars hockey team better than any other?" She jumps back away from me as I near her, my eyes narrowed.

"You're asking for it, you know."

"Asking for what, exactly?" She's laughing now, knowing exactly what she's up to.

"I'm much bigger than you are," I remind her. "And faster."

"Only on skates."

"Shall we put it to the test? Because I promise once I catch you, I'm not letting go."

I reach out for her, and she jumps back, shrieking as she runs toward the kitchen. I chase her around the island, both of us laughing like little kids. She heads for the stairs, but I catch her before she can climb too far and pull her off with my arm hooked around her waist. She cackles as I grab her waist and fling her over my shoulder, spanking her ass playfully along the way.

"You'll never get away with this, Milo Landric."

A maniacal laugh makes its way out of my mouth as I toss her onto the couch and hover over her, mesmerized by her simple beauty. My stiffening cock giving me all sorts of ideas.

"You want to try this one more time? Who is your favorite team?"

"Anahei—" I cut her off with a sloppy, wet kiss, shoving my tongue between her warm lips even as she giggles against me. Her body starts to writhe though, so I know I'm affecting her.

"Not good enough, Charlee. Tell me again." This time, I sneak my hand up her shirt smoothing my thumb over her nipple. She gasps, but still laughs.

"Milo... yes."

"It wasn't a yes or no question. Who is your favorite hockey team, Charlee?" Before she can answer, I suck her nipple into my mouth, and she moans. "Did I say Anaheim? I meant Chicago. Totally Chicago."

"That's my good girl." I lick her nipple one more time before trailing kisses down her abdomen.

"Milo."

"Say it again, Charlee. Who's your favorite team?" I tug at her sweatpants until they, along with her purple satin panties, are on the floor by the couch.

"Red Tails," she breathes as I spread her legs and hitch them over my shoulders. "I love my Red Tails."

"Fuckin' right you do. Let me remind you why."

I spread her with two gentle fingers and then lick through her end to end, connecting with her clit stroke after glorious stroke. Her eyes roll, and her back arches off the couch.

"Oh my God, Milo!"

CHAPTER 15

Charlee

> Me: This has been the best couple of days holed up with Milo during his break. I know he's probably itching to get back on the ice, but now that we've finally crossed the line that was keeping us apart, I don't want to let him go.

> Rory: Aww... Look, Carissa! Our girl finally caught the feelings! *heart emoji*

> Carissa: AAAAHHHHH!!!! YES!! Tell us EVERYTHING! Don't leave anything out!

Me: He's cozy and warm and safe and everything I've ever wanted in a partner. In the past few days, we've apartment hunted—something I know he didn't want to do but did it for me anyway, we've read together, and to each other, we've watched hockey and talked about hockey. We've flirted and teased each other immensely and oh my God, the sex.

Rory: Ok we're gonna talk about this apartment hunting later but tell us about the SEX!!!!

Me: Listen... If there is one thing I want to both scream to the world about Milo Landric but also keep as a super-secret only to myself it's this: Milo Landric eats pussy better than any man I've ever known.

Rory: In other words, he's a super sucker.

Carissa: The perfect pussy eater.

Me: OMG, YES! He knows how to claim the clit.

Me: Oh, and to put a cherry on top of this sexy sundae, Milo is packing some major heat. It's right up there with all the cocks mentioned in the books I edit. Let's just say no matter how we're intimate, I am guaranteed to be screaming his name in the end.

Carissa: SOOOO happy for you!!!

Rory: Ditto! Once the boys get back on the ice we need to get together. I swear to God if I have to hear Dex and Hawken discussing hockey stats one more time at the dinner table, I'm going to jump out a window. *eye roll emoji*

Carissa: LOL It's a date!

Rory: Oh great. And now they're talking about their dick sizes. OMG someone tell me that men actually do grow up at some point.

Carissa: *looks to Charlee*

Me: *blinks*

Rory: *opens window, tosses out hockey puck, waves to boys as they jump after it*

> **Me: LOL! That'a girl! *wink emoji***

It's Milo's first morning back at the arena after their small break, and I'm up before dawn. Wanting to send him off to practice in high spirits, I brew his coffee and then take a few quiet moments for myself, going through my morning yoga. I start with my favorite beginner poses, taking time to warm up and stretch my body, and then move into a few more difficult positions.

I move from the boat pose into the upward-facing dog, stretching my back in preparation for my next move. After all the sex we've had these past couple days, it feels good to stretch out my body, noticing muscles that haven't been used in a while. Once I'm sufficiently warmed up, I position myself carefully into the camel pose—essentially a backbend, and a great stretch for my abdomen, my chest, and my quadriceps.

"Jesus, fuck." Milo's morning voice rumbles like soft thunder from the kitchen counter. I didn't know he was awake, let alone sitting there watching me. "You should warn a man before you do that, Goldilocks."

"What's the matter? You can't handle a little yoga?" I can't exactly turn my head to look at him, but I'm smiling anyway.

His voice gets closer. "Not when you're wearing nothing but my jersey and those sweet red panties."

"Well, enjoy the show."

"It's a fucking good show," he growls. I internally high-five myself. Though I wasn't expecting it to happen during yoga, this was exactly the kind of show I was hoping to give him this morning. I knew he would find it sexy if I wore his jersey without pants before sending him off to work. Gives him something to think about while he's on the ice.

Milo steps over to where I am and smooths a hand up my

jersey, connecting with my breast. I nearly slip and fall out of my backbend, but he holds my weight with his other hand. "Maybe we should see how good at yoga you really are."

"What does that mea—"

He gently tugs my panties until they're over my hips, then pulls them the rest of the way down my legs where they drop at my feet. "Oh my God!" I kick them out of the way. "Milo, I can't—"

"Shhh. Don't move, babe. Just breathe."

He starts at my breast again, smoothing over my nipple and then sliding his hand across the curve of my torso and down to my thighs.

"Do you think you can spread your legs wider?" Milo's request isn't really a question as much as a challenge so I give it all I can, my body already humming with what I know he's going to do.

"Breathe babe. Breathe for me."

"But Milo..."

"I told you breakfast is the most important meal of the day. And when it's staring at me like this, looking so fucking delicious, how can I refuse?"

He positions himself on his knees between my thighs and buries his face in my warm, wet center. Like he's licking an ice cream cone about to melt down the side, he swipes his tongue through me, tasting me.

Savoring me.

And then he devours me.

"Christ, Milo!" My legs begin to shake, and my arms are weak, but he continues his assault, his tongue swirling around my clit until I'm so worked over, I can barely see straight.

"Milo! I can't hold on. I'm going to fall."

"I've got you." He wraps his arms firmly around me, his palm bracing my lower back as I lift out of the pose. His hand planted firmly on my bare ass, he kisses me with more longing than I anticipated given what we did last night...several times over.

"The bird."

I peer up at him. "What?"

"That bird pose. The one you did the very first day you were here."

"Yeah."

"Can you do that pose again?"

I picture the pose in my head, knowing exactly what he's asking me to do, and glance down at his crotch. Just as I suspected. Palming his erection through his shorts, I peer up at him. He hisses out a breath.

"Fuck."

"And what do you want me to do the crow pose for?"

His eyes are heated as I squeeze his cock in my hand. "For me. Because you look sexy as fuck in that pose, and because the very first time I saw you like that, I had dirty thoughts for the entire damn day. I need a new mental picture to take with me to practice. I want to see you like that again...but without your panties this time."

That's enough reason for me.

I'm wet just thinking about it.

Bending my knees slightly with my palms on the floor, I spread my fingers wide and press into the tips of each finger. I bend my elbows straight back and bring my legs up until I'm standing on the balls of my feet. Lifting my knees to rest on the back of my upper arms, I bring my weight forward to balance myself and find my center. Using my inner thighs for as much support as possible, I hug my feet closer to my butt.

"Fucking gorgeous, Charlee."

Milo lowers himself below me, so if I fall, I know I'll fall on him and won't be injured. He reaches up and places his hands on both of my inner thighs and strokes me with his tongue once again.

"Jesus, you taste so fucking good."

"Milo..." God, he makes it so hard to breathe because all I want to do is fuck his brains out, but he laid down this gauntlet, and I sure as hell don't want to disappoint him.

"So good, babe."

I feel him leave my body and stand up behind me, hearing his shorts fall to the floor in a small heap.

Oh God!

I close my eyes and focus on my center of gravity, pulling myself up instead of weighing myself down on my arms. Milo's hands rub up my back, and when they come back down, his thumbs rub over the globes of my ass, kneading, stretching, preparing. He drags a finger over my back hole and groans. "Christ, Charlee. You make me so fucking hard."

"Milo," I gasp my body humming with anticipation.

"One day, babe. One day I'll claim this as mine. But not like this."

Thank God! I wouldn't be able to hold myself up.

He steadies my wobbly body against his, lining himself up with my glistening entrance, and slowly pushes inside me.

"Ahhh, Fuck, Milo! I'm so... Oh my God! I'm so full like this."

"It's tight, babe. So, fucking tight. You all right?"

"Yeah." I nod. "Take my hair, Milo. Hold my hair."

"Fuck." He takes my ponytail and wraps it around his hand, pulling my head back slightly. With his other hand on my hip, he slowly pulls out of me and then thrusts back in. "Motherfucker, Charlee. Your body was made for me."

"I'm beginning to think that too, Milo. Please. More. Give me more."

As I steady myself and give my trust over to Milo, he pushes into me again and again and again, each time a little harder than the last, until we have created a perfect rhythm, working together to chase our finale.

"You are exquisite." He lets go of my hip long enough to spank me, the feel of his fingers hitting so close to my clit lighting a fire inside me.

"Milo!" I scream.

"Take me, Charlee. Take all of me, you fucking sexy woman."

"Yes! Yes. Oh, God. Keep going. Just like that."

Finally, he lets go of my hair and grabs my hips with both

hands, his cock plowing into me while his arms take most of my weight, and it is fucking glorious.

"Milo, I'm going to come..."

"Yes, baby. I want to feel you tighten around me. Squeeze the shit out of me. Come all over my cock." He reaches down with his thumb to pad against my clit, and my entire body trembles.

"Milo! I'm going to fall! I can't... I can't..."

"Yes, you can, babe. I know you can. Feel me. God, I'm filling you up. You're taking every inch of my cock right now, and it is beautiful."

His words are my undoing. I spasm uncontrollably around him, squeezing him until he loses control and comes right after me.

"Oh, fuck. God damn... Ahhh."

He doesn't collapse on me as he usually might. Instead, he takes all my weight and lifts me in his arms, satiated and exhausted, and carries me to the couch. He lays me down and kisses me from forehead to feet.

"Charlee, that was..."

"I know." I give him a tired smile.

"I don't want to go to practice. I want to stay here with you. Let's go back to bed."

"You can't do that, and you know it."

"Yeah, I know. But I'm going to miss you like fucking crazy today."

"I'll miss you too, but I promise I'll be here when you get back."

"Dressed like this?"

I smirk. "No promises. I need to shower."

"Come shower with me. I've got time."

"You really want that?" I peer up at him.

His brows furrow. "Of course. Why wouldn't I? Come on, I'll wash your hair."

A swoony whimper escapes my mouth.

Freshly fucked and now he's offering to wash my hair?

Pinch me. I must be dreaming.

CHAPTER 16

Milo

"Are you sure you're okay with this?" I ask Charlee while we're in the car. "Sophie can be a ball of energy sometimes."

"Of course, I'm sure." She nods. "I've been looking forward to it since you asked yesterday."

When my sister called and asked if I might be willing to come hang out with the kids tonight since it's a no-game night for me, I was more than willing to say yes. I don't get to see my niece and nephew as often as I would like during the season, and since Charlee's come into my life, I haven't done the best job of keeping up with weekly FaceTimes.

"It'll be nice to kick back and relax with them this evening," I tell her. "Henry's a cuddle bug most of the time, and Sophie makes me laugh. That little five-year-old is a spitfire with pigtails."

Charlee grins. "Good. I love kids and haven't gotten to play with any in a while. I'm totally game for whatever the night throws our way."

"You better not speak too soon, Goldilocks. It could be a long night."

We pull into my sister's driveway off a large cul-de-sac. No sooner do I open Charlee's door and offer my hand than the front door of the house opens, and out pops my favorite five year old.

"Uncle Lo!"

I beam at my favorite pigtailed pipsqueak and open my arms wide, knowing full well she'll be running into them. "Sophie!" She indeed jumps into my arms and I pick her up, squeezing her tightly in an Uncle Milo hug.

"How's my Sophie?"

She doesn't answer me, but instead eyes Charlee in that way that says, *who the fuck are you*? "Uncle Lo, who is that?"

"Sophie, this is my special friend. Her name is Charlee. I invited her to come play with us tonight. Is that okay with you?"

She cocks her head and gives me her best little grin. "Is she your *girl*friend?"

Charlee and I both laugh at her tone. "Yes." I nod. "Charlee is my girlfriend."

"It's nice to meet you, Sophie." Charlee smiles at her. "Your pigtails are very beautiful."

"Mommy did it!" Her eyes grow wide, like she just thought of the best idea. "But I can do yours and give you a whole makeover."

"Oooh." Charlee matches Sophie's expression. "I think that sounds wonderful!"

My sister makes it to the front steps as we walk up toward the door.

"I think she's a little excited, Uncle Milo. Long time no see."

"Meghan, this is my girlfriend, Charlee Mags. Charlee." I gesture to my sister with my chin since Sophie is still in my hands. "My sister, Meghan."

Meghan looks between me and Charlee and claps her hands excitedly. "Oh my gosh, Charlee! I'm so excited to finally meet you. My brother has kept you under wraps long enough." She nudges me with her elbow. "It's about time, butthead. What have you been waiting for?"

Meghan has always been that sister who loves me unconditionally. We may have had our fair share of fights growing up, and I may not have always been the nicest to her over the years, but when push comes to shove, all she's ever wanted was to see me happy.

"You know how it is for me, Meg. Once the media gets wind, it'll be everywhere. I wanted to get my fill of alone time while we had the chance."

What I wouldn't give for a long stretch of alone time with Charlee.

Naked with nowhere to go.

"Well, I'm glad you're here, Charlee," Meghan tells her. "It's really good to finally see my brother happy. Please come on in. Make yourselves at home." I carry Sophie upstairs, where we see her little brother, Henry, watching one of his favorite television shows. When he sees me, he smiles and gets up to give me a hug.

"Hey little man! Whatcha watchin'?"

"Shaun Sheep!" He points to the screen.

"Whoa. Shaun the Sheep? He's my favorite!" I give him a kiss on the forehead and introduce him to Charlee. He takes to her right away, grabbing her hand and climbing up on the couch to sit next to her.

"You guys okay here?" I whisper to Charlee. "I'll go check with Meg for any instructions."

"Absolutely. I think we're perfect."

"Be right back."

I step around to the kitchen where Meghan is flitting around putting everything in its proper place so I don't have to do anything out of the ordinary. Not that I can't handle it, obviously. But she's a mom, and moms like to know where their things are. I get it.

"There's a sippy cup in the fridge for Henry that he can have with supper. I made them chicken tenders, mac-n-cheese, and there are grapes here for them. You'll have to quarter them, though."

"No problem."

"Sophie is getting over a little stomach bug, so she may not be super hungry, but there's plenty of food for her too. Or even applesauce if she prefers. As long as there's something in her."

"Gotcha."

"Other than that, ummm..." She looks around. "I think that's it."

"You ready, babe?" Meghan's husband, Denny, comes around the corner. "Oh hey, man. Didn't hear you come in. Sorry about that."

Denny gives me a fist bump and a hearty smile.

"Hey Den. Just got here."

"Thanks for watching the kids tonight." He grins at Meghan. "I can't remember the last time we actually got to go out for an evening."

"Yeah, well, don't rush back. Charlee and I will take care of everything."

"Charlee?"

"His girlfriend," Meghan tells her husband with an eyebrow wag. "My little brother finally has a sweetheart."

"That's awesome, Milo. Congrats."

"Thanks, man. Yeah, she's something else."

I introduce Denny to Charlee and then see the happy couple out before closing the door and making my way back to Charlee and the kids, who have already claimed her as theirs.

I might be a little jealous.

But also, my heart is filling up by the minute, seeing her with both of them snuggled up next to her on the couch.

I bet she'll be a great mom someday.

However that happens.

Once the animated show is over, Charlee and I serve the kids dinner, making small talk with them as they eat their meals. Henry is a tank and eats every morsel of food put in front of him. Sophie, on the other hand, has been a Chatty Cathy this entire time so she's taking longer to finish her food.

"Few more bites there, Sophie," I remind her, nudging her food with her fork.

She leans over to me and puts her hand up to her mouth. "Pssst, Uncle Lo."

She's anything but quiet as she tries her best to whisper. It sounds more like a growl and makes me want to laugh.

"Yes, Sophie?" I whisper back to her.

"I forget her name." She points to Charlee, who smiles and winks back at me.

"Her name is Charlee."

Sophie gasps. "There's a boy who is Charlie in my class at school!"

"How about that!"

"Charlee, are you a boy?" she asks her, making me snort.

Charlee shakes her head. "Nope. I'm a girl. But sometimes people have names that could be for a boy or a girl."

"Is there...umm..." Her little brows pinch. "Is there any boys named Sophie?"

"Hmm, I don't know any boys named Sophie, but there could be somewhere."

"I like your name, Charlee," she says, popping a quartered piece of grape into her mouth.

"Well, thank you very much. I like your name, Sophie."

"Charlee, after I'm all done, can I fix your hair right up?"

Charlee chuckles. "Of course you can. Do you think you can give me pigtails like you have?"

"Oh yes!" She shakes her little head, her long blonde curls swishing back and forth on the sides of her head. "Just like mine. It'll be perfect, darling," she says like she's some diva celebrity.

After dinner, Henry and I play with a few of his toys while Sophie plays with Charlee's hair, turning it into what she calls a beautiful hair masterpiece...which would be relatively accurate if we're relating it to a Picasso or perhaps Salvador Dalí.

"Uncle Lo! Doesn't Charlee look amazing?" she asks as both girls strut out to the living room.

Charlee's beautiful long hair is in two...let's call them piles, on her head. One pile of hair is bound on top of her head with a tiny pink barrette, and the other sits near her ear on the opposite side, accessorized with a sparkly purple clip. She gives me a proud smile, turning as if she's on a runway, and I beam back at her, my heart growing three sizes for her. The way she's played with Sophie tonight. Snuggled her. Laughed with her. Read to her, and now letting her put her hair in all types of "amazing" looks.

She's the perfect woman.

Kind.

Generous.

Playful.

Motherly.

"You look absolutely breathtaking," I tell her. Standing from where Henry and I were playing on the floor, I give Charlee a peck on the cheek and then pick up and squeeze Sophie. "And you look beautiful too, pipsqueak!"

She giggles when I put her down and grabs my hand.

"Your turn, Uncle Lo."

"My turn for what?"

"I have to fix you right up next."

"Oh, I think my hair might be too short for fixing up, Sophie." I push my fingers through my hair to show her it's not nearly as long as hers or Charlee's.

"I can still paint your nails and do your makeup. Come on."

Charlee giggles next to me. "Oh, Sophie, you know what? Why don't you bring your things out here, and then Henry and I can watch you fix up Uncle Milo. How does that sound?"

"That's a great idea! I'll be right back!"

Sophie runs down the hall and I teasingly glare at Charlee.

"You're dead to me."

She's not the least bit affected. She merely snorts in laughter. "Oh, you love it. Don't deny it."

"Pretty sure I love Sophie. I don't think I love what I know she's about to do to my face."

"Don't worry your pretty little head, Uncle Milo. I'm sure she'll make you look amazing!" Charlee widens her eyes and spreads her fingers in a set of jazz hands, just like Sophie does when she says it, and I can't help but laugh.

"Are you having fun?"

"Are you kidding? This is a blast."

I reach over and press my mouth to hers, gliding my tongue across her soft lips.

"Good."

Sophie comes skipping back into the room with her box of goodies. "Okay, I'm ready, Uncle Lo."

I plop down on the floor so I'm at her height. "All right, cutie pie. Do your best work."

She spends a few minutes brushing my hair, which admittedly feels fucking good, but once she realizes it really is too short for ribbons and bows, she gives up and moves on to my face. She places her hands on my face, contorting my cheeks this way and that, saying things like, "Love it. Love it. Yes. Okay. I can work with this."

Fuck, she makes me laugh.

She picks up her makeup, which I have to assume is either Meghan's old makeup or things she doesn't use, and begins to turn my face into an artistic masterpiece.

"Uncle Lo, does Charlee live with you?"

"She does live with me, yes."

"Are you gonna get married?"

Wow. Tough questions from the five-year-old tonight.

"Well, I don't know yet. Maybe we will. Would that be all right with you?"

"Do I get to come?"

"Of course, you would get to come."

"Then yes!" She beams, jumping up and down before resuming her work. She's very quiet for a few minutes, but I can see the wheels turning in her little head. She's either a genius artist or there's a little guinea pig in her brain, literally running on a wheel stirring up all the thoughts inside.

"Do you love Charlee?"

"Of course, I do."

It's a simple answer and one that falls unequivocally out of my mouth before I hear what I'm saying. When I look over to gauge Charlee's reaction, she's snuggling Henry, but her cheeks are pink. There's no way she's not listening to this conversation, but I don't push it for now.

The fact of the matter is, I do love her.

I've had a silly crush on her for well over two months now, and that crush has turned into something more. I want to be around her every chance I get.

I love seeing her smile.

Hearing her laugh.

Watching how well she gets along with the guys and with Carissa and Rory.

The way she smells.

The way she tastes.

The fact she trusts me makes me love her even more.

Yeah. I guess that's it.

I love Charlee Mags.

Sophie, humming as she finishes my glamour look, catches my eye and says, "I love her too."

"Oh my God! What did she do to you?" Meghan's reaction when she and Denny get back is just as I expected it would be.

"What? This?" I gesture to my face. "I'm an artistic masterpiece. Don't hate me because I'm beautiful."

Meghan laughs with Charlee, and Denny gives me a proud dad fist bump.

"Gotta hand it to you, man, she made you look prettier than she's made me on several occasions. Must be the blue eye shadow. She's always used pink with me."

"Well, when you have this hair and these eyes, how could she pick anything other than blue?"

He nods. "You're so right. The girl is a genius."

Meghan grabs my hand and holds it up. "And she did your nails too?"

"Hell yeah she did." I flip them off to Denny's amusement. "I made her take her time on this finger so I could show it off the most."

"Milo, you definitely win uncle of the year. I hope you took pictures."

Charlee pats my chest with her hand. "Oh, don't worry. We did a whole photoshoot. I'll make sure you get all the photos."

"I have some makeup wipes if you want to wash all that off before you leave."

"And deny other drivers on the road the moment of horror when I pull up and smile at them? I don't think so. I'll wash it off at home."

Meghan cackles. "You're fantastic. Thank you guys so much for hanging out with the kids. I'm sure they loved spending time with you."

"Hey, anytime. I'm just glad I had the night off. Next couple nights are busy with games, so this was a good time to see them."

"Good luck tomorrow night. We'll be cheering for you."

"Thanks! See you guys soon!"

I open the car door for Charlee, and she slips inside. Once we pull onto the road, I rest my hand on her thigh. It feels good to finally be able to hold her like this. To claim her as mine. "Thanks again for going with me tonight."

"You're going to make a great dad someday, Milo," she says, looking out her window. "You were great with them."

"I don't know. Maybe someday, but I'm content with my life as it is. And I'm happy to have you in it too."

She gives me a shy smile but doesn't say much else.

"Hey." I squeeze her thigh.

"Hmm?"

"You all right?"

"Of course."

"You're quiet."

I see a smile working across her face and she finally turns her head. "Well, I guess I'm a little verklempt because right now, you totally look prettier than me, and I think I might be a little jealous about it." A giggle rises through her, and I can't hold back my chuckle. Soon we're both laughing over the ridiculousness of my appearance, but I wouldn't change a thing. I will never be the one to stifle a child's creativity.

CHAPTER 17

Charlee

Ugh, I have never felt sicker in all my life.

Literally.

Who gets a stomach bug in their late twenties?

Me. That's who.

I thought vomiting was done when I was a kid. I thought vomiting adults were just those who drank way too damn much the night before and therefore did it to themselves.

Nope. Wrong again.

Apparently, even adults can catch the stomach flu.

I was fine yesterday when Milo left for their game in Vancouver, but at some point this afternoon, something smacked me hard, and I've been down for the count ever since. My body feels as though I have ten-pound weights strapped to my arms and legs. I'm hot and then I'm cold. Sweating and shivering. And I don't want to get up off the tile floor of the bathroom for fear I'll vomit all over Milo's home. As it is, I feel bad about slipping on his favorite Wile E. Coyote hoodie when I saw it downstairs, but I was missing him, and his scent is all over it and I couldn't stop shivering, so two birds, one stone, and all that.

I haven't kept much of anything down today, having thrown up three or four times, but I've tried to sip water where I can. I probably should've grabbed some crackers on my way upstairs, but what's the point? I lost track of time a while ago when I fell asleep after climbing the stairs to my room, so I have no idea what time it is. It's dark outside so that at least gives me a clue.

I left my phone downstairs, but hell if I have the energy to go get it, so there it will stay for the night. I'm exhausted, and if I try to make it downstairs, I'll have to sleep down there. I don't know if my fever is so high I'm hearing things or if the door to the penthouse just opened and closed, but then I hear the familiar jingle of Milo's keys, and I know he's home. What I wouldn't give to be able to run to him and wrap my arms around him, but instead, my stomach gurgles, and my body lurches, and I'm leaning over the toilet once again.

I hear him call for me a couple times, but there's no way I can respond at the moment. The sound of his voice gets nearer, so I have no doubt he'll find me.

"Charlee? Oh shit."

With one arm over the toilet bowl, my head hanging over the rim, I try to shoo him away with my other hand.

"Get out of here, Milo. Whatever I have, you can't catch this. It'll be better for you if you stay away from me. I think I have a stomach bug."

"I know you do, babe." His warm hands pull my hair back as I dry heave.

Seriously, it's not like there's anything left in there.

"Meghan texted me earlier tonight. Said Henry caught what Sophie had so it's possible you and I could catch it. I'm so sorry, Charlee."

"Better me than you," I mumble. "I'm fine though, Milo. I'll be fine. You should go."

"Not a chance, babe. I'm not leaving you." He wets a washcloth and hands it to me to wipe my face, and then places his wrist on my forehead. "Jesus, Charlee. You're burning up." He grabs another cloth from the shelf behind him and wets it for the back of my neck. "Have you taken anything?"

I shake my head, leaning against him now that I think my body is done trying to flip itself inside out. "Can't keep anything down to bother trying."

"I get it, but we need to get this fever down so you can sleep."

He reaches up to my medicine cabinet. "Do you have Tylenol in here?"

"Somewhere. I think."

He searches through a few bottles of over-the-counter medications until he finds what he's looking for, then pops open the cap. He shakes two pills out onto the counter and then fills the cup on my sink with water. "Here. Take these."

I do as I'm told, and then he lifts me into his arms from the floor, his warmth a relief from the chill in my bones. He lays me down in my bed, lifting my legs as he pulls down the covers and then cocoons them around me.

"Did you win?"

He peers down at me. "You're vomiting up your insides, burning up on the outside, and freezing on the inside, and you're still worried about whether or not we won?"

"Is that a yes?"

"That's a yes, babe." He kisses my forehead. "We annihilated them five to zero."

"Good. You should go, Milo," I say with heavy eyes. I can tell I won't stay awake much longer. "I don't want you to get sick."

"I'll be right back."

He steps into my bathroom for a moment and brings out my small white trashcan, positioning it next to the bed. "Just in case." Then I hear his belt buckle and the whoosh of clothes coming off. He pulls down the covers enough to slide in behind me.

"Milo..."

He pulls me against his chest. "I'm not leaving you, Charlee. I'll be right here if you need me."

"If this fever breaks overnight, I'll be a sweaty mess."

"Then I'll be a sweaty mess with you, babe. It's nothing a shower and some fresh sheets can't fix."

"But you might catch—"

"Shhh. It's okay, Charlee. I won't catch anything. I get germs from the kids all the time. I'm around them a lot more than you. Plus, I'm amped on so many vitamins it would take a lot to bring me down. Don't worry about me."

"Milo." I turn and rest my head on his chest, my leg curling into his, trying to warm myself with his body heat.

I seriously don't know what I did to deserve Milo Landric, but he has somehow become my prince charming.

The perfect man.

Jared would've made sure we weren't in the same wing of the house for days if I was sick, and here's Milo climbing into bed willingly, to hold me while I sleep. While I sweat. While I vomit into a bucket.

How did I get so lucky?

"You're too good to me, Milo."

He kisses the top of my head and trails his hand up and down my back, soothing me. "I meant what I said the other night, you know. To Sophie."

I don't respond right away because I know what he's referring to. I didn't know what to say then, and I don't know what to say now. Well, okay, that's a lie. I know what I want to say in response. I guess I just...haven't yet.

"Do you love Charlee?"

"Of course, I do."

"I love you, Charlee. And there is no place I would rather be right now than right here with you in my arms. Sick or not, I don't care, because I'm in love with you. And I would do anything for you."

I try to sit up so I can look him in the eye, and he pushes one leg out of bed. "Do you need to throw up again?"

I shake my head. "You really love me?"

His body relaxes, and a smile crosses his face. He tilts his head and pushes my hair behind my ear. "I love you even when you have a stomach bug. I love you even though you probably have vomit breath. I love you even though we'll both wake up in a sweat puddle in the next few hours." He chuckles softly. "You look adorable in my sweatshirt, by the way. It's not too...purply on you."

"Milo—"

"But most of all," he continues, "I love you for the compassionate, caring, friendly, kind, funny, beautiful woman you are. I think I've loved you for a long time. I don't usually believe in things like fate or destiny because I've worked hard for my successes, but I've dreamed of falling in love with a woman like you, and then you literally knocked on my door. You were my dream come true, Charlee, and I'm so in love with you."

Even in a fevered state, I can muster a smile. "I'm in love with you too, Milo. And I want to say a bunch of nice things to you like you just did, but..." My eyes droop a little more. It's getting harder and harder to keep them open. "I'm so exhausted."

He huffs out a quiet laugh and pulls me down against his warm body once again. "It's okay, babe. Even Goldilocks gets sick sometimes. I'll be right next to you all night. I promise."

I slide my hand over his naked torso, my fingers curling to grasp on to him even though there's nothing there but muscle to hold onto. "I love you, Milo."

"I love you, too. Sleep now." I feel his lips on the top of my head one last time before my brain clouds over and I doze off for the night.

"Aww, he took care of you? How freaking sweet is that?" Rory exclaims over lunch a couple of days later. Spring break has her feeling fancy-free this week. Together, we're soaking up the city with Carissa, who took a couple days off while the guys are training.

"I honestly don't know how he didn't get sick. The man clearly has an immune system of steel, but yeah. He took wonderful care of me. Made sure I ate and drank. Washed my hair for me when I woke up a sweaty mess. Washed and changed my sheets. You name it, he did it."

"Did he read to you again?"

"Several times." I nod.

Rory swoons. "He totally loves you."

"Who loves who? What did I miss?" Carissa hangs her purse from her chair and takes a seat at the table. "Sorry I'm late."

"Milo loves Charlee."

Carissa gasps. "Oh my God! Did he finally say it? Because Colby and I have a bet going on how long it's going to take him to say it."

"Hmm." I narrow my eyes. "What's the bet?"

She shrugs. "Oh, it's totally of the oral variety. I think he's already said it and Colby thinks he'll hold out a bit."

"Well, you can tell Colby to get on his knees because he has indeed said it. More than once in the past few days."

"Eeek!" She throws her arms around me in a hug. "I knew it! I could see it on his face! He was missing you like crazy in Vancouver."

"I was missing him too. I even wore Wile E. Coyote while he was gone."

She rears back in shock. "You did not!"

"I so did. Milo thought it was adorable even in my fevered pukey state."

"Aww you poor thing. Feeling all better?"

"Much."

"Kids are the worst, right?" Rory laughs. "You love them fiercely even when they pass their evil little germs your way. Like, shouldn't we be old enough to fight those off by now? What is that magic they carry?"

"I don't know, but if there's a magic cloak or shield to keep me from ever vomiting like that again, I'm willing to pay top dollar."

"Same girl!"

Carissa orders herself a diet cola when our waitress stops by and then leans forward on the table, her brows wagging at me. "So, are you planning anything for Milo's birthday?"

"Actually, I was thinking about doing something for him, but thought I would discuss it with you guys first."

"We're all ears."

"I want to do something fun for him. But I think we should include the guys as well, you know? They're basically his family."

"Oh yeah." Carissa nods. "The guys won't want to miss it, and they'll totally invite themselves if you don't, so you may as well."

"All right, how about a party at Milo's place on Sunday? I'll do a huge nacho bar with all the fixings since that's his favorite. Since they don't play again until Tuesday and it's a home game, they'll have Monday to recover from any late-night shenanigans."

"Sounds like a plan." Carissa nods. "I'll tell the guys when I see them back at the arena. Do you want it to be a surprise?"

"And what are you going to get him?" Rory asks.

Rory's question makes me smirk because I've had a wicked idea floating around in my head about what to get Milo.

I narrow my eyes and bite my bottom lip, trying to hide an ornery smirk. "You know what, Carissa? Yes. Let's make this party a surprise. Don't let Milo know. Tell the guys to show up by six-thirty."

Rory nudges me with her elbow. "Girl, what is going on in that little head of yours?"

I give both of my friends a wink. "A little birthday surprise for the man who has everything."

"Uh-oh," she laughs. "I can't wait to see this."

CHAPTER 18

Milo

"Good morning, birthday boy."

A sleepy grin broadens across my face. I roll over a bit and grab Charlee's arm and pull her across me until she's straddling my waist.

"That's better," I growl, my voice still hoarse. "Good morning to you."

She shifts her body a smidge, and I'm already hard beneath her. She lifts a brow and rubs her hands down my chest. God, that feels good.

"Already?"

My chuckle is deep. Soft. "Always."

I am always hard for her.

I can't get enough of her.

I'll never get enough of her.

I slide my hands under her T-shirt and find she's completely naked underneath. What luck! Oh, the things I want to do with this body. A bit of mischief in my gaze, I lift her shirt off and then lay back admiring her body.

"So fucking beautiful."

She gives me a loving smile. "It's crazy to me how far I've come since living with...you know who." She doesn't like to say his name. "He never looked at me the way you look at me."

"I hope you feel how different I am from him. I hope when I look at you, you feel desired. Cherished. Loved. Because you are absolutely all those things and more."

"That's exactly how I feel when I'm with you. I never felt truly loved for who I am." She shrugs. "I was merely a baby carrier to him...until I wasn't. And then I was nothing."

I smooth back her hair and cup her face in my hands. "To me, Charlee, you are everything."

She leans down and kisses me softly. "And you make me feel it, hear it, and know it every single day. I'm so grateful for you." She kisses me again, only this time I bring my hand to the back of her head and hold her to me, my tongue pushing through her lips, deepening our connection. Showing her how much I love and care for her.

Her nipples drag against my chest, and fuck, she makes me so goddamn hard.

"So, I have a plan for the evening," she says when we finally separate. She lifts up, trailing circles around my chest with her nails.

"Oh yeah?"

"Mmm-hmm. It involves nachos. Maybe a little hockey. Maybe a few...other things."

"I like the sound of...other things."

"Yeah?"

"What kind of other things did you have in mind?"

"You'll see." She winks, and a whole new level of intrigue and excitement washes over me. The woman I love has planned something for my birthday. Whatever it is, I have no doubt I will love it.

"But until then, you get to make the call for the rest of the day. Whatever makes you happy."

"You. Naked. On every surface of this penthouse. That would make me happy."

"I think that can be arranged, if you think you can keep up."

She makes me laugh. "Babe, I'll put the straw in the juice box more times than you can count today, don't you worry. But there's one thing I need first."

"Anything."

I lay my head back and gesture for her to move.

"Take a seat on my face. I'm ready for breakfast."

She raises her brows. I think I may have shocked her. "You're... serious?"

I grab her hips and pull her up my body while slipping myself down at the same time until she's positioned above my face, right where I want her. "Of course, I'm serious. Sit the fuck down, Goldilocks. I'm famished."

I help her out by pulling her down on top of me so her sweet pussy rests on my mouth.

Holy fuck, she smells good.

Spreading her with my hands I trail my tongue through her folds, her body tensing as she gasps, and then melting against me as she lets out a loud moan.

"Oh God, Milo."

Hearing her moan my name makes me smile every goddamn time.

That's right babe. I know what I'm doing.

I drag my tongue back and forth, swirling it around her clit and then flicking it several times in a row until her body starts to writhe over me. Bringing my hands to her ass I tap her puckered hole with the pad of my finger, and she nearly shoots off me.

"Milo! Fuck!"

Her pleasure makes me chuckle. "Not done, babe. Need to clean my plate."

"It's too good," she cries. "Babe. Oh my God."

"Sit." I ease her back down on my face and lick through her faster.

Harder.

More pressure.

Her moans grow more intense, and her body starts to move forward and back.

"That's a good girl," I praise her. "Feel my tongue. My mouth. Take the ride. Fuck my face. You taste so goddamn good."

My tongue dives inside her licking, eating, devouring.

Relentless as she shifts her pelvis, rubbing along my beard, my nose tapping her clit every time she thrusts forward. "Milo... God, yes!"

Motherfucker, I think I'm harder than I've ever been. I bend my knees and grab my cock, palming it in my hand, knowing damn well I won't even make it inside her before I blow my load.

Charlee's legs start to shake, and her moans become louder and longer until finally, she cries out, "*Oh, fuck.*"

I'm eating her faster and harder, lapping up every damn drop she gives me as she rides out a long orgasm, and it's so fucking hot. My balls tighten, and my own legs start to tremble, and as I take one long last lick through my girl, I squeeze my cock and come all over my stomach.

"Mother fuck. Christ."

Charlee carefully untangles herself from my body and lies next to me, a satiated and happy smile on her face. I turn my head toward her, catching my own breath as I come down from the buildup.

"Never have I ever come while eating out a woman. You, Goldilocks, are intoxicating, and I would do that again in a heartbeat."

She leans up and kisses me, tasting herself on my lips. "I love you, Milo Landric."

"I love you too, Charlee."

She nuzzles my nose with hers, and I playfully spank her ass. "Come shower with me. And then we can do this all over again on the dining room table."

"What is it?"

"Open it!" She smiles at my curiosity after handing me a wrapped gift.

"You shouldn't have gotten me anything, babe. You are all I want. All I need."

I step up to kiss her, and she pushes on my chest with a giggle. "Yeah, yeah. I knew you would say that, but I think you'll like this. I mean, I hope you'll like it. I know I'll love it."

When I glance at her, she winks at me.

"Oh, so this is a gift for both of us?"

She lifts her shoulder and grins. "Maybe."

Something for both of us.

What did she do?

I pull back the wrapping paper and open the unmarked box, amused and excited about what's inside. Removing the smaller box inside, I read the front.

"A remote-controlled starfish cock ring."

When I glance at Charlee again, she's biting her bottom lip, visibly pleased with herself.

"Have you ever used one?" she asks me.

"Can't say that I have, no."

Though I'm now very intrigued.

"Does it scare you?"

My brows furrow. "Fuck no, it doesn't scare me. I think this is amazing." I wrap my hands around her. "My girl likes to play, huh?"

"Your girl likes to play with you. I've never used toys before, other than a vibrator, but with you..." Now she gives me a shy smile. "With you, sex is both intimate and fun. So why not? I thought it would be something to make the evening a little more exciting."

"You want me to go put this on right now?"

She nods. "Mmm-hmm."

I peer down at the box. "And this little remote..."

"Goes in my pocket."

"So, you can zap my dick anytime you want, huh?"

Her laugh is maniacal, but the happiness and excitement on her face is fucking worth it. I'm so head over heels for this girl. "I don't think zapping is the right word. But yes, that's the idea. I promise to be somewhat nice."

I pull her harder against me and kiss her sweet lips. "You

don't have to be nice, babe. But you should know the minute you make me hard, I'll be bending you over the coffee table, or the couch, or the kitchen sink. Or if you're lucky, all three."

"I can't wait." She kisses my chin and then swats my ass. "Now give me that remote, and then be a good birthday boy and put that sucker on while I get the nachos ready."

I excuse myself to the restroom so I can take a quick look at this new toy before putting it on. Ripping the package open, I take a glance at the picture explaining how best to wear it. There's a ring for my dick and a ring that secures around my balls. The vibrating part is a starfish-shaped, soft silicone material with tiny massaging tentacles on one side.

"Holy shit, this completely covers my balls once I slip it on?" I smile to myself. "There's no way this isn't going to feel good."

I take the silicone rings and stretch them a bit and then work them both on, placing them exactly where they need to be.

Fuck me. This should be fun.

I pull up my boxer briefs and joggers and discard the box under the bathroom sink just in case I need it later, and then make my way back to the kitchen.

"Well, is it on?"

"Yeah, baby. It's on."

"Shall we try it out?" She holds the small remote in her hand, smiling at me proudly.

"Give it your best shot."

She presses on the remote, and the vibrator starts off on the softest setting.

Buzz Buzz Buzz.

"Holy fuck." I take a deep breath and let my head fall back. "Babe, that feels amazing."

Ding dong!

What the fuck?

"Perfect. Our guests are here!"

My face falls. "Wait, what? What guests?"

She tries her best to hide her giggles, but she's failing. "Why

SUSAN RENEE

don't you go answer the door, birthday boy."

"Fuck. Me. You did not just make me put this thing on knowing we're about to have company."

Laughing still, she wraps her arms around my neck and kisses me sweetly. "I sure as hell did." She steps on her tippy toes and whispers in my ear, "Think you can handle the challenge, Landric?"

"I think you better be ready to touch your toes when this night is through, Mags."

I hear her cackling as I swing open the front door and find Colby, Carissa, Dex, Rory, Hawken, Quinton, and Zeke standing on the other side.

"Happy birthday, man." Colby offers me a fist bump followed by our typical bro hug, and then everyone else follows suit.

"What is she laughing at?" Rory asks with a smile when she hears Charlee laughing in the kitchen.

"Trust me. You don't want to know." Suddenly, my face grows serious, and my eyes roll. "You had better not fuckin' know. Do you know?"

"Know what?"

"Charlee?" I shout over my shoulder.

"What?"

"Does Rory know?"

"No!" She giggles.

"Does Carissa know?"

"No!" She fucking giggles again.

"I want to know," Dex says, walking into the kitchen and giving Charlee a quick kiss on the cheek.

"What's going on? What are we knowing?" Zeke asks.

"Nothing." I shake my head and wave my arms. "Nobody is knowing anything."

"Uh-oh," Colby says, his arm around his smiling wife. "This has to be good. Your face is red, Landric."

"Is this about sex?" Hawken turns himself around, studying my living room. "Did you guys have sex today or something?"

I nod. "It's my birthday, dumbass. What do you think?"

Quinton shakes his head. "Well, I don't know big guy. Your girl is standing up and walking on her own two feet, so maybe it wasn't that good. Your age giving you a problem, Milo?"

Dex's brows practically rise right off his face. "Oh, is that what we're knowing? Milo's dick isn't working right? Do you have dick dysfunction?" He leans in. "Nothin' to be ashamed of. They make pills for double D you know."

"Oh, for fuck's sake. My dick works perfectly fine, thank you very much."

"Maybe we shouldn't be asking you." Carissa winks. "Hey, Mags! Does Milo have dick dysfunction?"

"I am happy to report that's a big negative. There is absolutely no dysfunction whatsoever...in Milo's dick...or his tongue."

"TMI!" Zeke covers his ears and shakes his head. "TMI! I don't need to know what Milo does with his tongue."

I don't know why I'm proud to hear her say it, but hearing her talk about me just made me feel all warm and fuzzy.

This is such a weird conversation.

"Well, there you have it then." Carissa shrugs. "Case closed."

Smiling at my surprise guests, I raise my arms. "Who wants nachos?"

I lead everyone over to the kitchen counter, where Charlee has laid out several dishes of nacho toppings and a crock pot full of taco meat. I glance over at her, and she winks at me, my soul feeling more love for her knowing she remembered my favorite food and coordinated this entire evening for me.

She even puts a hockey game on the big screen for us to watch, and we've been shouting at it ever since.

"Ooh, well played Legeaux." Quinton claps his hands. "That's his second goal of the game."

Zeke lifts his beer to his lips. "Yeah, but Anaheim's on a power play now, and that's Magallan's strong suit...well, when he's not the one sittin' in the sin bin."

Colby shoves a loaded nacho into his mouth and nudges me

next to him on the couch.

"How lucky are you that your girl allows you to watch other people play hockey after being away from her all the time because you play hockey?"

"Don't give her too much credit, Colb. She lets you think she's a supportive girlfriend, but she also has a crush on Magallan."

"Hey! I heard that!" Charlee says from the kitchen where she and the girls are giggling together.

Buzz. Buzz.

A light vibration hits my balls, causing me to lean forward on the couch, my elbows on my knees.

Fuck.

I shake my head, trying not to laugh at my girl.

It feels good, but this is not the place, and if the guys knew what was happening right now, they would never let me live it down.

Deep breath.

I can do this.

Do not get hard.

Do not get hard.

Do not get hard.

I can't believe I'm wearing fucking joggers.

Jeans would at least hold me in a little better.

"She tried to tell me her favorite team was the Anaheim Stars. Can you believe that?"

Every guy in the room turns to scowl at Charlee. They're teasing, of course, but still.

"The audacity." Dex shakes his head.

Memories of our romp on this very couch, eating her into submission over her favorite hockey team float happily through my head.

"Right? I had to work my magic to get her to change her mind."

Buzzz. Buzzz.

"Shit." The vibration in my balls sends my body into a sudden spasm on the couch. I nearly toss my entire plate of nachos onto Colby's lap.

"What the hell, Milo? You okay?" he asks.

"Yeah. Fine. I'm fine. Just a little leg spasm or something."

What the hell am I going to do when she turns this fucker up even more?

"Oh, man. Those are the worst." Zeke shakes his head. "I get them at night sometimes when I'm dehydrated."

"Anaheim's got it going on right now," Hawken says, his eyes glued to the action of the game. "I can see us facing off in the playoffs this year."

"You may be right," I answer, trying to drive attention away from what's going on in my crotch. "If they win the next two and we beat Seattle."

Seattle.

They're our last game of the regular season and one of the biggest games of the year for us. For more than one reason obviously.

Jared McClacken is Seattle's center, which means he and I will face-off on the ice. And I swear to God, when we're out there I'm going to tear that man to shreds for what he did to Charlee.

"Come on, Morgan! Pass the fuckin' puck!" Dex stands up when Anaheim loses possession and circles back. Morgan finally passes to Richiez who passes to Hutchinson, and the puck is back in Anaheim territory. "There you go! Keep the stick low."

Magallan shoots and misses, but circles the goalie's net until he has a second attempt, and this time he does not miss.

"He shoots and scores!" Dex shouts, giving everyone a high five.

Buzz. Buzz. Buzz.

Buzz. Buzz. Buzz.

Fucking hell.

I can't stand up.

If I stand up right now, the entire room will see my fucking boner.

I lower my plate and let my head fall back for a moment, a sheen of sweat breaking through my skin.

"You good, man?" Colby asks again.

I gesture to my nachos. "Hot pepper. Fucker was hotter than I expected." He chuckles and I lean back enough to peek at Charlee, who is stifling a laugh.

She has me so goddamn hard right now. I can barely stand it.

When I think it's safe to do so, I finally stand up to throw away my plate.

Buuzzzz.

"Fucking hell." I freeze right where I am to ride out the unbelievable sensation going on in my nether regions, but the moment I try to take a step, Buuzzz.

Oh my God.

"What the fuck is up with you, Landric?" Colby laughs. "You look like you're trying to hold in a shit."

I'm trying to hold in something, that's for sure.

I throw my hand out to my side, shaking my hand with a stupid ass grin on my face. "I'm good. I promise."

It's too late though. Colby's reaction has drawn the attention of the rest of the guys.

"What's this? Milo's holding a dookie?" Hawken asks with goofy grin. "If you need to shit man, just do it. Release the beast."

The beast is definitely in need of a release.

"You know, that's another thing that happens with age, I hear," Quinton teases. "Old people can't control their flatulence. End up crop-dusting the whole damn room as they walk across it. If you need to fart, Milo, let 'er rip. Nothing you haven't done before."

"You guys, I promise I'm good. I think I—"

Buuzzz. Buuzzz. Buuzzz.

My eyes roll back in my head, and I try to hold my breath through the unbelievable sensation.

"Oh my God."

Dex chuckles softly, watching me from the other side of the

couch. "I don't think he has to shit, boys." He turns to look back at Charlee, who is covering her mouth to hide her victorious smile. He nods his head toward her and then turns back to us. "I think this birthday boy's got a different issue going on."

She still hasn't turned off the damn vibrator stimulating my nut sack. I think she might be trying to kill me. My damn legs are like JELL-O, and if I'm not careful I could seriously jizz in my pants like a fucking teenager. I shake my head in laughter because if I don't laugh, I may damn well cry.

"Fucking birthday shenanigans. She got me, guys. I'm sorry, but I'm going to need a damn minute."

They all break out in hearty laughter, finally realizing what I'm dealing with. So now I don't feel badly about maneuvering myself to the kitchen island, where I can hide my embarrassing hard-on.

"Can I get you anything, babe? Another beer? More nachos?" Charlee smiles like a doting housewife, but my mind is a goddamn blur. All I can think about is bending her over right here, right now, and fucking her brains out in front of everyone until she screams so loud every tenant in this building knows my name.

"Yeah, actually." Coming up behind her, I place my hands on her waist and turn her around. "I could use your help in the wine closet if you don't mind. I want the guys to try that whiskey I showed you."

"Oh, yeah? Which one was that?"

"Just come on. You can help me grab the glasses."

She giggles as I direct her down the short hallway and into the wine closet, closing the door behind us.

"You seem a little tense. Everything okay?"

I yank my pants down enough to free my cock, and then pull down her leggings until they're around her ankles. "Tense is an understatement, Goldilocks. Call me a weak man if you want, but you won't be thinking that in about three seconds. Bottom shelf sweetheart. Grab on and don't let go."

I hold on to her waist as she bends over and grabs hold of the bottom shelf, and then I waste no time. "This is going to be fast and hard, and you're going to take me like the goddamn good girl you are because you have driven me absolutely fucking insane and I need you."

"Take me, birthday boy." She wiggles her ass at me. "Take all you want."

I don't wait for her permission before I line myself up with her pussy and dive right in, bottoming out against her, the vibrator against my balls now stimulating her as well.

Her mouth falls open and she loudly whispers, "Oh, fuck!"

"Yeah. I know. That's what you've done to me, babe."

I pull out and thrust back in, giving her a taste of her own medicine. "Are you all right? Is this okay? I don't want to hurt you?"

"I'm perfect, Milo. I promise I won't break."

"You make me so goddamn hard. I need you, Charlee. God, do I need you." Pulling out once again, I slam into her, repeating my movements over and over until I find my pace. That inevitable speed where I lose all control and can think of nothing but blowing my load inside her.

"Fuck, yes."

Her gasps are quiet but steady as she holds tight to the wine shelf. From this angle I can penetrate her deeply, my balls slapping against her. The next time I pull out, I tug on the cock ring I'm wearing until it's off and on the floor, and then I fuck her as fast and hard as I can until we're both breathing through our tandem orgasms.

Catching my breath against her back, I rub my hand up and down her spine and kiss her lower back before pulling out of her and looking around for something to help clean her up. To my relief there are a few tea towels on another shelf, so I grab one and help her before standing her up and pulling her leggings back up her legs.

She's all smiles when she turns back around. "Happy birthday, Milo."

Leaning forward, I tip my forehead against hers. "This has been the most unforgettable birthday I've ever had. Not one in my whole life compares to today. Thank you for this, Charlee."

"It's my pleasure, Milo." She snickers. "Well, and yours, obviously."

She wraps her arms around me, and I squeeze her against my chest. "God, I love you."

"I love you too, birthday boy."

Elias: Hey man! Sorry it's a little late, but happy birthday. Would've been there but Josie sprang a small fever (teething). But I heard your night was a whole vibe. Sorry we missed it!

Hawken: LOL

Dex: Hehe a whole vibe!

Zeke: *wink emoji* That's an understatement, Nelson!

Me: Clever. I see what you did there.

Elias: What, no video? LOL

Me: Smh No fuckin' way would I allow a video of me with a birthday boner to be released into the universe.

Dex: Hmm, but I bet you could get a cool sponsorship for the cock ring that did it for you, man!

Quinton: Oooh that's a great idea! *Googles cock ring sponsorship by hockey players*

Zeke: Oh my God can you even imagine the poster they would have to make for that advertisement?

Hawken: *GIF of Loki saying Oooooh Me Likey*

Me: You all can have at it. There will be no cock ring endorsements from me.

Dex: *whispers* But you do endorse it, right? #askingforafriend

Me: LOL Oh HELL YES. You're all getting cock rings for Christmas.

Dex: *GIF of little kid in Penguins jersey screaming YESSSSSSS*

Elias: Sounds like Charlee has had quite the impact. She got you good!

Me: Oh, don't let her fool you. In the end, she made out pretty well too. *wink emoji* But yeah. She's an amazing human.

Colby: Milo is so in luuuuurve.

Hawken: Figures the guy who reads the smut books is the guy who falls in love with his roommate. According to Rory, those kinds of storylines happen all the time.

Dex: *raises an eyebrow at Hawken* You talking about smut with my sister?

Hawken: *gives Dex the middle finger* Yeah. Giving her recommendations for circle time reading at school. LOL

Elias: Well, I'm thrilled for you, Milo. It's good to see you finally happy.

Me: Hey Elias, you coming to the big game?

Elias: Hell yes! As long as Josie's all right, I'll be there! Best of luck to all of you. I have no doubt you'll emasculate Seattle.

Me: Oh, there will definitely be an emasculation happening tomorrow. Before the puck even hits the ice.

Elias: Just keep yourself in check and don't do anything stupid.

Me: No promises.

Elias: That's what I'm afraid of.

CHAPTER 19

Charlee

"You know you don't have to come if you don't want to, right? Never in a million years would I force you or expect you to be there." Milo kisses my forehead, his fingers pushing through my hair.

I peer up into his autumnal brown eyes and smile at his need to keep me protected.

"I want to be there, Milo. For you. For the guys. This is a big game, I know that."

"Are you worried?"

Ugh. The dreaded question. It's not that I haven't been thinking about this day since I came to Chicago, because I have. I knew at some point, Jared and Milo, both being centers, would end up facing off on the ice. Although Jared doesn't know about Milo or that we're together now, Milo knows about him. And that could be enough to set things off.

"Worried? No. Not at all." I shake my head. "That asshole can't do a thing to me in the arena, nor would he even try. He's way smarter than that."

Milo scowls. "Let's not give him too much credit."

"And as of now, he has no idea you and I are together. How would he ever find out? It's not like I'm going to see him up close today. Daveed hasn't told him. You guys aren't going to tell him." I pat his chest. "So, as long as you keep your cool around him on the ice, and by keep your cool, I mean show him up at every turn, then the game will be smooth sailing and we'll be celebrating the night away."

He smiles at me and wraps me in his strong arms. "Naked celebrating?"

"Any kind you want."

"What if I decide to get kinky?"

A smirk plays across my face. "Then I'm here for it." Playfully, I spank his butt. "Now get out of here. Jada will be here soon. We'll see you at the arena."

"Promise me you'll come by the locker room before game time."

"Why? So you can check on me and make sure I'm not shaking in my boots?"

"No." He shakes his head. "So I can watch you walk away with my name scrawled across your back."

"Ah. You like that, do you?"

He licks his lips. "More than you fucking know, Goldilocks." He gives me one lazy, hot, panty-melting kiss, and then grabs his bag and heads out the door, leaving me to fantasize about the many different ways we might celebrate the win when we're alone tonight.

"Jada!"

"Oh my gosh, Charlee!" She wraps me in a bear hug, and I close my eyes, reveling in the comfort of the arms of my best friend. "Girl, you look amazing! How the heck are you?"

When we separate, I close the door behind her. "I'm...well, I'm fantastic."

"Yeah? Tell me everything!"

"I'll fill you in on every detail, but I'm starving. You good to grab some food before we go to the arena?"

"Lead the way, babe."

We take an Uber to the arena district and find a Mexican restaurant to hop into, deciding to avoid Pringle's for now. We'll celebrate there later tonight.

We're led to a booth near the back of the restaurant and are served a heaping bowl of tortilla chips and salsa. We order margaritas and a bowl of queso because it's a sin to eat chips without all the cheesy goodness. Once we've placed our dinner orders, she leans across the table, an expectant look in her eyes.

"Tell me everything. Leave nothing out. Start from the beginning."

Her excitement makes me laugh. "Well, most of the beginning stuff you already know."

"Right, right." She nods. "You fell asleep in his bed like a little Goldilocks, and he covered you up and was so sweet."

"And now he calls me Goldilocks. It's like...his thing," I say, dipping a chip in the cheese.

"Oh my gosh! He has a pet name for you? How cute is that?"

"Yeah. I admit, hearing him say it makes me smile."

"He gives you the warm fuzzies."

I nod. "Yeah. He does."

"Okay, so what else?"

"Uh, I met his family not too long ago. Well, his sister and brother-in-law, and his little niece and nephew. We babysat one night, and it was so much fun." I start to laugh and tell Jada all about Milo leaving Meghan and Denny's house in all that makeup and then pulling up to cars at stoplights. God, it was the funniest thing, and now she's cackling as well.

When she regains composure, she shakes her head, grinning at me. "I knew it."

"What?"

"I knew the two of you would hit it off."

"How did you know?"

She shrugs. "I think somewhere in my brain, I knew the two of you had a lot in common, and that at the heart of it all, you're both really good people who just want to love and be loved. He's the perfect guy." She puts her hand on her chest. "I mean apart from Daveed, obviously."

"Obviously." I smile back at her.

"Milo Landric has always been that cinnamon roll kind of guy, you know? Someone you can depend on. Someone who hypes you up and makes you feel like a million bucks."

"A golden retriever." I nod.

Jada tilts her head and chuckles. "Yeah, he's totally a golden retriever." She watches me for another second and then says, "You love him."

"I do, yeah."

"Have you told him?"

I nod.

"Has he said it back?"

I pop another chip into my mouth. "He said it first."

"Ahhh!!!!" She claps her hands. "This is so great!"

"Yeah. It's been sort of a dream come true since I left Seattle. Other than the fact I haven't found a place yet, everything has been going so well. It's almost scary. Like at some point, the other shoe has to drop, so I keep looking up at the sky, waiting."

Jada's brow furrows. "Don't be ridiculous. You deserve this. You both do. Revel in it. Does he even want you to get your own place now?"

"Oh, no. He does not." I roll my eyes teasingly. "If Milo has his way, I won't be going anywhere, but..."

"But what? Are you scared to make it official with him?"

"No, not at all. I guess I feel like I want to be able to make it on my own first, you know? I don't love that I went from living with one pro hockey player to living with another. And really, I went from living with my brother, to living with a pro hockey player, and now Milo. People will think I'm some sort of freeloading whore."

"Okay, first of all, the word whore will never be used in a sentence that also includes your name. And secondly, let people think whatever the hell they want. It's nobody's business but yours, and the tabloids will say whatever the hell they want to say anyway, trust me."

"Oh, I know."

"Have you guys had the talk?"

I bring my eyes up from my margarita and catch her staring at me.

"Yeah. We have."

"And?"

I tap my fork against my plate, recalling the night I told him about the ramifications of my cancer. "He felt awful that I was carrying such a heavy weight on my shoulders and never said anything, but he also wasn't the least bit worried about it."

She sits back against the booth, a satisfied smile on her face. "See? This is one time I'm happy to say I told you so."

I wrinkle my nose. "But what if we get really serious and he changes his mind? Milo deserves to be a dad. He'll be a great dad."

"Did you ask him that?"

"Not in so many words. He reassured me there was more than one way to have kids."

Jada leans forward and grabs my hand, squeezing in comfort. "And he's not wrong. Babies don't have to be pushed through your vagina to be your babies, Charlee. You know this."

"I do."

"And your eggs are still frozen, right?"

"They'd better be."

"Then please don't push him away because you can't physically carry them yourself. Where there's a will, there's a way. Where there's a will, there's modern medicine. Or fostering or adoption. If you want to be a mother, and Milo wants to be a father, I have no doubt you will find your path to that goal."

"You're right. I know you're right. I think I'll always be anxious about it until we cross that bridge and make it safely to the other side, you know?"

She takes a long sip of her margarita. "Understandable. But Milo is a good man. He's not Jared."

"He's definitely not Jared."

When our food arrives, we stop talking about relationship

fears and spend the rest of our time laughing over Milo's latest birthday present as well as Daveed's newest sexual kink in the bedroom. A conversation between two best friends that makes me feel like we've never been apart.

***

"Signed, sealed, and delivered," Jada says to Milo.

"Thanks, Jada." Milo gives her a fist bump.

"I'm going to find my man. I'll meet you in the suite, Charlee."

"Sounds good."

She starts to walk away and then turns back quickly. "Good luck out there, Milo. Hope you play a great game. But also..."

"Yeah, yeah. You hope we don't win."

"Bingo!" She laughs and continues down the hallway and around to the away team locker rooms.

"Landric, you're next in the press room," the coach announces. "Foster, you're up after Landric."

"Walk with me." Milo takes my hand and leads me down the hall outside of the press room while he waits his turn. "Good time with Jada?"

"Oh, yeah. We had tons to catch up on. We went for Mexican at that place around the corner, and it was like we'd never been apart."

"Good. I'm sure you needed that reconnect. You look beautiful, by the way." He eyes my outfit of tight black jeans, black heels, and his jersey. My hair pulled up so everyone can see his name scrawled across the top.

"Thank you." I squeeze his hand. "So, are you feeling good about the game? All loosened up, stretched, and ready?"

"As ready as I'm going to be, yep."

"Good. You're going to have an amazing game. I can feel it. Score a goal for me?"

"They're all for you, baby." He leans down and lightly tugs at my chin as he kisses me, his tongue brushing lovingly against my lips. I grasp his jersey and moan into him. He responds with a groan of his own, and damn this is a kiss I would totally sink into if we were anywhere else other than right outside the press room.

"Well, well, well...look what we have here."

That voice.

It sends shivers up my spine and causes my entire body to stiffen.

I know that voice.

There's a part of me that doesn't even want to turn around, but I know I have to. I have to face him. I have to show Milo I'm okay. And I have to show Jared that he doesn't fucking scare me.

Not with Milo by my side.

Milo stiffens as well but stands tall, his arm wrapping around me, pulling me against him.

"What do you want McClacken?"

He does a once-over on Milo holding me and shakes his head, huffing out a laugh, but he's not laughing when his eyes land on me. Ignoring Milo all together at this point, he says, "What the fuck are you doing, Charlene?"

Milo's hand tightens on my side. "Her name is Charlee, asshole."

His brows shoot up and he laughs. "Is that what she told you?"

"Shut the fuck up, Jared," I sneer.

He glares at Milo and me, noting his arm wrapped tightly around my waist. "You know, I'm beginning to think center hockey players might just be your kink. What would your brother think about that?"

I cock my head, emboldened by his question. "And what would he think about asshole men who hit women for pleasure?"

Out of the corner of my eye, I register Milo's gaze on me. He probably has a million questions right now.

Fuck Jared for being here.

Fuck him for doing this to Milo's head right before a game.

Fucking fuck!

To my pleasure, Jared huffs a breath and steps back, his eyes darting between Milo and me again. "My hand slipped."

"Oh, your hand slipped right into her eye socket. That's amazing aim for a mere slip." Milo shakes his head. "Wow, McClacken. You're a sad case of bullshit."

"Believe whatever you want." Jared shrugs. "It's my word against hers, and let's be honest. I'm the superstar here. My money goes a long way, and you...well, you had a mental breakdown and left. Who knows what happened to you between there and here. Not to mention, it appears you left me." He fakes a ridiculous frown. "Alone and heartbroken, and now here you are, in the arms of another star hockey player."

That's not how it happened at all, fucker.

"Tsk, tsk, Charlene. I guess that makes you a professional puck bunny...or do you prefer hockey whore?"

Milo's face grows red, and he grabs Jared's jersey, pushing him up against the cement wall behind him. "You call her a whore one more time, and I swear to God I will fucking rip your shriveled-up worthless nut sack from your body and slam it down your throat."

"Hey, whoa. Milo, what's going on?" Colby, Dex, and Zeke are behind Milo immediately.

Where did they come from?

Carissa is with them and wraps a protective arm around me while Colby steps between Milo and Jared. Zeke wraps an arm around Milo's waist, pulling him back.

"Come on, man. Let's save it for the ice."

"He's not worth being banned from the game." Dex glares at Jared. "Besides, at least on the ice, knocking his teeth out will be seen as an accident."

Colby gestures down the hall with his chin. "Get the fuck out of here, McClacken, or I'll join Milo on his castration endeavors."

He stares Milo down for a brief moment, and then smirks. "See you at puck drop, Landric." His smirk fades as his gaze slips to me. "Hope you rot in hell, Magallan."

"Fuck you, Jared!"

An attendant from the press room steps out, noting the

group of us standing there. She glances at each of us, undoubtedly questioning what's going on out here, and then clears her throat and gestures to Milo. "Mr. Landric, they're ready for you."

"Fuck." He huffs. "Be right there, Sarah."

The woman closes the door behind her, and Milo stares at me.

He looks mad and he looks confused, but most of all, he looks hurt.

I have so much explaining to do, I know, but there's no time now. This couldn't have happened at a worse moment. He has to do his interview, and then they have to be on the ice to warm up.

"Are you okay?" he finally asks, though he's not the mushy, compassionate lover he was just ten minutes ago.

I nod because if I try to make words come out of my mouth, sobs might come with them, and I don't want that right now so I nod silently.

"Charlee, I—"

"Mr. Landric?" Sarah opens the door once again. Milo looks completely put off, but he's never mean to the staff.

"Yeah."

I do the only thing I can think of to help get his head back in the game. Stepping up beside him, I kiss his cheek, squeeze his arm, and then whisper, "Thank you, Milo."

His brow furrows. "I'll see you after?"

His question knocks me off guard, as if he thinks I'll leave him.

As if Jared's comments are getting to him.

Fuck.

"Yeah. Of course. I'll meet you right back here."

Carissa loops an arm through mine. "We're going to go get our seats. Have a great game, gentlemen!"

He watches me for a second and then follows Sarah into the press room, questions immediately being thrown at him before the door even closes. Carissa blows a kiss to her husband and then turns to walk me down the hallway away from the chaos.

"What the hell happened? Tell me everything."

CHAPTER 20

Milo

Love is such an unfair game.

You spend so much of your life alone, that the moment you meet someone you feel a connection with, your heart starts to pump a little faster. Grow a little larger. Love a little more. Until you get to the point where you can't imagine yourself living your life without that person.

That connection.

That smile that takes your breath away.

And then, one moment happens between you that has you questioning everything.

Maybe our connection wasn't as real as I thought it was.

What the fuck happened outside the press room?

My team didn't give me a single minute to let my mind wander during our warm-up on the ice. We were focused, confident, and never once glanced at Seattle's team. I refused to give McClacken the time of day out there.

But now that we're sitting back in the locker room, about to make our way to the tunnel, my thoughts are wandering.

Why did he call her Charlene?

Is that her name?

Why would she tell us something different?

Is Magallan her last name?

Is she related to the player?

"She has to be," I whisper.

"Has to be what?" Quinton, Dex, and Hawken are seated nearby, overhearing my mumble.

"McClacken called her 'Charlene Magallan.'"

Dex shrugs. "So? He's a stupid douche."

"Yeah, but...do you think..."

Quinton raises a brow. "You think she's related to Oliver Magallan?"

I nod. "It makes a lot of sense. She knows a lot about hockey. Knew the stats for all the Anaheim Stars."

Hawken narrows his eyes and nods. "She does kind of resemble him, now that I think about it."

"Fuck. How could I not have seen it?"

"Hey." Colby claps me on the shoulder. "What difference does it make if she's related to another player? What does that change?"

"What if it changes everything?"

"But does it?"

"I don't know. I haven't thought about it much yet. I'm figuring it all out. I'm processing."

"Then stop jumping to conclusions. You're letting McClacken mess with your head, and that's exactly what he wants right before this game. This game, Milo, decides whether we move on or not."

"Trust me. I'm well aware."

"Okay. And he just fed into your biggest weakness."

"How so?"

"Your heart, Milo," Hawken states. "He's trying to discredit Charlee and make you question everything about her right before you face-off."

I swallow. "But what if he's—"

"You really going to believe that asshat over the person who has allowed herself to be vulnerable in front of you since the very beginning?" Colby asks with an arched brow. "Do you not remember she showed up with a fucking black eye from that guy? Do not side with him, Milo. It will not end well for you if you do."

I release a big breath.

He's right.

"To the tunnel, gentlemen!" Couch announces. "Let's play a strong game!"

Hawken steps up next to me as we waddle up the hallway on our skates. "Something to think about, man."

"What's that?"

"Maybe you're looking at this from the wrong perspective."

"What do you mean?"

"You read all those smutty romance books, right?"

I huff. "Sure, but I hardly see how—"

"So how are you not looking at this situation like one of those books?"

My brows raise, and I nearly smirk at my colleague. "What do you know about romance books, Malone?"

"Ugh." He rolls his eyes. "Rory has them lying around Dex's place. I may have read one out of complete boredom. But anyway, that's not the point. What if McClacken is the antagonist in this story? The one who will always mess with your head, and you're the hunky hero that has to figure out the heroine's puzzle?"

Wow. For once, Hawken is speaking my language and making a lot of sense.

"All right, I'm following."

"Let's say Charlee Mags isn't her real name. First of all, so fucking what? You know Charlee the person. She's more than just her name."

"Yeah."

"So maybe you should be asking yourself—"

"Why she would change her name," I finish his thought.

He nods. "Bingo."

I clap my friend on his shoulder. "Hawk, I've never appreciated your advice as much as I do right now. Thank you."

He smiles. "Anytime, man."

"Hands in!" Colby shouts as the team huddles together.

"Clean game, guys." He stares at me. "Let's take them out, bring home the win, and then playoffs, here we come! What do we say?"

"Hustle, hit, and never quit!"

"PUT YOUR HANDS TOGETHER FOR THE RRRRED TAILS!"

As the announcer pumps up the audience and introduces the team we skate onto the ice in perfect formation as the crowd explodes in cheers around the arena. I look up to the suite where the ladies are and see Jada, Charlee, Carissa, and Rory all cheering us on. My chest tightens, and for a moment, my breath leaves me as I lock eyes with Charlee. She's a long way off, but when she blows a kiss my way, I catch it, watching as a smile spreads across her face.

Charlene...Charlee...I don't care what her name is or what she wants it to be.

I love her.

And that's all that matters.

After introductions and the national anthem, it's time for the first of many face-offs of the game.

Laser focused and refusing to allow McClacken to rile me, I take my place at center ice for the puck drop.

"Charlee," McClacken laughs under his breath. "I can't believe you were dumb enough to fall for that one, Landric."

I glare at McClacken, and then a thought hits me like a ton of bricks and I nearly fall on my ass.

She changed her name because we all would've known who she was.

She changed her name because she wanted to fucking hide.

Because she needed to feel safe for one damn minute.

And I provided her with a safety net.

I gave her every comfort she needed.

I gave her the respect she deserved.

I gave her my kindness and friendship.

And then I gave her my heart.

"God, what else did she make you believe?" He chuckles.

We take our positions, waiting for the ref to drop the puck. Before he does, I smirk at the asshole across from me. A veil has been lifted, and I can see things as clear as day.

"Well, Jared, she told me your dick is the size of a fucking baby carrot."

And with that, the puck hits the ice, and I slam it away from him toward Colby, who shoots it down the ice to Malone. Daveed intercepts for Seattle, but Dex is on the inside and hooks it off to Quinton, who stops, pops the puck, and scores in the first minute of the game.

"Fuck yeah!" I pump my fist and join the team in a group hug, congratulating Quinton on his goal and then I'm off the ice for the next shift.

"You doing all right?" Colby asks when he sits down next to me, his water bottle dripping into his mouth.

"Fuckin' fantastic. That was a great shot for Shay."

"It was." He smiles. "But that's not why I was asking."

"I hear you. You're right. Nothing changes the way I feel about her. I don't give a fuck what she wants to be called. I completely understand why she made the decisions she made. She did it all for her safety, and who can blame her?"

"True."

"I mean, had Daveed called and told me that Oliver Magallan's sister needed a place to stay, I still would've said yes, but she doesn't know that."

"Correct again."

"Hell, maybe Magallan doesn't know what she's been through. Maybe they don't talk. That's a discussion for the future. But for now, I want to win this fucking game and then celebrate with my girl, so she knows how much I love her."

"Nelson, Landric," Coach calls out. "You're up."

Colby elbows me and gives me a wide smile. "You're cute when you're in love, you know that?"

I laugh as he throws a leg over the side of the wall and hits the ice. "Fuck you, bro."

We make it through the first period tied one to one and begin period two with another face-off between me and McClacken.

"You know she's damaged goods, right, Landric? Or did she not tell you that either?"

"Fucking mention her again and I'll break your—"

The puck drops, and my stick slips in my hand, giving McClacken the upper hand. They pass the puck through their team several times over as the Red Tails try to control their defense. Zeke keeps an eagle eye on every movement around him and defends the goal like the expert he is. Quinton rebounds their goal attempt and shoots it back to Hawken, who sends it back to me. McClacken is on me in an instant.

"She's a barren bitch, you know." He jabs at my stick, trying to make me lose control, but I try my best to ignore his immature comments, even though my blood is starting to boil. I swear to God if he continues this behavior, I'm going to lose my cool and beat the hell out of him. He circles me, driving me toward the wall. I know I need to get out or risk being checked. The asshole bellows a laugh, and then hooks me with his stick until I lose control of the puck, he mumbles, "She can't have kids, but she sure can swallow them decently enough."

"You son of a fucking bitch!" I turn around and charge after him in a fit of rage, but Colby is there along with a referee to hold me back. The whistle blows, and the referee calls a hooking penalty against McClacken. With a fucking smirk on his face, he heads over to the sin bin for his obligatory two-minute sit.

Serves him right.

"You good?" Colby shouts at me.

I nod. "If he makes it out of here alive, it'll be a fucking miracle."

"He's doing it on purpose. You know that. Keep your cool, Milo. You'll be fine."

We go into the two-minute power play as a force to be reckoned with. I look down the ice—my best friends ready and waiting. The puck drops, and the Red Tails have two minutes on the ice with one more player than the Sea Brawlers. This is what we're good at. This is what we live for. If there's anything our team does well, it's taking full advantage of a power play.

This time is no different.

Like the guys know exactly what I need, we pass the puck between each other all the way down the ice, avoiding Seattle's attempts to intercept or rebound. Dex takes it around the goalie's net and passes to Quinton, who passes back to me. I slip it quickly to Colby, who acts as if he's about to try for a goal. Seattle swarms him, but he manages to slip the puck back to me just in time. I shift my weight from one leg to the other and slap my stick hard into the ice, sending the puck to the left of the goalie and right into the corner of the net.

"MILOOO!" The crowd goes wild calling my name as I raise my arms in triumph.

"That's right, Landric!" Dex shouts, skating over to wrap his arms around me. "You're a fucking *beast!*"

"Let's go!" Quinton shouts, giving me a high five and tapping my helmet.

Colby joins us, all smiles. "McClacken can choke on his own dick. Let's bring it home, boys!"

I glide past the penalty box where the asshole sits and flip him off for good measure.

Fuck him.

At the end of the two minutes, Zeke taps his stick on the ice, letting us know the power play is ending and McClacken is back in the game. It's not even time for another face-off before he's on me again, taunting me with everything he's got.

"You know, if you think about it, you're a damn lucky man, Landric," he says, stealing the puck away and shooting to one of his teammates. I race after it, and he's on my tail the entire time. "I mean she's the ultimate puck bunny, you know? You can stick your dick in her, fuck her all you want, and you'll never have to pay child support."

That's it.

The nail in the coffin.

The straw breaking the camel's back.

Whatever it needs to be called.

But I am done.

And.

All.

I.

See.

Is.

Red.

I turn so fast I'm nearly dizzy as I round on McClacken. Grabbing his jersey, I spin him on the ice and throw him to the ground. I tear off his helmet and deliver my strongest uppercut, his head falling back against the ice.

"Fuck you, you fucking cunt piece of shit goddamn son of a bitch bastard!"

He fights back with a blow to the side of my face, but it's not forceful enough to faze me with my adrenaline as high as it is. I punch him again and again and again. My rage finally coming to center ice.

"Is this how you like it? Huh? You get off on hitting women, fuck face?" He tries to hit back, but he's at a disadvantage right now, and no way in hell am I letting up until I've had my fill.

"Well, get off on this, you fucking sorry pint-sized dick." I kick him as hard as I can in his tiny little nut sack, even though I know it's protected. He must feel something, because he curls over when my skate makes contact. Then, I grab him by his hair and punch him solidly in the eye three times before a referee, Colby, Dex, and Quinton finally pull me away.

"Enough, Milo."

"He's down, man."

"Easy there, killer."

The ref blows his whistle and calls me out for game misconduct, officially ejecting me from the game. As pissed off as I am at that call, I feel zero remorse. This time, the punishment is well worth the crime. I have more than enough faith in my teammates, and have no doubt they'll pull out a win, and we'll be on our way to the playoffs. And if for some reason they don't, I can live with that too. The guys might be disappointed, but they'll forgive me. Any one of them would've done the same thing. They all know I needed that.

At least now I can shower in peace and be ready to hug my girl.

CHAPTER 21

Charlee

"Oh my God!" Carissa gasps.

Rory looks on with wide eyes. "Wow. He's really going at him."

All four of us stand in the suite watching Milo and Jared fight. We all saw this coming. Jared hasn't left Milo's side for most of the game. There's no way he wasn't taunting him with whatever bullshit he decided to spew.

Poor Milo.

Putting up with all this because of me.

What could Jared be saying to him?

What did he say to set him off like that?

It's rare for Milo to get so mad he rages like this during a game. He's always been protective on the ice, but he's usually the level-headed one.

I watch as Milo takes a punch to the face, and my chest constricts. I know the crowd loves it when players fight, and there are certainly times it's all for show, but this...this is not for show. This is personal.

He's down there right now taking a blow for me.

He's fighting for my honor, I'm sure of it.

He's defending me when I'm right here.

I should be defending myself.

And now he's putting his game on the line.

It's not like Jared doesn't deserve it, but still.

This is quite the fight.

"If Milo's not careful, he'll kill him," Rory mumbles beside Carissa.

Carissa gestures toward Colby. "Colb will pull him away before that happens. They're just letting Milo get rid of some aggression."

"Listen, even I think the fucker's got what's coming to him," Jada says. "But Milo's about to get his ass kicked out of the game."

No sooner does she say that than the referee blows his whistle, the guys are pulled apart, and Milo is ejected from the game.

Shit.

The crowd roars because Milo is a fan favorite and nobody wants to see him thrown out of such a high-stakes game.

And now, suddenly, I feel like the smallest person in the arena.

It's my fault he was taunted.

It's my fault he got angry.

It's my fault one of the favorite players on the team is leaving the game.

It's my fault he could potentially be walking off the ice for the last time this season.

Please, Red Tails, win this one for him.

What if he's mad at me?

I wouldn't blame him.

A lot of shit was thrown at him before the game even started. He undoubtedly has questions.

"I should go," I tell the girls, wiping my sweaty hands on my thighs and standing from my seat.

"What? Nuh-uh." Jada shakes her head. "Everything is fine. They had their moment, and now the game plays on. There's only one period left."

Gesturing down to the ice, I try not to cry. "Jada, that all just happened because of me." I grip my chest, trying to rid myself of the tingling sensation going on inside me. "Jared told him my name isn't Charlee. He used my fucking last name, and God only knows what he said to him on the ice. I'm certain Milo is reeling from all the unknown. I'm sure he feels like I've lied to him. He deserves an explanation. I owe him that much."

"Wait, wait, wait." Rory raises her hand, her brows furrowing. "Charlee isn't your real name?"

I glance at her, swallowing my pride and releasing a deep breath. "No. My name is Charlene."

"Charlene what?"

"Charlene Magallan. Look, I promise you guys I'll explain everything, but right now I need to get to Milo. I need to make sure he's okay."

"I can take you down if you want," Carissa offers, but I shake my head.

"No. It's okay. You guys stay and enjoy the game. I'll run down to the locker room and see if I can talk to him. I'll meet you down there when the game ends."

"All right, you know where you're going?"

"Yeah. See you in a few."

I make my way from the topmost floor, where the suites are, to the basement, where I know I'll find a man who may very well not want to see me right now.

And that crushes me.

I make it down to the bottom floor, but rather than turning in the direction of the locker room, something inside me pulls me the opposite way. I stop about fifty feet down the hall and close my eyes, bringing a shaky hand to my face, my fingertips brushing against my lips. My legs feel weak, and I have a sudden urge to sit down, but I don't.

A few random people pass me in the hallway. Most pay me no mind, but one does stop to make sure I'm okay. I wave her on and assure her I'm fine, but in reality, I think I'm anything but fine.

What the hell, Charlee?

You're fine.

Stop being so dramatic.

I palm the cement wall behind me and force myself to take three deep breaths. On the last breath, I choke out a sob as my mind takes me back to what I'm now realizing is the trauma I suffered during my time with Jared.

"You stupid bitch."

"Why are you so fucking forgetful?"

"Nothing but a hockey whore."

"Damaged goods."

"If you can't have children, what good are you?"

"Is that what she told you?"

I thought I could handle this.

He hit me, and I left. Easy peasy.

I did all the right things. Or so I thought.

Jada brought me to Chicago, and I found myself at the kindness of another man who gave me everything I could have ever wanted. His protection, his home, his friendship, his heart, and then he gave me his love.

So why the fuck am I standing in this basement and not running to him?

Because trauma drama is real.

My mental health is real.

And I need a damn minute.

I take a moment to look both directions down the hall and steel myself to do the one thing I promised I wouldn't do. Because when push comes to shove, I need a moment.

I hope everyone will understand.

I have to pray Milo understands.

Frustrated with myself, I wipe my tears and head back the way I came to find a way out of the arena. Quickly looking on my phone for the nearest Uber, I direct the driver to the penthouse and ask him to wait while I run inside to pack a small bag and write Milo a note.

I need to be alone.

I need to sit in my feelings.

I need to think.

And at some point, I need to forgive myself.

CHAPTER 22

Milo

Fucking McClacken.

I can usually handle a lot of trash talk on the ice between players. I'm a level-headed guy, after all. But no way in hell was I going to let him talk about Charlee...Charlene...whatever her name is like that. Fuck, he's a piece of work.

The idea that Charlee was ever intimate with that asshole makes my skin crawl. It also makes me want to take her home, lay her out on my bed, and reclaim her over and over again until McClacken's memory no longer exists in her head.

I spend the last period in my workout shorts and watching the game on the closed-circuit televisions in the player's lounge, while a few men stand around outside making sure I don't try to get back on the ice. Like that would happen.

I know I should be paying attention to what's going on in the game, and I've kept tabs for the most part, but my mind is focused on Charlee. The look on her face when we parted was crushing, and the fact that we didn't have time right then to clear the air and talk was frustrating as fuck.

But we'll have tonight.

Two more minutes and she'll be down here in my arms, and we'll be able to celebrate what looks to be our biggest win of the season. The guys are pulling out a victory, no thanks to me, and I'm damn proud of them for it. I worried for a while I would have damaged their gameplay, but we're a band of brothers. We carry each other through personal struggles, and these guys have been by my side this entire time. I couldn't ask for a better group of friends and teammates. And I'm proudly hugging each of them when they step into the locker room.

Dex gives me a fist bump and then pulls me in for a hug. "McClacken was an ass for the rest of the game, but don't worry. I hip-checked him whenever I could. He'll be feeling it for days."

"Atta boy, Dexter."

"Hey, Milo!" Zeke gives me an elbow bump, still dressed in all his pads. "Nice play out there, man! Sorry I didn't get to see you before you left."

"Zeke, you were the man out there tonight." I clap him on the back as I wrap my arms around him.

"Thanks, man."

"Nice shiner, Milo." Quinton winks at me.

"Yeah, yeah. I let him get one in, but that was it."

Not unlike Charlee.

I take a moment with each player, thanking them for their efforts and apologizing for being ejected from the game. Not one of them gives me any grief over it though.

"Pringle's?" Quinton shouts. "You're all coming, right?"

I nod. "Wouldn't miss it."

"Fuck yes. Hawk owes me a beer," Dex says, laughing.

Hawk smacks Dex's ass with his towel. "What the fuck for?"

"Because I'm amazing. Duh."

"Don't worry, guys," I announce. "First round is on me. Now, if you'll excuse me, my girl should be waiting for me by now." I pat a few guys on the shoulder on my way to the door and then swing it open, ready to wrap my arms around Charlee and make sure she's okay.

But she's not here.

My brows pinch when I spot Carissa and Rory waiting along the wall without her.

"Did she run to the restroom?" I ask them.

Carissa gives me the same confused look. "No. She's not with you?"

"Why would she be with me?"

"Because she said she was coming to see you."

"When?"

"Uh, second period. Right after you were ejected."

"Are you sure?"

Rory nods. "Yeah. We even asked if she wanted one of us to go with her and she said no."

"Fuck," I mumble. "Where could she have gone?"

"Could she be with Jada?"

I snap my fingers and point at Carissa. "Yes! That's probably where she is. I'll run over and check their side."

Though why she would want to risk a confrontation with McClacken again is beyond me.

Fighting my way through the throngs of press staff, arena staff, and all the people traveling with Seattle's team, I finally find myself outside their locker room and spot Daveed and Jada.

"Hey guys, is Charlee with you?"

Jada's shoulders fall. "You mean she's not with you?"

My head falls back in frustration. "Fuck. Where the hell did she go?"

"I'm so sorry, Milo. She was worried about you and said she was going to see you."

"Well, that never happened. So, what the fuck could've happened between the top-floor suites and here?"

Jada shakes her head. "Do you want me to help you look?"

"Uh, no, that's all right. I'll text her and see if she answers. If you hear from her, will you—"

"I swear, you'll be the first person I call."

I play through every scenario as I head back the way I came.

Did she fall and get hurt somehow?

Surely, she would've let someone know to come find me.

Did she get stuck talking to someone?

Who does she even know who wasn't with her already?

Could she have been kidnapped?

Charlee is much smarter than that, and security is tight around here.

"Hey, Landric!" I run into Dex and Quinton in the hallway. "You coming to Pringle's?"

"Yeah. I just need to find Charlee. We'll meet you guys there!"

"Great. See ya, man!"

I wave them off and head to the parking garage, thinking maybe she needed a quiet moment outside, but when I reach my car, she's nowhere around. Pulling my phone from my pocket, I check for any messages from her, and then shoot her a quick text just in case.

Me: Hey. You okay? Where are you? I can't find you.

I wait for her reply, but nothing comes, so I run back into the arena because the last thing I want to do is leave if she's still in the building. As the clock ticks by with no sign of her, the sinking feeling in my stomach grows.

She ran?

Why did she feel that was necessary?

Is this my fault?

Am I the asshole?

Where did she go?

Christ, if anything happens to her, I'll never forgive myself.

Chicago is not the safest city to simply take a walk through at night.

After a full hour of waiting around and texting everyone to see if maybe she showed up at Pringle's I get in my car and head home, no longer in the mood to celebrate anything. I want to be alone.

Scratch that.

I want to be where Charlee is.

When I open my door, I know she's not here. I can feel her absence. Emptiness surrounds me. The penthouse is dark except for a small light in the kitchen. I throw my bag down where I always toss it and head to the small liquor cabinet in the kitchen, where I pull out a bottle of bourbon. A gift from Elias, I grab a glass from its rightful cabinet and turn to pour my drink but stop short when I see a piece of paper on the countertop with Charlee's handwriting scrawled across it.

Milo,

I'm not running. I just need a minute. Tonight was overwhelming, and I'm not as okay as I thought I was. Staying at a hotel for the night to clear my head. I hope you can forgive me. I'm so sorry, Milo.

Love,

Charlee

"No, no, no, no, no." I groan. "She's gone to a hotel?" Her note in my hand, I lean back against the counter and inhale a deep, steadying breath, wishing like hell she were with me right now so we could clear the air and get through this together.

I mean, I'm relieved she's not running, and I'm glad she's safe and doing what she needs to do for her own mental health, but at the same time, I'm aching to see her.

Talk to her.

Touch her.

Be with her.

If she's hurting, I want to make sure she's all right.

Did she seriously not tell anyone where she was going?

What if she needs me?

I can't possibly stay here tonight, wondering if she's okay.

I need to see her.

Staying at a hotel tonight.

"Fuck, that could literally be anywhere. How would I ever have a chance of finding a needle like Charlee in the haystack of Chicago?"

There have to be three hundred hotels in the city alone. I'll never get to her. I'll be searching all night. I pour my glass of bourbon and bring it to my lips, about to toss back the warm amber liquid and wallow in my disappointment when a thought crosses my mind.

"I love staying at the Palmer House."

Yes!

She told me that once.

She loves that place for its old-world charm.

That has to be where she is tonight.

Lowering my glass back to the counter, I forgo my wallowing and grab my keys instead. I need to get to my girl, and I'm certain that's where she has to be.

"Good evening." I greet the gentleman behind the desk with a calm and friendly smile, even though I'm anything but calm on the inside.

"Evening. Welcome to the Palmer House." The guy's eyes rise from his computer screen, and his expression changes completely.

"Aren't you..." He tips his head, studying me. "You're Milo Landric."

"Yes."

He beams happily and offers me his hand. "Wow! It's amazing to meet you in person. That was a wild game tonight." He leans toward me, his hand cupped over his mouth. "Nice uppercut, if I do say so myself. McClacken is a jerk."

"He's a lot more than a jerk." I shake his hand.

"Well, what can I do for you, sir?"

"How would you like a pair of tickets to our first playoff game?"

"Whoa! Are you serious?" He laughs. "Like, really serious?"

"Hell yeah, I'm serious. I'm about to ask you for a big favor. I know it's a big ask, but if you can come through for me, I'll gladly get you to a playoff game as a thank you."

"Anything you need. What can I do?"

I take note of his name tag. "Your name is Caleb?"

"Yes, sir."

"Caleb, listen, I know this is a big ask, and if someone were asking around about me, I would be pissed, but I was hoping you could tell me if someone checked in here this evening?"

"I might be able to do that." He nods. "Do you have a name?"

"Her name is Charlee Mags," I tell him. "M-A-G-S."

He types her name into his computer and frowns. "I'm sorry there's no name matching that in our system."

"Dammit," I whisper, tapping the counter with my finger as I try to think.

"Wait. Try one more?"

"Sure."

"Charlene Magallan. M-A-G-A-L-L-A-N."

"Magallan..." Caleb shakes his head again. "I'm so sorry. That name isn't showing up either."

Fuck!

"You're sure?"

"Absolutely. List goes from Mable to McClellend. There's no Magallan."

My head falls in disappointment. "Damn. All right, thank you for your help, Caleb. Oh, if you'll give me your full name and number, I'll make sure you get your tickets."

I wait while he writes his information on the back of a small business card and hands it to me. "That's incredibly generous of you, Mr. Landric. Thank you so much."

"Sure thing. Thanks again." I want to smile but I can't make it happen. I really thought she would be here. It's the only place in town we've talked about. I take a minute to look around the lobby, just in case she's sitting at one of the lobby tables or something. I know it's a long shot, but miracles happen every day. As I watch people coming and going, my phone dings in my pocket.

Daveed: Jada wants to know if you found Charlee.

Me: Not yet. She left me a note though. Said she needs a night alone to think and is staying at a hotel but didn't say which one. Jada wouldn't know, would she?

Daveed: She said probably the Palmer House.

Me: Yeah, I'm here now. She's not here.

Daveed: I'm sorry man. At least you know she's all right.

Me: Physically, I guess so. But mentally? She's dealing with some shit, and I hate that she's putting it all on herself.

Daveed: Give her time. Jada said she's crazy about you. I don't see her leaving you any time soon. Maybe she needs to breathe.

Me: Yeah. I guess. Thanks Daveed.

Pocketing my phone, I release a deep breath and head for the door, mumbling to myself, "Where are you, Goldilocks?"

And then I stop in my tracks.

What if...

She wouldn't...

Would she?

Worth a shot!

With one last shred of hope in my chest, and because I read those mushy romance books and swear I've read something like this before, I turn around and walk back to the check-in counter where Caleb is still standing.

"Okay, one more, and I swear I'll go if it doesn't work."

He smiles. "Anything for you, Mr. Landric."

"All right, humor me here. But would you please look for a Goldie?"

"Last name?"

"Locks. L-O-C-K-S."

Caleb glances at me. "Goldilocks, sir?"

"Yes."

"I don't even have to type that name in to tell you she is indeed in the building. I'm the one who took that name when she checked in and thought maybe she was a celebrity using a fake name. Happens a lot."

Fuck yes!

I found her!

This feels better than any goal I could make!

"She is a celebrity, my friend. She's a celebrity to me. Can you please tell me what room she's in tonight?"

"Absolutely. One moment." He types away and then looks up at me. "She's in four-thirty-six."

"Four-thirty-six," I repeat. "Got it. Caleb, you are a lifesaver." I pull a wad of cash out of my pocket, not giving a damn how much is there, and slide it across the counter to my newest hotel friend. "Thank you so much!"

"It's my pleasure, Mr. Landric. And congrats again on tonight's win."

"Thank you, Caleb! See you at the playoffs!"

I ride up the elevator, thinking of all the things I want to say. The questions I want to ask her. I want to make sure she doesn't think I'm upset with her and tell her I understand completely why she didn't tell me everything from the get-go.

The elevator dings, and the doors open on the fourth floor.

Charlee's room is located near the end of the hall, tucked away in the corner. Standing in front of her door, I lift my hand to knock, but something stops me.

I just need a minute.

Those were her words.

Tonight, was overwhelming...

My hand lowers with each thought as I come to the realization that it doesn't matter what I need. It doesn't matter what I want. Though the drama of the night was confusing and frustrating for me, it was more than that for Charlee.

It was a reminder of the trauma she suffered.

Whether she sees it that way or not.

"Shit."

Nothing about this night is about me.

It's all about her.

My Charlee.

She needs a minute, and I need to respect that.

I love her enough to give her space when she asks for it.

I love her enough to respect her boundaries.

Stepping away from the door, I pull out my phone and tap out a quick text allowing myself that small compromise, so she hears from me that I love her, before I head back home.

> **Me: I love you. I just wanted you to hear that/see that from me personally. I'm so sorry for what you've gone through and are going through now. I'm sorry it was a rough night. Take whatever time you need, and know if and when you're ready, my arms are open and waiting to hold you. Sending you a good-night kiss.**

I press send, and a few seconds later, I hear the glorious sound of her phone dinging, alerting her to my text. Watching my screen, I see when my message is marked read.

Okay.

She's really in there.

That's all I need to know.

Now, I can take a deep breath and relax.

CHAPTER 23

Charlee

"Well, long time no talk, sis. To what do I owe the pleasure?" My brother smiles at me when he answers my FaceTime call. I haven't talked to him since Christmas. We used to be so close, but once his hockey career took off, he got swept up in the chaotic schedule of it all, and we lost touch.

Last time we chatted, I was with Jared, and didn't want to tell him we weren't the happy couple my family thought we were. Honestly, I didn't want to tell my hockey star brother that my hockey star boyfriend was a verbally abusive asshole, but I couldn't afford to move out and didn't want our breakup in the media. What a shock to my family that would've been.

"Hey, Ollie." I watch his happy expression change to one of concern. His brows furrow, and he winces at his screen as if he can't see me clearly enough.

"Char? Are you crying? What's going on?"

Swallowing down a sob, I answer his question the best I can. "I need to tell you something, Oliver."

"All right. I'm listening. Are you okay?"

I shake my head. "At this very moment, no, I'm not okay."

"Char, I can hop on a flight and be in Seattle in—"

"I'm not in Seattle."

"Oh. Right." He shakes his head. "I forgot the team is in Chicago tonight. Did you travel with them?"

"No."

"Oh. Okay. Then where are you? Are you in trouble?"

"I'm not in trouble, Oliver, no. But I need you to know I left Jared. I left him several months ago."

"Thank Christ." He sighs. "That man is a fucking douche, and I never liked him."

"What?" I try to laugh through a few tears. "You guys always got along so well."

"Negative," he says. "I tolerated him because I love you, and you looked happy. So, what changed?"

I stare up at the ceiling, willssing myself not to cry, but lying here talking to my brother, the one member of my family I was closest to growing up, there's a comfort factor surrounding me that makes it hard to rein in my emotions.

"Char?"

"He hit me, Oliver."

My brother stares into his phone, blinking. "I'm sorry. Did you say he hit you? Like, he fucking hit you? With his hand?"

"With his fist. And yes."

"Goddamn son of a fucking bitch, I will kill that man."

"He hit me once, Ollie, and then I left. Daveed and Jada helped get me out. He had been a dick to me for months once he found out I couldn't carry his children."

"Motherfucker... Why didn't you call me, Charlene? I could've come to get you. You could've moved back in with me."

"Because I just wanted to be me, Ollie. I wanted to get away to a place where I could be me and not Oliver Magallan's little sister. No offense, but I lived in that shadow for years and I never knew if people liked me for who I was or if it was merely that I was related to you. I needed to get the hell out."

"So, where are you now?"

"Chicago."

"Okay. Do you need money? I can send you money."

I shake my head. "No, Ollie. I don't want your money, but I think I need your advice."

"Anything you need."

"When Jada brought me to Chicago, I temporarily moved in

with Milo Landric because he had plenty of space and is a friend of Daveed."

"Milo Landric... Oh shit. Did Jared know? They faced off tonight, you know. Were you there?"

"I was."

"Did Jared see you?"

"He did."

"I saw the fight. It's our night off, so I was watching. Are you telling me that fight was because of you?"

I release a heavy breath. "Yes."

"Fuck, Char."

"I know, Ollie, and now I don't know what to do. This could damage Milo's reputation, right? He's not a huge fighter. Definitely not the way he fought out there tonight. What if the media makes him out to be some sort of monster?"

"They won't do that."

"How can you be sure?"

"Because it wasn't the biggest fight in hockey history, I can assure you. Will it go viral online? Yeah, maybe. But even you know fights happen so often in hockey that they're rarely paid attention to for long. I really wouldn't worry about it. Landric is a good guy. He knew what he was getting himself into, I'm sure. What was McClacken saying about you to set him off?"

"I don't know."

"What do you mean you don't know? Are you home now?"

"No. I'm in a hotel."

"What for?"

I release another audible sigh. "Because seeing Jared tonight, although I was with Milo, it brought the trauma I ran from back to the surface. I need a night alone, you know? To process everything."

"Milo was defending you?"

"Yeah. I would assume."

"Does he have feelings for you?"

Ugh. It's been a while since I've had this type of conversation with my brother.

"Yes. He does. He's a wonderful guy, Ollie, and he's treated me with nothing but respect since the day I showed up at his place with a black eye."

"Jesus."

"I love him, Ollie. I don't want to hurt him, and I don't want my past to hurt his future. It's an unfair game for him to have to play."

"If he loves you, why is he not there with you right now?"

"I told you. I needed a night to myself. I couldn't do anymore peopling tonight, and staying with him would've meant going out to celebrate with loads of people, and I got overwhelmed with anxiety and needed to take a step back. I left him a note so he knows where I am."

"Still," he mumbles. "If I were him, I would be there."

"Well, thank God you're not him because you're my brother." That makes him smile.

"So, what are you asking me? What kind of advice do you need?"

"Do you..." I sigh. "Do you think I need to make a report against Jared?"

"That's not something I can answer for you, sis. That's a personal decision that only you can make, but if you're thinking you need to do it to save Landric's reputation, don't. That would be the wrong reason. This isn't about him. It's about you."

"But if I do it, the media will turn on you as well. The brother who didn't protect me. You know the media will stir the shit pot."

"I don't give a rat's ass what they have to say, Char. Again. This is about you and how you feel. Your past. Your body. Your truth. In the end, you have to do what's right for you, and to hell with everybody else. And I guarantee you, if Milo is half the man he's known to be, he will tell you the exact same thing."

"I knew I needed to see your face tonight."

"It's been way too long."

"Agreed. So, what are you going to do now that the season is over?"

"Uh, it looks like I'll be flying to Chicago to watch some Red Tails playoff action with my sister."

I chuckle at my brother's suggestion, remembering how we used to watch hockey games together as kids, always yelling at the television. "I think that would be a blast. It'll be good to see you."

"Ditto." There's a lull to our conversation, almost awkwardly so, and then he asks, "You sure you're okay? I can be on a plane first thing in the morning."

"Yeah, I'll be okay. I'm kind of missing Milo already, but I know a night away is good for me."

"Take the time. Relax. Sleep. Cry if you need to. You deserve that. Your feelings are valid."

"Thank you, Oliver."

"Anytime, sis. Call me if you need me."

"I will. I promise."

"G'night."

"Night."

Freshly showered and wrapped in the hotel's soft, white bathrobe, I sink down onto the plush bedding of my hotel bed. I'm exhausted from crying, frustrated with myself for not processing my feelings over the last few months, only to feel the brunt of them tonight. I don't know if I believe in fate or destiny or that everything happens for a reason, but if it does, maybe I needed to run into Jared one more time. Maybe I needed to be able to stand in front of him and tell him to fuck off. Maybe I needed him to see me happy with someone else.

Someone who loves me for who I am, instead of hating all the things I'm not.

Someone who appreciates me.

Someone who cares about my happiness.

Someone who wants to share this life with me.

Ugh, and now I feel guilty for not being by Milo's side tonight after all he did for me. I sincerely hope he's out celebrating with the team—it was as much a win for him as it was for the rest of the guys.

My phone dings on the bedstand so I pick it up and smile when I see Milo's name on my screen.

> **Milo:** I love you. I just wanted you to hear that/see that from me personally. I'm so sorry for what you've gone through and are going through now. I'm sorry it was a rough night. Take whatever time you need, and know if and when you're ready, my arms are open and waiting to hold you. Sending you a good night kiss.

> **Me:** I needed this message from you tonight. Thank you, Milo. I love you too, and I feel bad I'm not by your side tonight celebrating. I owe you so much. If I could give you that good night kiss in person, I would.

> **Milo:** Then open the door, Goldilocks. *heart emoji*

"What?"

I stare at the door to my room and then look down at my phone, wondering what he meant by that last message.

Does he really mean...?

I climb out of the bed and pad over to the door where I lean up to look into the peephole.

"Oh my God," I whisper to myself. With shaky hands, I unlock my door and pull it open, and there he is. Milo Landric, leaning against the opposite wall, still in his suit, his hair disheveled, his body tired, but his eyes filled with love, empathy, and compassion.

"Charlee."

The sigh in his voice when he says my name brings me to tears, which quickly turn into gigantic sobs and before I know it, I'm vomiting all the words out of my mouth as quickly as possible.

"My name is Charlene Magallan, and yes, Oliver Magallan is my older brother, and I'm so sorry I didn't tell you everything from the very beginning. I just wanted some time to be me. Just me. Not some superstar's sister, and not some other superstar's abused and weak girlfriend. I wanted to be me, but I promise everything else I've ever told you about me is true. I really do love you, and I really am sorry I left you alone tonight when you should be celebrating, and if you think you can—"

Milo stops me by wrapping me up in one of his warm, comfy bear hugs, lifting me and carrying me inside, the door closing behind him. "Shhh. It's okay, Charlee. Everything is going to be okay." He holds me while I crumble against him, sobbing, my body trembling. "Let it out, babe. Let it all out."

How does this man know what I need before I know I need it? How does he know how to give me everything I could ever want with a simple hug? A simple murmur in my ear? I'll never understand what I did to deserve him, and that thought makes me weep.

"I thought you would be mad," I whimper, my voice muffled by his chest.

He smooths his hand up and down my back. "Never, Charlee. I'm mad for you, not at you."

"Stay with me," I cry, grabbing at his dress shirt with both hands. "Please stay with me."

Milo wraps a hand under my legs and lifts me into his arms. He carries me to the bed lays me down, and reclines next to me, never once letting go.

"Shhh." He smooths my hair back from my face as I snuggle

into his chest, still sobbing uncontrollably. "You're not alone, Charlee. You can let it all out. I won't leave you if you don't want me to."

"I don't want you to go."

"I didn't come here to take over your night alone. Well, maybe I originally did, but when I got to your room, I realized what you need isn't about me. It's about you, babe. I just needed to know you were safe and then I was going to leave."

"Please don't. I need you, Milo."

He presses his lips to the top of my head, lingering there for a moment. "I'm here, babe. I promise I won't leave you. I'll hold you while you cry it out, and then I'll hold you while you sleep. I'm here for whatever you need."

And that's exactly what he does.

No more words exchanged.

Only hiccups of a wounded soul.

Steady breaths of a calming influence.

A comforting embrace.

And an impervious shield of love and compassion surrounding me as I close my eyes and drift to sleep.

CHAPTER 24

Milo

I don't think I've ever been happier to have been defeated in the second round of this playoff season than I am this time. No more games to play equals more time to spend wrapped up in Charlee. She's always been one hundred percent supportive of my having to be away during playoff games, but that doesn't mean it doesn't suck ass every time I have to go. I like sleeping next to her every night, knowing I, too, am not alone anymore. I have someone to share life with, and I don't plan on ever letting her go.

In fact, with a little help from the guys along with my sister, I have some pretty big birthday surprises in store for my girl today. I've been at work behind the scenes and I may have told Charlee a few fibs here and there, but I'm certain it'll all be worth it when she sees what I've been up to. I find her snuggled in her favorite chair, her laptop on her lap as she busily works on book edits. I sneak up behind her and lean in, my lips warm on the back of her neck.

She jumps with a gasp. "Oh my God, I didn't know you were there."

"What are you workin' on, babe?"

"Removing the thousands of ellipses from this author's manuscript because she uses them too often."

I kiss down her neck and around her clavicle. She clearly doesn't mind it because she turns her head to give me more room. "That sounds terribly boring."

She chuckles. "To you, maybe."

"Mmm..."

"But it's my job, and I love my job so..."

Pushing her hair back, I press my lips behind her ear and then nibble on her earlobe.

"Think you can step away for a little while?"

She inhales a deep breath and sighs when I drag my hand softly through her hair.

"For you? Anything."

"Actually, it's for you."

"Oh?"

"Save your work and then it's time to go."

"Wait, what? Where are we going?"

"If I told you that, it wouldn't be a surprise, would it?" I wink at her and walk to the front door where I slip on my tennis shoes and wait for her to do the same. She slips on a pair of sandals, throws her long dark hair into a clip at the top of her head, and grabs her sunglasses.

"All right, I'm ready."

I tug her against me and kiss her rather fiercely, tongues colliding, lips moving, moaning into her mouth when she grabs my biceps. I'm a sucker for her when she touches my arms. We pull apart, and I nudge her nose with mine. "I love you, Charlee Mags."

She smiles. "I love you too, Milo."

"Happy birthday. You look amazing."

"Thank you."

The night we ran into Jared McClacken was rough for her, and therefore, me as well. I don't like to see her unhappy. I made sure she knew that I understood why she made the decision to change her name and didn't blame her even a little for anything that had gone on between Jared and myself. She asked what he said to me on the ice, and so far, I've refused to answer her question. I'll be damned if I'm going to let his words hurt her any more than they already have. I'll take his comments to my grave, and I don't regret that decision at all.

We all know now that Charlee is really Charlene Magallan, sister to Oliver Magallan of the Anaheim Stars—a super nice guy by the way, who has since thanked me several times for looking out for his baby sister. But I will forever call her Charlee because that's who she is to me. My Charlee Mags. The not broken but slightly bent and always beautiful woman who showed up on my doorstep that one February day.

We drive for a short while outside the city to a modern blue Cape Cod style home on a rather large piece of land. If I had to guess, I would say it's sitting on about four acres.

"What are we doing here?"

"You'll see." I get out of the car, make my way around to open her door, and help her out. Hand in hand, we start toward the front door but are met by a smiling middle-aged couple as they come around the side of the house.

"Welcome, Mr. Landric," the gentleman says.

"Thank you very much, Mr. Olentangy." He shakes my hand, then Charlee's when I introduce her, as does his wife. She waves us on.

"Why don't you come on back, we have them outside for some fun in the sun."

Charlee looks at me questioningly, but I simply shrug and toss her a wink. She sees what we're here for soon enough. As we round the corner to the back of the house, there sits a beautiful set of golden retrievers and their nine puppies.

"Oh...my...gosh!" Charlee gasps, covering her mouth in shock. She turns to me. "A puppy? Are you kidding me?"

"No jokes, babe. And how about puppies?"

She rears back. "Wait, we're not adopting all of these babies, are we?"

"No." I laugh. "How about two? So they can keep each other company? And keep you company when I'm away?"

"But..." She tilts her head, watching them run around and play in their pen in the backyard. "What about when I find my own place? Would we each take one? I don't feel like we should separate them. They'll be bonded."

"Babe..." I cock my head and smile at how cute she really is.

"You know you're not going anywhere, right? You're stuck with me. Where you go, I go. Plus, it's like you said, we can't separate the puppies, so..." Yep. That's right. I'm all about using her own words against her if it gets me what I want.

And I want my girl with me. Always.

"You really want that?"

My brows lift. "You don't?"

"No, I do, I just—"

"Then it's settled." I kiss her forehead. "We're bonded. They're bonded. Choose two."

"Where would we walk them in the city?"

"Lots of people own dogs in the city. Don't worry. I have a few ideas."

An excited smile spreads across her face, and my chest warms knowing I put it there. "Oh my God, we're getting puppies! Best birthday ever!" She very nearly cries at the overload of cuteness but instead, she claps her hands and follows Mrs. Olentangy into the pen to meet the parents.

She spends time petting the mother dog and rubbing behind the ears of the father and then she plops down on the ground a few feet away from them. The puppies run, waddle, and roll to Charlee, sniffing and lunging at her. My God, she is in puppy heaven. I laugh as they overwhelm her with love and kisses as she coos at all of them. Eventually, they start to scatter, but one of them snuggles its way into her lap and has fallen asleep, while another continues to lick her arm and nudge her hand for pets.

"Looks like those are the ones," Mr. Olentangy announces. "In our experience, humans don't choose their puppies. Puppies choose their humans."

I look on as Charlee picks up the second puppy and snuggles it in her lap along with the first one, nuzzling them both and showering them with kisses on their heads.

"Milo, we can't possibly take them home today. They look so little."

Mrs. Olentangy puts a collar on each of the two puppies so

others know they're spoken for. "That's right," she says. "They need about two more weeks with their mama and then they'll be ready for their new homes."

I wrap an arm around my girl. "Which means when we get back from our vacation, we can come pick them up."

"Oh, man! I was really looking forward to vacation but now I'll be wishing for the next two weeks to fly by."

The Olentangy's laugh, and I kiss her on her cheek. "You might feel differently when we land in Key West."

Charlee and I spend a little more time bonding with our two puppies and I leave two of our T-shirts with Mrs. Olentangy so the pups can snuggle with them and become acquainted with our scents. We thank them profusely and say our goodbyes.

"Okay, that was the best surprise I could've ever received!" She leans over and kisses me. "Thank you, Milo."

"I'm glad you approve. But we're not done."

"We're not?"

I shake my head. "Nope. More birthday surprises to come. You gettin' hungry?"

"I could definitely eat."

"I've got an appetite for a good burger. That okay with you?"

"Yeah." She nods. "A well-grilled burger sounds amazing right now."

We drive another twenty minutes or so toward Colby and Carissa's, eventually pulling into the driveway of an immaculate, stately house a few doors down from them. A deep gray with white pillars, porches, and stairs, there is a definite nautical vibe to the home, but what appeals to me the most is the relaxed atmosphere inside the house as well as around the perimeter. A place where Charlee and I could host our families and friends for a lakeside party, but also one that allows us to feel cozied up together in front of the fireplace.

"Whose house is this? It's gorgeous."

Phew. That's what I needed to hear.

I turn the car off and pull the key from the ignition, smiling at Charlee and opening my door. "You'll see."

Taking her hand, we make our way together to the front door where I stop and hand her a key.

"What's this?"

"The key to the door."

"Why do you have it?"

"Because it's yours. I'm giving it to you. You'll need one."

Her jaw drops, and she looks back and forth between the house and me.

"Are you even fucking serious right now?"

I give her a half-cringe, half-smile. "Don't be mad, okay?"

"Why? Why would I be mad? What's happening?"

"I thought maybe we could, you know, move here."

"Here?"

"Yeah."

"Here? As in this very house?"

"Yeah."

Her brows shoot up. "You bought this house?"

"I might have."

"You might have, or you did?"

"Happy birthday, Goldilocks."

"Oh my God, Milo! I bought you a fucking cock ring for your birthday, and you got me two golden retrievers and a full-blown house?"

As she says the words, the front door swings open, and Dex rolls his eyes. "Trust me, Charlee, a cock ring is so much better than a house." He winks. "Now, would you two love birds get in here? We're starving, and the burgers are ready."

The look on Charlee's face right now makes me bark in laughter. Her mouth falls open, and her eyes bulge as she blinks several times at Dex.

"What the—"

"Happy birthday, Charlee!" Carissa exclaims as she and Rory step outside to pull her into the house. "Come see your new house!"

"Oh my God." Rory shakes her head. "Wait till you see the

master bedroom closet. You will shit your pants!"

Carissa adds, "And there's even a place for your yoga already set up. It's amazing!"

Rory leans in and whispers loud enough for us all to hear her, "Ooh, though I may need you to explain why there are handles screwed into the floor next to the yoga mat. I wasn't aware those were needed for yoga."

Charlee nearly chokes, and my face turns beet red. Rory simply pats Charlee's shoulder and then turns her head back to wink at me.

Thanks for bringing that up, Rory.

Once Charlee and I take the grand tour, my second time around as I'm the one who planned the move, we meet all our friends outside, where Colby is busy grilling burgers for everyone.

Charlee pulls me aside, her arm linked through mine. "When did you have time to do this?"

I lift my shoulder. "Plane rides. Lonely hotel nights during playoffs. It wasn't too hard to keep from you. And I only had to fib to you twice about having practice and a promotional meeting with Carissa."

She smiles and swats me playfully on the arm. "I can't believe you did this for me."

"I did it for us," I tell her, pulling her into my chest. "It's the perfect place to raise a family, whatever that might look like for us in the future. There's plenty of room for the dogs, and the neighborhood is tightly secured which will make me feel better when we're away. Though, I'm not giving up the penthouse, so we can always stay in the city when we want to."

"Wow, Milo. I don't know what to say."

"It's not a ring, but you should know that's coming too when I find the perfect opportunity."

She kisses my cheek and whispers, "What if I slip a ring on you first and ask you to marry me? Would you say yes?"

"Hmm," I tease with a smirk. "Wouldn't be the first time you've slipped a ring on me, babe. If you're asking my cock to marry you the answer is a resounding yes."

"That's what I like to hear, Landric." She spanks my ass, my dick twitching in response. "The honeymoon starts tonight."

Ready for Milo and Charlee's Epilogue?
Join my newsletter at authorsusanrenee.com

Want more of the Chicago Red Tails?
Keep reading for an excerpt of Dex Foster's story in
Beyond the Game.

Chapter 1

Dex

"I think I'm in a someone-needs-to-fuck-me-out-of-this-mood-I'm-in kind of mood."

Hawken nearly spits out his beer. "Don't look at me, man. You know I love you, Dex, but I don't love you enough for that."

I turn to him, dismayed. "You mean to tell me you wouldn't fuck me if my life literally depended on it?"

His brows raise. "Does it?"

"No."

"Then no. I might consider it, if, and only if, we were literally the last two human beings on this earth, but other than that, my dick paddles for the pretty pink canoe."

"Thanks, I guess." I roll my eyes.

"Why the hell are you in a mood, man? We're in Key West. We just spent the day at the beach, and now we're sitting here enjoying paradise while drinking. What could be better than that?"

"Pussy," I state. "Petting pussy. Eating pussy. Fucking pussy. I'm good at two things in this world. Hockey and sex. And right now, I don't have either of those two things."

"Aww, are you fuckstrated, big brother?" Rory steps up to the bar overhearing Hawk and me talking. I almost laugh at her made-up word, but I don't, because she's right.

"Hell yes. I'm fuckstrated. I came here for the sun, the sand, and the sex."

"Okay, so what's the problem?" Hawk asks, taking another sip of his beer.

"Nobody knows who I am down here."

Rory frowns. "And that's bad because...?"

"After games, the bunnies come out to play. They just want to fuck a hockey player to say they fucked a hockey player so it's easy pickings. But not one person has recognized me since we arrived in Florida. It's a little annoying."

Rory laughs. "You pitiful thing. I'm sure you'll find some willing piece of ass eventually. You might just have to work for it this time." Her eyes grow huge, and a smile widens across her face. "I know. The nerve of these Florida women, right?"

"Ugh. You're so annoying. Why did you come down here again?"

She smirks. "To help plan the best beach wedding I have ever seen. You must admit, it was outstanding. And Charlee looked like a fucking goddess."

I sip my beer and nod in agreement. "That she did."

It was a beautiful wedding, and really, I couldn't be happier for Milo and Charlee.

Rory pinches my cheek the way our grandmother would after not seeing us for long stretches of time. "And yes, Dexter. You made the cutest flower girl I have ever seen."

"Damn right he did." Hawk laughs, clinking his beer bottle with mine. "Those petals aren't easy to toss on a windy beach."

"You can say that again. I had to stretch for the job and everything."

"Well, if anyone deserves to get laid tonight it's you, big brother. Do you need some help? I could pick a couple hot ladies for you. There are a few sitting by the pool right now."

"Get outta here." I shove her teasingly, but Hawk catches her before she falls backward. "I don't need a wing-sister. I can catch tail all by myself."

"Good." She straightens up. "Hawk, I need a partner for pool. Will you help me kick Colby and Carissa's asses?"

"What?" I perk up. "Why wouldn't you ask me? I'm your fucking brother. We're blood."

"Because you're way too fuckstrated. Duh." She rolls her eyes. "Go get laid. You'll feel better." She gestures toward a small group of women dancing by the pool. "Seriously, if I were you, I would opt for one of those." She pats my shoulder with excitement spread across her face. "Oooh, and you should totally use your old pick-up line from high school. You know that Transformer one!"

"Shut up, Rory. We don't talk about the Transformer pick-up line anymore."

"Oooh," Hawken laughs. "This is one I haven't heard! What's the Transformer pick-up line?"

She waves him off. "Something about being Optimus Fine."

She laughs, and Hawken cackles as I rub my forehead, my annoyance for my sister growing by the second.

"Oh, fuck, please use that one, Dex. Let me know how it goes."

"Come on," Rory says to Hawk as she steals him away. "We have a game of pool to win. Catch you later, Sexy Dexy." She winks and laughs as the two of them walk away.

"Do not call me Sexy Dexy!"

She cackles even louder as they round the patio to the bar. Shaking my head in laughter, I finish off my beer and am about to order another when a woman steps up to the bar next to me. She orders a Sex on the Beach and a Long Island Iced Tea, and then turns to me.

"Hey."

"Hi." I give her my best smolder, but she giggles in response.

"Yeah, that won't work too well on me, big guy. I like to lick pussy too." Her smile and wink make me laugh out loud.

"Fuck, nobody has ever said that to me before."

"I mean, don't get me wrong. It's a sexy smolder for sure. And it would work on my friend over there if you're interested." She gestures to a woman lounging by the pool in a black bikini, her golden hair piled creatively on top of her head. I can't make out her exact features from here, but at first glance, she doesn't appear to be a troll.

I cock my head. "Are you trying to set me up with your friend?"

She shrugs. "Depends."

Well, this is interesting.

"On?"

"Are you a nice guy?"

"Uh, I'm literally the nicest guy. Like, ever."

She smirks. "Why don't I believe you?"

"Ugh, okay. In all honesty, my buddy, Milo is literally the nicest guy, but he just got hitched, so he's off the market. If you'll allow me to be nice guy by proxy..."

That makes her laugh. "All right, so you're a nice guy. We'll go with that. Is nice guy single?"

"Fuck yeah. Nice guy doesn't commit. He's nice to everyone."

"You good in bed? Or are you just, you know, average?"

I laugh at her question. "Uh, I'm more than good. Trust me."

"You know that's what they all say, right?"

"And you know there isn't a guy on this earth who is willing to admit he's just average, right?"

"Fair point." She laughs again and raises her plastic cup to clink with my empty beer. "Look, I invited my friend to Florida with me to celebrate her divorce from a nasty-ass piece of cheating shit."

Narrowing my eyes, I stare down the woman who is now double-fisting the drinks she ordered. "So, you want me to pity fuck her? Is that what you're asking me?"

"Uh, no." She scoffs. "She doesn't need nor want anyone's pity. She's happy to be moving onward and upward. I'm merely suggesting you hit on her. Make her feel sexy. Maybe boost her confidence a little before she starts her life over again. It's always nice to go on vacation and feel noticed, right?"

She's not wrong.

Wasn't I just saying something like that?

"And hey, if things work out and you both get to experience a little non-committal playtime. What's the harm in that?"

She slides the Sex on the Beach over to me. "This is hers. I'm going back to our room to shower and pack. It was nice meeting you, nice guy who is supposedly good in bed."

"Yeah." I nod, watching her walk away from the pool area and back toward the elevators. "Nice to meet you too..."

My eyes shift to where the woman's friend is sitting by the pool, but she's not there now. I spy a girl in a black bikini heading toward the very bar I'm sitting at, and holy fucking shit, I am one lucky son of a bitch.

Tendrils of her hair fly around her face in the wind. Her skin kissed by several days in the sun. She's not one of those stick-thin Barbie doll types. On the contrary, this woman has curves in all the right places for a man like me, and she walks with confidence, which I love to see.

I'm merely suggesting you hit on her. Make her feel sexy.

Maybe boost her confidence a little before she starts her life over again.

Seems easy enough.

I guess it's now or never.

Just as she makes it to the bar, I meet her and blurt out, "If you were a Transformer, you would be Optimus Fine."

What.

The.

Fuck.

Did.

I.

Just.

Do.

Oh my God!

Did I seriously just throw her the Transformers pick-up line?

Fucking Rory!

My feet plant firmly in place, my body goes rigid, and I swear my dick just shriveled up and died of disappointment. This is the end of my life. Tomorrow's headline will read *"Twenty-nine-year-old man dies of dick disappointment when using Transformers pick-up line on hot chick."*

Fuck me.

Blondie laughs as my cheeks redden. She places her hand on

her hip and tilts her head. "So, what if I prefer Bumblebee?"

I shake my head, still horribly embarrassed. "I am so sorry. I-I-I want to say I don't know where that even came from except it's totally my sister's fault, and I swear I'm usually a whole lot smoother than this. I'm slightly mortified right now."

She laughs again and my chest lightens. "Don't be. You got my attention, didn't you?"

"Uh, yeah." I chuckle to myself if nothing else. "I guess I did." I slide her drink toward her. "Look, I don't ever recommend taking a drink from a strange guy, but your friend just ordered this for you and then said she was heading to her room to shower and pack. She asked me to give it to you. I promise I'm a nice guy."

"You're safe ma'am," the bartender adds. "I made the drink and I've been right here the whole time."

She reads the guy's nametag. "Thank you, Barry."

"You're welcome, ma'am."

"See? Told you. I'm a nice guy." I gesture to Barry the bartender for another beer, catching the pretty woman's eyes floating up my body taking note of the tattoos on my chest and shoulder. I don't miss the few seconds her gaze lingers on my lower abs either.

Yep. Check me out baby.

"So, my roommate left me, huh?"

"Looks that way, yeah. She said you wanted to soak up the last of the sun before you leave tomorrow."

"She's right. I wanted to watch the sunset."

"They're definitely beautiful here." I offer her a hand. "I'm Dex."

"Tatum," she answers. "Care to join me?"

I clink my cup with hers. "Sure."

I follow her out to the beachside patio, where she steps into one of the open hot tubs. I step in behind her and take her hand so she doesn't slip. She sits along the edge, where we can see the ocean and admire the colorful canvas the sun is painting for us right in front of our eyes, and I maneuver myself next to her.

"So, where are you from?" I ask her, trying to make small

talk.

"Michigan."

"That's quite a distance from Key West."

She smiles. "Damn right it is."

"Uh-oh." I chuckle. "Something about that response doesn't sound good."

"Nope, it's all good now." She shakes her head.

"Oh, okay. Good. Are you here for a reason?" I already know the answer, but she doesn't know I know.

She returns my question. "Are you?"

"Uh, yeah. I am. My buddy just got married. We're down here on a group vacation."

"Ah. Well, you might want to avoid me then."

As if.

"Why do you say that?"

"Because I'm here celebrating my divorce."

"Celebrating, huh? So, this is a divorce you're happy about?"

She nods emphatically. "Fuck, yeah. Now. He's nothing but a lying, cheating piece of shit."

"Cheater? Ugh, what a fucking twat monster. I'm sorry that happened to you."

"No, twat monster would be my best friend who was fucking him in our bed when I walked in on them."

"Oh shit!"

"Yeah."

"Wow. What did you do?"

"What could I do? He tried to tell me it didn't mean anything, which pissed her off, and she tried to apologize out the ass, but it was too late. I told them both to burn in Hell."

I shake my head. "Nothing wrong with that. Cheers to doing what you needed to do."

She clinks her cup to mine once again. "And then when he went to work the next day, I threw every one of his belongings outside on the front lawn, flushed the house keys and moved out."

"Oh shit. That's savage. Way to go, tiger!"

"Thank you. It happened months ago. The divorce only just became official, thank God. It's good to finally feel free."

"I can imagine."

"Ever been married, Dex?" she asks.

"Hell no."

Her brows raise. "Oh, touchy subject, huh?"

"Nah. Just not sure I'm marriage material."

"Meaning you don't want to commit."

I tip my beer to my lips. "Somethin' like that." Wanting to get the subject off me, I throw more questions her way.

"What do you do?"

"I'm an elementary school teacher. I was teaching second grade, but I actually just interviewed for a new position teaching first grade."

"So, new freedom, new job, new life, huh?"

She swallows a sip of her drink. "That's the plan."

"Have you done anything fun here on your trip?"

"Yeah, of course. We snorkeled, we shopped, we spent time on the beach. I read a couple books, we danced our hearts out at a few clubs, and now here I am, watching the sunset on my last night here."

"Good for you," I tell her. "Sounds like you knew exactly what you needed and you went for it."

She looks out at the ocean. "Yeah, I guess."

Her demeanor changes slightly. She doesn't make eye contact, but continues to sip her drink, staring out at the water.

"If you've had such a momentous week, why don't you look happy? Is it because you're heading home tomorrow?"

"That's part of it, sure."

"What's the other part? Can I ask?"

Her cheeks redden and she shakes her head. I think she's embarrassed. "It's stupid. You'll just laugh at me...or think I'm weird."

I lift a few fingers. "Scout's honor. I won't laugh."

"Were you actually a Boy Scout?"

"Fuck no. But I promise I won't laugh. Consider me a stranger you can tell anything to. Because after tonight, you won't see me ever again so what does it matter?"

"True."

"See? I'm all ears. Tell me your regrets."

She gazes out at the ocean one more time and then tips her cup back gulping the remainder of her drink. My brows rise as I watch her drink down the colorful liquid. Her swallow is impressive, and suddenly, I'm imagining her swallowing something else.

"I regret coming here and not hooking up with someone."

Is she serious?

Or is this some sort of joke?

Did Rory put her up to this?

"Uh...did you have someone in mind, or...?"

She shakes her head. "No. Obviously, it was just the two of us traveling together. But I had this fantasy that I would come to the Keys and meet someone who would like...rearrange my guts, if you know what I mean."

My brows lift, but I try to control my reaction because fuck yes, I know what she means.

She lifts her face to the sky as she breathes in the sea air. "I was hoping for this..." She rests a hand on her chest, drawing my eye to her two beautiful breasts, clad in small pieces of black material. "Soul-destroying orgasm like I've never experienced before. A reward for leaving my lying, cheating husband, you know? A night of epic sex and everlasting memories to take back home with me. Something positive to think about instead of how Mr. Douche ruined my life."

Holy fuck.

Did her lesbian friend really exist back there at the bar, or was she some sort of guardian angel?

Suddenly, my mouth is dry and I'm finding it hard to swallow.

"He didn't ruin your life, Tatum."

"No?"

I shake my head. "If things hadn't happened the way they did, you wouldn't be sitting here with me right now. In fact, what's his address? I think I need to send him a thank you note."

She laughs heartily. "For what?"

Fuck this.

I'm going for it.

"For giving me the opportunity to show the woman who once loved him what an epic night of sex is supposed to feel like. How much her beautiful body deserves to be pleasured." I lean in a little closer and murmur, "What it feels like to orgasm so much and so hard that she forgets her damn name."

The small gasp and heavy sigh that comes from her mouth have my dick so hard I could bend her over this hot tub and rearrange her guts right the fuck now. But all these people around might cause a problem.

Tatum's face reddens, and she shakes her head. "You don't have to do that."

"Do what?"

"Pretend you're coming on to me. It's sweet of you though." As the sun finally sets, she stands, turning toward the beach and picking up her drink. "I should probably go."

What?

No!

She can't go!

I stand quietly behind her and thank the gods that it's dusk enough to not be noticed by copious amounts of people. I wrap an arm around her waist and pull her against my chest, my hand resting on the warmed skin of her abdomen. "Who said anything about pretending, Tatum?"

"Dex..." she breathes.

"I happen to think you're a goddamn knockout, and I would be honored to make every single one of your fantasies come true before this night is over."

She slowly lays her hand on top of mine as I feather my fingers over her wet skin. "What are you saying, exactly?"

"I'm saying, you want a night of epic sex. Soul-destroying

orgasms and memories you won't soon forget, and I can give that to you."

"Why should I trust you?"

"You shouldn't." I kiss the side of her neck. "But I promise you I'm not a creep. If I wanted to pull one over on you, I would've done it already with your drink, remember?"

She contemplates my reasoning for a moment, and then turns her head. "Anything I want?"

"You name it, sweetheart."

"I don't want gentle."

"Good. I'm anything but."

"I want you to press me up against the wall and..."

"And what, Tatum? Finger you until you can't stand anymore? Get on my knees and lick your sweet pussy until you're shaking? Or simply lower you onto my massive dick and drive into you until you're literally screaming."

"Oh my God. That sounds...wonderful."

I reach for her other hand and bring it behind her, placing it over my hardened cock. She palms me, her gasp not taking me by surprise. It's not the first time a woman has reacted this way.

"Holy shit, you're pierced?"

She turns and looks down at my crotch currently covered by my swim trunks. I merely smirk and smooth my thumb over her cheek. "Only one way to find out. Are you with me, Tatum? Tell me you want this, and I'll make it a night you won't soon forget."

"I'm all yours."

"You're not mine, sweetheart. But I'll absolutely ruin you for any man who comes after me." I offer her my hand. "Let's go."

Continued in *BEYOND THE GAME*...

OTHER BOOKS BY SUSAN RENEE

The Anaheim Stars Hockey Series
What If We Do (novella): Jilted Bride
What If I Told You: Best friends to Lovers
What If I Knew You: Coach's Daughter

The Red Tails Hockey Series
Off Your Game: Angry Meet Cute
Unfair Game: Strangers/Roommates to lovers
Beyond the Game: One Night Stand/Surprise Pregnancy
Forbidden Game: Teammate/Best Friend's Sister
Saving the Game: Fake Relationship
Bonus Game: Single Dad/Nanny

The Bardstown Series
(Prequel) *I LOVED YOU THEN*: Second Chance at love
I LIKE ME BETTER: Enemies to Lovers/workplace
YOU ARE THE REASON: Second Chance
BEAUTIFUL CRAZY: Friends to Lovers
TAKE YOU HOME: Boss's Daughter

The Camel Club Series
Smooch: One Night Stand/Strangers to Lovers
Smooches: Single Mom/Ex's Best Friend
Smooched: Fake Relationship/Surprise Pregnancy

The Schmidt Load Novella Series
You Don't Know Jack Schmidt
Schmidt Happens
My Schmidt Smells Like Roses

Stand Alone Novels
Hole Punched: Strangers to Lovers/Hidden identity
Total Ship Show
(part of Love at Sea multi-author series)
Kamana Wanalaya for the Holidays
(She-grinch/sunshine trope)
No Egrets: Grumpy Sunshine
(Part of the Tuft Swallow Multi Author Series)

The Village series
I'm Fine
Save Me
*The Village Duet comes with a content warning.

Solving Us
Surprising Us (a Solving Us novella)

ACKNOWLEDGEMENTS

I know Milo isn't always the typical jock you read about in other sports romances but I really needed to write him as the super nice guy who would give anyone the shirt off his back. He's not a grump and he's not a diva. He's not a conceited jerk and he's not a bad boy (though he has his desires). He's just...Milo. I needed a golden retriever for this book and he did not disappoint in my mind. I hope you enjoyed him as much as I did.

I tend to lean heavily on several people during my writing process. This job can be a lonely one when you're sitting at home by yourself, writing books by yourself and marketing them by yourself so please allow me to thank a few key people without whom I would simply not be able to do what I LOVE doing.

My alpha readers, Jenn, Jennifer, Kristan, and Stephani, you are proving to me over and over again that I made the right decision in reaching out for your help. I know I can get needy and will lean on you during those times when my fear creeps in so THANK YOU so much for being my rocks! For reading when I need you to, and for always giving me your honest opinions as I move through the world of hockey romances.

Brandi, Kandy, and Sarah, my team of ladies who are always there to not only be my friend but to talk me through issues whether they be story related, cover related or life related. THANK YOU so, so, so much for always being a never-ending group of encouragers.

ARC readers, you make me smile on a DAILY BASIS! Man do I love and hate sending you things to read!! You are the BEST cheerleaders and although it always scares me that you might not like what you're reading, you never fail to send me your hugs, smiles, and virtual high fives. You boost my self-esteem whether you know it or not. You know how to make a girl feel loved when she's the most vulnerable.

To my TIKTOK following, SERIOUSLY FUCKING THANK YOU FOR every single message, like, comment and share. It has been an absolute pleasure getting to know so many of you and I can't wait to experience more booktok craziness because there is so much fun to be had! Some of you come up with the best one-liners to start my books and I am here for it!!

To my readers and friends, THANK YOU for continuing to read my books. Thank you for continuing to share my words and THANK YOU for continuing to talk about my books. It only takes a spark to light a fire and I appreciate every one of you for being that spark for me!

KEEP IN TOUCH

Website: authorsusanrenee.com
Instagram: @authorsusanrenee
Twitter: @indiesusanrenee
Tiktok: @authorsusanrenee or @susanreneebooks

ABOUT THE AUTHOR

International bestselling author, Susan Renee wants to live in a world where paint doesn't smell, book boyfriends are real, and everything is covered in glitter. An indie romance author, Susan has written about everything from tacos to tow-trucks, loves writing romantic comedies but also enjoys creating an emotional angsty story from time to time. She lives in Ohio with her husband, kids, two dogs, and a cat. Susan holds a Bachelor and Master's degree in Sass and Sarcasm and enjoys laughing at memes, speaking in GIFs and spending an entire day jumping down the TikTok rabbit hole. When she's not writing or playing the role of Mom, her favorite activity is doing the Care Bear stare with her closest friends.